ASGARD AWAKENING

Asgard Awakening, Book One

A VeilVerse story

By Blaise Corvin

Table of Contents

Also by Blaise Corvin

*Note: Some titles are scheduled for launch in 2018 or 2019

<u>Artifice Universe</u>

Delvers LLC

1. Welcome to Ludus
2. Obligations Incurred
3. Adventure Capital

Nora Hazard

1. Mitigating Risk
2. Competitive Advantage
3. Accounts Payable

Delvers LLC (Cont.)

4. Golden Handcuffs
5. Hostile Takeover

<u>VeilVerse</u>

Asgard Awakening

1. Asgard Awakening

Yggdrasil Universe

Secret of the Old Ones

1. Luck Stat Strategy
2. Airship Privateers

Written with Outspan Foster

Anthem of Infinity

1. First Song Book One
2. First Song Book Two

For my loved ones and their infinite patience.

Foreword

Hello readers! This book is classified as GameLit.

You might be curious what GameLit actually is. GameLit, a larger genre umbrella, is any fiction with game mechanics or that takes place in a game. RPG GameLit, or LitRPG is a subgenre of GameLit where stories include some sort of linear progression for characters that is significant to the plot of the story. These types of stories have been extremely popular in Russia and other countries where they are called LitRPG. They're just now making an impact in the West!

RPG GameLit is usually a funky mix of Fantasy and Sci Fi. The settings can vary, but what most GameLit novels have in common is a world that most gamers can immediately relate to.

Asgard Awakening is definitely GameLit, and some would classify it as RPG GameLit/LitRPG as well.

This series is also Harem Lit, a subgenre of literature that includes polyamorous relationships with a single lead.

***

For everyone who enjoys this book and the VeilVerse in general, you have William D. Arand to thank.

Will and I go back a ways. We started writing at around the same time, but he beat me to it. In fact, I read his books (Otherlife) before I had published anything yet. We have very different styles, and even approach writing itself from different directions, but our friendship has really been based on a mutual love for writing and literature from the get-go.

A while ago, Will approached me with an idea for a shared universe. As far as I know, nothing like the VeilVerse has been done before, especially by indies. There have been other collaborative universes, like Star Wars EU, Dragonlance, and Michael Anderle's large library of work. But as far as I know, two authors have never created a new universe from scratch and then proceeded to write /separate/ books in it right off the bat.

This is an exciting time to be a writer, and I feel honored to have been part of this project.

The cool thing about the VeilVerse universe is how readers can simultaneously read the adventures of two very different cousins, marooned in two different worlds. Furthermore, other writers may join us in the future with tales of their own veils.

In closing, I want to sincerely thank everyone for coming along with me on this journey. I've always wanted to add a series like Asgard

Awakening to my growing library of work, and there was no better author than William D. Arand to join in this new endeavor.

Please remember to leave a review, even if you only post a few words. Every little bit helps!

***

I really had a lot of fun writing this book. If you'd like to visit my website, the URL is http://blaise-corvin.com/

I also have a writer's note in the back of the book with a whole mess of links.

If you'd like to connect with me on Patreon, the link is http://www.patreon.com/BlaiseCorvin.

My reader group on FB is at:
http://www.facebook.com/groups/BlaiseCorvinBooks/

I hope you enjoy your time on Asgard with Trav!

The Veilverse Universe is owned by Blaise Corvin (that's me!) and William D. Arand.

Asgard Awakening follows the adventures of Travis Sterling. To read about his cousin Ash, please check out William's series, Cultivating Chaos!

Prologue

Stars twinkled amidst the inky vastness, handfuls of glittering sand thrown across the darkness of infinity. The uncaring vacuum of space was remorseless, offering no warmth or safety, but the Traveler remained untouched. Ages had passed. The Traveler had not spent much time actively thinking for quite some time. All that remained had been a single purpose, a single destination, all driving towards one thing. Hope.

Despite traversing the void for an eon, the bodiless entity had never lost focus. Revenge and knowledge—the ancient drive still remained strong. The Traveler should have stopped existing long ago, merely dissipating into the cosmos, but the hope born from forbidden knowledge still burned, combining with an iron will to create energy from nothing.

These days, the Traveler was not much more than a moving, glittering shadow with a general plan to exist again. A great deal of luck would be necessary. Uncertainty made the Traveler nervous.

So much time had passed that sacrifices had been made, of course. All knowledge and power came with a price, and this mission had never been an exception. With steadily decreasing options, the price had grown.

Something had changed, though, providing new direction. Blowing gently, the winds of fate had stirred long-forgotten memories. The Fates could be cruel even as they granted a break. To most, energy was better spent adapting than questioning unattainable knowledge. But to the Traveler, no knowledge was ever truly unobtainable.

It had taken a great deal of time, but the Traveler had been able to read the new shifts in the mystical patterns of the cosmos, and had adjusted course. This would probably be the best, last chance to complete the mission. To live again.

Suddenly, a newcomer joined the Traveler, a bright glow amidst the endless shadow. The Traveler sensed something familiar from this Spark, a resonance. Family. The Spark was not directly connected to the Traveler but was connected to another. A son? The Spark had a name, a relationship. Grandchild.

The Traveler had not expected to meet another on this journey, much less family. At first, the new addition was neither positive nor negative. The Spark was descended from a betrayer but was still Kin. Also, the Spark's energy was fading fast despite being newer, younger than the Traveler. The Traveler had sailed among the stars for far, far longer than the Spark, but had also been far mightier, to begin with.

As the two moved through the endless black, the Traveler

understood that the Spark was somehow heading toward the same destination. The two did not communicate, but over time, the Traveler took solace, a kind of grounding contentment in the Spark's presence.

Cracks, fissures had begun forming within the Spark's power. The Spark's glow was weaker now but still burned.

Whether the two would reach their destination together was in doubt, but after so much time, the Traveler decided that it would be good if the Spark succeeded too. Their end goals were probably similar, if not the same.

Everything about their destination, the timing, and even a kind of poetic parallel all practically reeked of the Norns' meddling. In some ways, it was fitting that a child of Loki would still be alive. *Live on, Little One*—the thought was selfless, different—this new thing begged to be explored. Perhaps later. Like the Spark's, the Traveler's strength was waning, just slower. Wisdom and knowledge would help the Traveler with piercing the Veil, but the Spark did not have these tools, these advantages. Youth and willpower may not be enough.

The Traveler knew the time had almost come; the end of the great journey was at hand. There was no more time to consider the Spark or to wonder if any other family still survived. Preparations had to be made, now. Weapons must be forged from memories, tools from thought.

Everything had a price, and what the Traveler planned would naturally have a high price indeed. But it must be paid. Any other path led to oblivion, and that would be unacceptable.

The Traveler crept towards the veil, waiting for the event, a window of time when it would be possible to save two lives for the price of self, to give up almost everything for a second chance.

Revenge and knowledge, knowledge and revenge.

Chapter 1

Pain lanced across Trav's back like fiery red stars. Lashings had become a part of life for the last three years, so he endured it, feeding the quiet flame of hatred burning in his soul. When the whipping stopped, he cautiously glanced back. The guard had finally lost interest in beating him, so Trav slowly got up to limp back to work.

He wasn't sure what the punishment had been for, but there didn't always need to be a reason. Recently, especially within the last couple months, the whippings had been more frequent. From the rumors he'd heard, Trav's captors were preparing for war.

What this actually seemed to mean for the slaves had been increased quotas of the red ore that they mined every day...and surlier guards. Trav didn't really care. Not much mattered anymore—Beth was gone. The entire world seemed to move slower; colors weren't as bright.

All the pain in his back slowly faded as he plodded through the glyph-lit tunnels. Many things had changed since he'd left Earth. One of his new advantages, something he had managed to keep a secret, was how fast he healed these days. The other slaves weren't so lucky.

The tunnel he moved down led deeper into the mine complex. He wouldn't have to travel much longer until reaching the point where most of the human slaves started feeling discomfort or pain. Mining the glowing red ore was dangerous work, and the stuff had a nasty aura—it eroded the health and energy of any human that got too close. The guards could tolerate being near it, but still usually avoided touching it at all costs.

Another of Trav's new 'quirks' was how he was seemingly unaffected by the ore in any way. Unlike his other changes, his ore-tolerance was an open secret among the other slaves. They all kept their mouths shut about it as a matter of survival, though.

The majority of the human slaves usually stayed up top, outside the mine, trying to eke out an existence and help keep everyone else alive. A number of slaves worked in the mine itself, helping cart out debris or dig new tunnels. But this deep, Trav didn't encounter many other slaves.

Some of the other slaves that came this deep were hopeless, just wandering. Others were lazy, disappearing this far down to kill time in the dark and escape work. Still others were courting death. Very few slaves were like Trav, venturing this far to actually work, searching for the rich ore veins to harvest large amounts of the mysterious red stone. Since the ore worked like a currency of sorts among the slaves and their masters, anyone driven to actually find the stuff in large quantities usually needed a favor for someone...or the quotas might have gone up.

It was always bad when the quotas went up. Always. Trav couldn't do everything on his own—there was not enough time in a day. Everyone was always punished en masse if the quotas weren't met. People died every time that happened.

Suddenly, the darkness to one side of the tunnel seemed to swell, and a big, unwashed man with a bald head stepped into Trav's path. The slave pushed him back, grunting, "Stop blocking my light, puke. Why did you bump me? Give me any food or anything you have in your pockets, and maybe we can forget about this, yeah?"

Trav vaguely remembered seeing the other man around and thought his name might be Duncan. *Is it Duncan?* Travis wondered. The man's thick, scraggly red beard had bald spots. 'Maybe Duncan' kept moving forward, no doubt expecting Trav to comply with the shakedown.

Not all of the human slaves had had their spirits crushed yet, but some of the unbowed took out their misfortunes on the others. That or they were just assholes to begin with. Duncan was big and accustomed to getting his own way, at least among the other slaves. Down here, he was probably trying to prey on others that were tired of living. Anyone that was searching for death probably wouldn't care too much about being robbed, after all.

Trav had never thought about it before, but it made sense and was probably another reason that troublemakers ventured down to this part of the mine. Trav had just never put the pieces together before.

Fighting in the mines wasn't actually forbidden, but the guards would beat slaves for doing anything that annoyed them—-which lately meant anything but work. However, the guard in this section of the mines was not anywhere nearby; Trav had just been beaten and knew where the brute was, after all.

The big, bearded slave shoved Trav backwards again and lunged forward to grab his shoulder, cocking his other hand back to punch. Before striking, he finally looked at Trav full in the face and realized exactly who he was trying to bully. With a swallow, the big man's fist dipped, and he took a hesitant half-step back.

Trav smiled without humor. "That was a mistake," he growled. Beth had always hated jerks like this. She'd used to say that the hell of their slavery was made even worse with how some of the humans treated each other. The fact that some people still had to act as guards against others, had to give up on rest to make sure nobody got raped or murdered at night...it was hard. Every time a new batch of slaves was brought in by their captors to replace dead workers or increase productivity, things...always got bad for a while.

And yet, despite the sheer number of predators among the remaining humans, nobody had ever actually tried to lean on Trav before, not even while he'd been mourning after his wife's death—not until now. There had been a reason for their respect. It seemed he might have to remind everyone about what that was.

Trav grabbed Duncan's hand on his shoulder in a vice-like grip, stepped back, and slammed his palm into the other man's hyperextended elbow. The break was quick and savage. Then Trav twisted the man's broken arm and kicked him in the ribs. All the while he wondered, *Is his name Duncan or not? This is going to bug me if I can't figure it out.* Trav finally let go of the bearded man's hand, and he crumpled to the ground, cradling his crippled arm and desperately stifling his bellows of pain. They both knew that if he made too much noise, it would attract the attention of the guards. That would be bad.

Trav thought the situation was ironic the environment that had allowed this asshole to treat the other slaves like shit was also what made him desperately hold in his screams, gritting his teeth, sobbing in agony. When he had been younger, Trav might have thought this was justice. Now he knew better; there was no justice. At the end of the day, everyone would still be slaves.

He stomped his foot down next to the writhing man's head, and the former tough guy flinched. "Hey, what's your name?" Trav asked.

"Fuck off, you dead son—"

Trav kicked the scumbag in his damaged arm, and the man recoiled, chomping down on a bellow, his throat convulsing. Then Trav conversationally said, "Wrong answer. What is your name?"

The bearded man gritted his teeth in pain and glared sullenly from the floor. "Duncan," he finally grated.

"I thought so! So, Duncan, you really fucked up. Which I'm sure you know by now, right, Duncan? See, since you were such a wonderful person to me, I can only assume you act like this to the others too when I'm busy saving everyone, including your worthless ass. Let's just consider this karma, okay? But if I ever notice you roughing up other people, much less doing anything worse, I'm going to kill you. Do we understand each other?"

"You think you're so tough, just because you're a freak. If we were back on Earth, I'd end that sm--"

Trav stomped down on the unwashed man's hand. This time Duncan let a whimper escape, almost a whine. Suddenly, the big man's good hand darted down into his unkempt clothing, then came up with a shiv. Trav managed to avoid the awkward attack, moving his leg to one side; then he grabbed the man's wrist in a death grip before slamming it against the rocky ground a few times. When the hand finally opened, Trav grabbed the shiv, slammed it into the wounded man's leg, then stood and flicked blood off the ugly, improvised blade.

The unwashed thug hissed in fresh pain, holding his good arm against the new wound. A pool of blood almost immediately started spreading in the dust. Trav said, "That was stupid, Duncan, very stupid." With a frown of distaste, he pocketed the shiv. Trav didn't usually carry a weapon; if the guards caught a slave with anything dangerous other than tools for work, all the slaves were punished for it. This was also why Trav had made the decision to take the shiv. He'd need to dispose of it somewhere.

Trav sighed and said, "You can just lie there for a while and have a nice rest. Hopefully, that wound on your leg won't get infected, right? Right."

"Fuck off, freak," hissed Duncan.

Trav shrugged. "So be it. Have a nice day," he said and began walking away.

"Too bad your little wife isn't here to see you acting all high and mighty. She acted really good for that monster, huh, freak?"

The words hit Trav in the back like red-hot darts, burning with regret and shame. He turned and just stared for a second, but finally shrugged. Why restrain himself? What was the point? His voice cold, he said, "So, so stupid. Your pride has such a grip on your balls..." The words trailed off as he plodded back, his feet heavy with intent. Duncan grinned nastily right up until Trav knelt and planted the shiv into the idiot's throat, then with another economical motion, slid the blade home through the bastard's heart.

Trav sprang backward, avoiding most of the sudden spray of blood that patterned walls and began puddling on the floor. The dying scum on the ground thrashed, his eyes bulging. Duncan stared in horror and accusation at Trav. He probably couldn't believe that a man that some of the other slaves called "Protector" had killed him so easily. Duncan's world had been one of fear, bluster, and threats.

It was true that at one time in Trav's life, he could not have imagined doing anything like this. The entire scene would have made him feel sick, given him nightmares. He would have felt sadness and remorse for killing another human being. Now all he felt was annoyance.

He'd seen a lot worse. Three years as a slave on Asgard had taught him lessons that would be burned into his soul for eternity. He'd learned other things too, secret things. Some of the secret things he knew were helpful, especially right now. A body in the mines dead by blade wounds would definitely bring the ire of the guards. Even the guards didn't usually kill healthy slaves outright on purpose. No, that power was reserved for their masters. The old hate welled up in Trav's heart, and he made a fist so tight his hand began to hurt.

Trav needed to make this death look like an accident, and to do that, he'd need to move fast. It was dangerous to run in the tunnels, but there was no time to waste. Luckily, he'd been down this way so many times, the bumps and ruts in the stone were familiar. He was one of the lucky ones. A lot of slaves didn't survive long enough to grow accustomed to anything except despair.

After heading deep enough, Trav did his best to ensure nobody would be caught in a cave-in. Then he ran up the other direction and did the same. Finally, he came back to the body and made a face. "Stupid bastard," he muttered. In another place, another time, he might have thought killing someone over words was wrong. But now, in this place, life was cheap, and sometimes he made hard decisions.

Duncan's actions had been so stupid, so aggressive. Killing the man would probably make Asgard a tiny bit safer for the rest of the slaves, and that was something worth killing for. Beth would have wanted Trav to keep caring. Her memory was one of the only things that kept him going, so he clung to it. He cherished all of Beth's dreams, what had made her special, like a drowning man struggling for air.

Trav stared up at the top of the tunnel and pulled up his Mystical Overlay, the name he'd come up with for the strange thing he could do with his fake eye. Just like his artificial sight, it worked right through his eyepatch. Now that Beth was gone, not another soul knew about his replacement eye. If he were to ever take his eyepatch off, the stone eye would glow a baleful red, and needless to say, avoiding notice would be impossible.

Attracting the attention of the guards was bad. Beth had learned that the hard way.

Trav swallowed at the sudden memory and focused on the present, running through the list of glyphs, sigils, and runes he could somehow remember. As far as he could tell from his three years on this world, the knowledge of runes had been lost long, long ago. Even glyphs were only used by the most powerful monsters that ruled Asgard like old Earth warlords. Sigils were incredibly rare, known only to the oldest or most powerful monsters, or Kin as they called themselves. Runes...well, he still didn't know how to use those, maybe he never would. One thing he was fairly sure of though, was that he might be the only person on this world holding rune knowledge.

Too bad he couldn't use it to save the other slaves and himself. Powerlessness was having great power he couldn't actually use...it was the story of his life.

Trav used the Mystic Overlay to trace a single sigil on the rock of the tunnel. Then he added a series of glyphs around the sigil with his mind. After that, he...channeled...through his arm and the dirty shiv to scratch out the symbols that he saw in his mind's eye. Glowing red lines appeared as he did so, and when the last symbol snapped into place, he began running up the tunnel.

The rumbles began almost immediately, and Trav hissed, hoping he hadn't overdone it. The tunnels were so shoddy, and the stone so easy to destroy with all the red ore nearby—even as careful as he'd been, he might have made a mistake.

Finally, after the crashing from behind stopped and a billow of dust caked him from head to foot in filth, Trav decided he was probably safe. He slowed down, panting, and leaned against a wall. Other slaves would come soon to check on all the commotion. Maybe the guards would come too. Trav didn't want to deal with either, so he looped around to another tunnel and started moving lower into the mines again.

Maybe he shouldn't have killed Duncan. Now the collapsed tunnel might need to be dug out, and that would put more lives in danger. No, what was done was done. There was no use worrying about it.

It was just too bad he couldn't kill a guard. Trav snarled, letting old hatred and all of the terrible memories he still carried run through his mind, warming him. This deep in the earth, the air was cool, but Trav's skin burned hot from a combination of raging emotion, and the energy from the stone he'd put in his eye socket a year before.

Of course, that was back when he had still been able to hear the voice. The voice had helped him, but now it was silent, gone, probably dead like everything else he'd ever trusted.

Trav plodded deeper into the bowels of the mines. He was aware of the irony in working for masters he hated, on a task he despised, to fetch materials he didn't understand, probably to be used as weapons. He desperately wished he could stop, to just give up like so many others had, but duty was heavy. It never went away, just got stronger.

He'd made a promise to Beth before she'd died. In hindsight, it'd almost been like she'd known what was coming. Trav had already thrown away a number of unnecessary things. Innocence, naivete, and even kindness in some ways. But there were aspects of who he was that he refused to give up, continuing to hang on through sheer stubbornness.

The inhuman bastards that had captured him would never beat Travis Sterling down enough to break a promise, not least of which one he'd made to the wonderful, gentle woman he'd called his wife.

The gloom pressed in from every side, but Trav forced himself out of his regrets and pain. Instead, he remembered Beth's smile, her grace, and the way she'd gone out of her way to reassure the slave children.

"Baby, am I doing okay? What am I supposed to do?" he whispered, his words carrying through the surrounding gloom.

No answer came. Beth was gone, and even the voice in his head had died. Trav was alone.

Chapter 2

Trav finally descended deep enough to start seeing specks of glowing red ore in the walls. Any of the other humans would be showing signs of pain or discomfort at this point. Trav thought it was too bad the ore was so dangerous—he thought it could be pretty, even mesmerizing.

Some of the other slaves called the stuff twinkledeath, or glow agate, but Trav knew its real name—emberstone. Of course, he also knew better than to name it out loud. The Kin never used the real name for the stone, and if they ever heard its real name, there would be questions.

The Kin, he thought and growled. Most of the slaves just called them monsters, and they weren't wrong. From what Trav had seen, Kin had many forms. Some seemed to be unique, or at least rare.

Privately, Trav had to admit that a few Kin he'd seen had been beautiful, at least in a dangerous, bestial way. Meanwhile, others like the hideous, rat-looking Dacith were obviously all part of the same group or tribe. The sad thing was, while the Dacith were the weakest and lowest rank of the Kin, the unsettling creatures were still far faster, stronger, and tougher than humans. The absolute weakest of the Kin could easily overpower a healthy, full-grown human male—meanwhile, most slaves were not healthy, not by a long shot. Rodent-faced Dacith usually acted as servants for their betters, but they still enjoyed mistreating the human slaves. The rules the terrible creatures seemed to be compelled by were all that saved the human slaves from being eaten or worse.

Trav's lips drew back from his teeth as he thought about his captors. His thoughts turned dark, his eyes glazed over and he almost tripped. *Not good—need to pay attention.* He was familiar with this part of the mine, but attention to detail was still important. If he were to get hurt, he would heal faster than a regular person, but if he had to take any time off, the other slaves would suffer.

Without Trav, more slaves would need to go deep enough to mine ore, and would slowly die. Well, they'd die quicker than they were already. Trav was a much faster worker for multiple reasons too, so without him, the others would be punished for not making their ore quota. When the slaves were punished, people usually died, especially the children. Some of the Kin seemed to live for the chance to kill or torment the slaves. Some, like the Dacith, stalked around like hounds straining at a leash, just waiting to be loosed.

Of late, the ore quota slowly kept getting higher...because of Trav. He was aware that his efficiency was the reason that the others couldn't survive without him now, at least in the short term. Of course, it was one thing to know that he was potentially making it harder on the others and himself, but it would be another matter to mine less ore and deal with the resulting suffering until quota levels were lowered.

Trav picked up a pickaxe he had left leaning against the wall sometime before. Since he was really the only person mining most of the time, he kept tools in every tunnel that he could just pick up to use, then leave behind again. The pick had been left near some crude, wooden ore wagons.

The way the slaves' mining process usually worked was simple. Travis would work to fill up the ore wagons and leave them behind. That way, none of the other humans ever had to touch the stuff, and their captors would see other slaves working. The slaves would slowly cart out the wagons to draw out the workday. Trav usually only put a few pieces of broken rubble and emberstone in each wagon so the other slaves could bring up more wagons every day, making the mine look busy.

This process had been working for over two years. The guards didn't like to come down this far into the mine since the emberstone scared them. All they really cared about was that the quotas were being met and their masters thought the lazy brutes were doing their jobs, so they usually hung around close to the entrance of the mine and randomly beat people.

If the guards ever did descend farther, there was always plenty of warning, and the connecting tunnels that had been dug by the other slaves had proved invaluable. As long as everyone looked busy, the guards assumed they were busy.

Trav's job was to mine the ore—nothing else. Everything the other slaves did was still important, backbreaking work, but Trav staying focused on the ore saved an untold number of lives every month.

After descending for another few minutes, Trav passed the strange fissure in the rock on the wall of the tunnel. The crack seemed to lead down, and every time Trav passed the opening, he could swear he felt a breeze. The workers that had dug this tunnel out a year before had claimed they could hear things from the hole, like growling or breathing. Trav was skeptical, but the gap was definitely something out of the ordinary.

There was a good chance that a natural cave was actually beneath the man-made mining tunnel. Trav thought it was unlikely, but he didn't know much about geology, and he was already in a fantasy world anyway. Compared to bird-headed or skeletal Kin with magic powers, a deep cave didn't seem all that unlikely.

Finally, Trav found a new vein of ore that had been unearthed at the rear of the tunnel. The slaves had already used the glyph-stamping tool to cast yellow-red light in this portion of the cave too. Trav wasn't sure when the Kin had created the glyph stampers. They'd been in use before he had been captured as a slave...he grimaced and focused on the task at hand. This day had already dredged up enough bad memories.

The tall, dirty man spat on his weathered hands and began swinging his pick. It was getting late, and most of the other slaves had already left the mine at this point. Trav was usually one of the first slaves into the mine, and the last to leave. The guards were so used to it at this point, they didn't always wait for him to be done for the day. He wasn't usually upset about the unfairness of it. Beth would have wanted him to keep caring, keep working. The other slaves had to live without his advantages.

Life was unfair, and Asgard was worse. All the other slaves got worn down by time, lack of food, poor living conditions, hard work, and exposure to the emberstone. Meanwhile, Trav was currently in the best shape of his life. He wore loose, layered clothing most of the time so the guards wouldn't notice anything out of the ordinary, but three years of hard labor had turned Trav's body into a mining machine.

His biceps contracted as he swung again and again, dislodging ore. The meager amounts of gruel, cornmeal, and mystery meat had somehow been more than enough to sustain him over the years. He knew it had to have something to do with the voice he'd heard before, but getting answers had been difficult in the first place. Now it was gone.

Just like the strange cave he'd passed earlier, hearing a voice hadn't been all that remarkable compared to being enslaved by monstrous Kin on another world.

Trav lost himself in the rhythm of his work for a while. He had a feeling the ore quota might go up soon—a new group of slaves had been added a week before. The situation was looking grim. Trav hadn't hit his maximum productivity yet and usually had to wait on new tunnels being dug anyway. But still, in less than another year, additional slaves would need to start directly working with the emberstone again. More people would die...well, faster. All of the slaves were doomed anyway.

"Fuck this," Trav hissed, the sudden surge of emotion making him vent out loud. There was nothing more he could do, though. Every day he tried to figure out how to use his tricks, his powers to help him save the other slaves—maybe even himself. But it was no use; the Kin were too strong. Trav knew he couldn't even use the full range of his strange abilities yet. He just didn't have the magical energy, or whatever it was he needed. Everything he could actually do now drew energy directly from the emberstone-laced rock and was really only good for causing cave-ins or helping the digging crews when they were not around to watch.

If the Kin ever found out about his abilities or knowledge, he was absolutely sure they'd dissect every inch of him. He didn't want to be eviscerated, which was at odds with his general plan to stay alive.

Suddenly, Trav thought he felt something. A tremor? His boots were crude. Basically, just bindings made with dirty cloth and rubber soles. Maybe he'd stepped on a mouse? He paused, and it came again. "Okay, I definitely felt that," he muttered. He began walking back up the tunnel, listening as hard as he could. Nothing else seemed amiss, but he was really far down in the mines. Then he felt another vibration.

"What the..." Trav shook his head, wondering if the whumping tremors he had felt had anything to do with the fool he'd killed earlier. That didn't seem likely, though. Cave-ins had a particular feel to them. The guards that had no doubt checked on the cave-in that day probably would have retreated to deal with it tomorrow. It wasn't like they cared about saving the lives of slaves.

The vibrations didn't feel like an earthquake, either. Something was happening. Trav felt a premonition and began hurrying up the tunnel, moving as fast as he could. He almost placed his pick against the wall on the way up, but thought better of it and kept it. Most of his life, moving up an incline in a cramped tunnel while carrying a heavy iron pick would have exhausted him almost immediately. However, working in the mines for the last couple years while infused with whatever the voice had done to him, and the emberstone sphere he'd crafted and used to replace his missing eye...

Thinking of the eye reminded Trav he could use it right now. The tunnels were dim, and he was trying to move quickly. He activated his darksight, allowing the eye to help him see more clearly even through the patch covering it. Trav didn't use this ability very often. Any time he used the eye, the emberstone glowed more brightly, and even with its covering, he worried about being discovered.

The voice had told him how to make the eye. In fact, that had been one of the last times he'd heard the voice, not long after Beth had died. Trav shook his head, focusing on the present. Bad memories had been crowding him all day, and he'd even killed a man. The bad omens should have been a clue that trouble was coming. Misfortune usually arrived in groups of three.

Trav began hearing strange noises about halfway back to the surface. All he could make out was muted, disjointed, distant, but his stomach dropped out. Something was definitely wrong. Had the Dacith finally gotten tired of just threatening? Had they actually attacked the slaves en masse? Trav began running, moving at a reckless speed through the tunnels.

The sounds he was hearing grew louder, and he somehow moved with more speed. When he started approaching the mine's entrance, he turned off his darksight ability from habit. Finally, he burst out of the mine's entrance and gaped in shock. What greeted his eyes was a scene he could have never imagined.

The Kin were under attack...from humans. He could only catch glimpses of the fighting, but what he saw was surreal. Men and women in Eastern-looking clothing fought toe to toe with some of the Kin, moving with inhuman speed and strength. Trav could only imagine that these were the Cultists the Kin grumbled about from time to time. *Humans can fight the Kin!? Wait, where did these guys even come from?*

An explosion in the distance brought Trav back to his immediate situation, and he finally registered all the noise around him. His eyes lowered, and he beheld pure chaos. Slaves and Kin ran everywhere, panicked. The crude ghetto that the slaves lived in was spread out around Trav, all the roads leading to the mines. The crude shacks were not much to look at, just cheap wood with hammocks strung inside, but some had been destroyed, and others were on fire. The thin, dry wood was going up like tinder.

Kin guards, easily recognizable in grey vests, directed screaming slaves away from the mines. One, a huge, leather-skinned, frog-featured ogre bellowed and casually back-handed a slave forward. The slave, an old woman, hit a wall and fell limp to the ground. The guard didn't even notice that he'd killed her; the beast had already turned away.

Trav felt the deeply buried rage flare. He started forward, about to do something stupid, when he was tackled to the ground by something. In a panic, he pushed away, his hands touching something soft, and quickly realized he'd been knocked down by another slave, a woman wearing the same type of mottled rags he was. She was pretty, sobbing, and young—-probably a teen. Her blonde hair was wild, chopped short like many of the slave women kept it. She was tall for an Asgard woman, maybe 5'6". The woman's chocolate-brown eyes met Trav's from behind a veil of tears.

The way the woman's clothes felt reminded Trav of his first day on Asgard. When Trav had first been captured, the Kin had stripped him and destroyed his old clothes.

Between the memories, the scattered fires filling the late-afternoon sky with smoke, and the explosions nearby rocking the ground, Trav didn't recover as fast as he normally would. He didn't even register he was still holding the girl up by her breasts until she was pulled off him by another figure. He blearily looked up and blinked, realizing that a Kin woman was holding the slave girl by the wrist.

The Kin woman's mouth moved with no sound for a moment, then the din of the surrounding violence came rushing back. "—to get out of here!" screamed the inhuman woman. She grabbed Trav's shoulder and pulled the unfamiliar slave. "We don't have any time to—"

A giant pillow made of hot blankets knocked Trav through the air, and his head spun like he was underwater. He hit the ground rolling and heard a voice at the back of his mind, something he had not experienced in a long time. The words came faintly but resonated with power.

GET UP, FOOL! BE STRONG! USE YOUR PAIN!

The voice made something inside Trav snarl, and he sprang to his feet. His ears rang, and he had to hold his head for a moment, but then he stumbled forward. It took a moment to realize he'd been thrown a fair distance back into the mine shaft he'd just come out of. He was lucky he hadn't split his head open. Stones and sediment were beginning to fall; the waning light from outside dimmed as the rubble fell faster.

Trav had seen enough cave-ins to know what was about to happen. He made a split-second realization based on previous experience—he wouldn't be able to escape the mine; there was only one hope of survival.

Frustrating flashes of fading daylight outside barely added to the light from the glyphs on the walls. Trav's eyes hadn't adjusted yet. The two women were just shapes in the dark, so Trav grabbed one wrist each and pulled them with him, down, deeper into the mine.

Rumbling filled his ears from behind, and the ground under his homemade boots trembled so badly that he almost fell a couple times.

Trav gritted his teeth and kept moving forward.

Chapter 3

Trav kept hustling long after being outside the area of the immediate cave-in. He'd seen stones from collapses come bouncing down a tunnel before, acting like cannonballs. There was no such thing as safety on Asgard, but there would also be no use in testing fate.

Finally, he began slowing and allowed himself to start machine-gun sneezing, reacting from running through all the dust in the tunnel. Where she was half standing, the young human girl groaned, but the Kin woman had recovered, yanking her wrist out of Trav's hand and growling at him. The woman's eyes shined in the dim light, and her posture made Trav think she was deciding whether to attack or not. Eventually, either pragmatism or curiosity won because she turned to look back the way they'd come. She laid her ears back and sniffed loudly.

Trav got a chance to study her as he held his side and panted. The Kin woman looked young, but Trav knew it didn't mean anything.

The Kin couldn't be judged by human standards.

The woman had canine features, but unlike some of her kind, she could probably pass for a girl in really good cosplay and makeup back on Earth. Her lithe, athletic body sported obvious muscle, but she had modest curves in all the right places. Trav had no idea what average Kin height was; it seemed to be completely random—this female was nearly as tall as he was, though. She reminded him of a college tennis player...well, maybe one that had been mixed with a really pissed-off wolf.

She had fairly normal, human-looking hands except for cuffs of fur at both wrists and dark, thickened nails. The lighting in the tunnel was dim and somewhat red to begin with, but the fur looked like a dark maroon color. A ruff of fur ran down the outside of each arm, and her ankles had cuffs of fur just like her wrists. She wore sandals laced up both calves; a white, airy tank top; and a thin, embroidered brown vest over it. Her feminine, embroidered shorts had been cut to allow her tail to poke through in the back.

The female turned back, and her eyes found his. Trav's stubborn nature combined with the adrenaline still coursing through his body made him bolder, more like his old self. He stood at his full height, matching her open stare with one of his own. Her eyes were slightly mismatched in color. Trav wasn't sure if she had been born that way, or if it was a result of whatever had put three parallel scars across her face, one running over her eye socket.

She had high cheekbones and gentle lines of fur on the outside of her face. The fact that one of her canine ears was damaged—maybe bitten off in the past—added to the scars across her face, combined to give her a fierce look. Her raised lip showing sharp canines helped with that too.

Suddenly all of her fire seemed to extinguish, and she lowered herself to sit against the wall. The Kin looked up at the ceiling and muttered, "We are dead, slave. That was the only entrance to this portion of the mines. Even I know that. I do not have the power to burst through all that stone.

"You can stop looking at me with lustful eyes. I don't care to take your life. Nothing matters now."

Trav frowned and cocked his head. Around Kin, he was usually extremely careful not to appear too strong or self-confident. But now, mirroring the energy that the Kin woman was giving off, he dropped all pretense of being bowed or broken. "What are you talking about?"

The Kin woman didn't look up. "I was trying to move the stupid slaves. Most of the Kin were fleeing from those damn Cultists." She snarled the last word. "My friend Tala-tala ran off, so I was alone trying to move the dimwitted humans away from the mines. Now it's too late, and we are all trapped in here."

"Why is it too late?"

"The red stone is a secret. Still, somehow the Cultists must have found out about it. The Skijorn council realized a long time ago that something like this might happen, and they prepared for it. In case of an attack on the city or on the mines, they would deny our enemies a single speck of red stone. These mines are all rigged to explode."

Trav's heart dropped. He dimly wondered why she seemed to be talking to him with more respect than the Kin usually gave humans, but the impact of her words shook him to the core. "How long do we have?" he asked.

"Probably only about twenty minutes."

"And the explosives?"

"They are tied into the glyphs on the walls somehow," the Kin said, gesturing. "Every tunnel will collapse. We are going to die. If this had been your fault, I would have killed you already, but the Fates do as they will."

The world narrowed to a point, all of Trav's senses terminating to a tiny dot, and he thought, *I'm going to die? All of this for nothing?*

Die. Die. Die. The words rattled around in his head. He'd never figure out how he ended up on Asgard. Nobody would remember Beth. He'd never see his family again.

The voice came again, barely a whisper, but both what it said and the heat it spoke with perfectly matched the sudden fire that filled Trav.

No! breezed the voice.

"No!" growled Trav.

The Kin woman seemed to lose even more energy, staring at the entrance of the mine, but Trav began to pace. He ignored the ongoing vibrations, the rumbles, tuning out the world completely. His thoughts raced as he ran through everything he knew about his potential abilities; he considered dozens of plans before rejecting each one.

As Trav stewed, he caught sight of a shard of rock against one wall, one of the handful of weapons he'd left scattered through the mines. He knew that this bit of rock was sharp and had emberstone on the side against the wall. He bent down to adjust a boot, and discreetly pocketed the makeshift weapon. There wasn't much emberstone on it, just enough for most humans to feel sick if they got too close, but Kin or human would feel pain touching it. If it were used to cut with, it would probably even kill a Kin.

Leaving the stones in tunnels had been the best he could do up until now. Slaves were regularly checked for weapons and keeping emberstone on him would raise too many questions since the stuff was lethal to most humans. It would have hurt the other slaves if he'd taken the ore with him into the slave camp, so that had not been an option. He hadn't been entirely unprepared for everything going sideways at some point, though.

Having the weapon in his pocket made Trav feel even more rage at fate. Why was he even here, trapped on this hell world? It was too soon to die. Giving up now would be letting the monsters win. Worse, it would be admitting Kraachias was right, and Trav would rather gnaw his own arm off than give his wife's murderer anything. The old hate welled up, and this time he didn't stop it. Trav let the venom and darkness keep growing within him, pushing away every doubt. He refused to die a slave!

From her place against the wall, the Kin woman suddenly jerked around, her eyes glowing as they focused on him. A half-formed plan had come to Trav, and there was no time to waste. The human girl was awake now, warily watching the two of them. Trav grabbed her wrist, and she gave a little squeak before complying. She stared at the

Kin woman, every inch of her posture screaming her fear.

"What is your name?" Trav growled at her.

"Asta...Lord," the girl stammered, speaking Waode, the native language of Asgard, and not particularly well. With those two words, Trav could immediately tell she'd probably been a slave all of her life. For a second, pity threatened to push his anger back a bit, but he stomped on it. Asta would die too if he didn't do something they all would.

The time for hiding his power had come to an end. He didn't have a choice anymore. It was also time to stop playing the meek slave. He needed the Kin woman now, and she needed to get on board, or Trav was going to get some very immediate real-world experience to determine whether the makeshift weapon in his pocket was effective or not.

"You, Kin, what is your name?" said Trav. He let the hate, the anger burn inside and glared at the canine woman, mentally daring her to attack.

She narrowed her eyes and studied him for a full three seconds before answering. "Narnaste," she finally said. "But you are a slave; you will call me Mistress."

"Yeah, fuck that," said Trav. "We are all about to die anyway. You are going to listen to me carefully, and do what you're told. You are going to follow me because sitting here holding up the wall while you wait for your death is a waste of your power. Alternatively, you can attack me right now, and I will kill you so fast it will make your wolfy head spin. It would be a shame to scar up the pretty hide any more, but I might be able to use your body dead or alive."

The Kin woman's eyes widened, and her eyebrows climbed into her hairline. Then her nostrils flared, and she regarded him through slits before slowly smiling, her teeth on display. "What is your name, slave?" she asked, her voice not much above a growl.

"Trav."

Narnaste touched her top teeth with her tongue before pronouncing, "Liar."

Trav's anger rose, but he was able to think clearly. Some Kin could use magic; he'd even seen it. His half-assed plan would really be easier if Narnaste cooperated. He made a face and said, "Fine. My full name is Travis British Sterling, but I prefer people call me Trav. My name is in a language called English, which you have no possible way of knowing, and includes a really stupid joke that my father thought was funny." It had been three years since Trav had spoken English. The last time he had talked about it had been with Beth, and it felt weird to even hear the word out loud again.

The Kin woman studied him a moment longer, cocking her head before announcing, "I am Narnaste Batastesdatter, first-born daughter of the Voidshield family, a branch of the Voidlines. Those who know me call me Narn. If my kind could see me speaking to you like this, I would be mocked, maybe disowned. But as you said, we are going to die anyway. Plus, I am curious. I don't smell any deceit from you, just anger and power. Something else, too."

Trav didn't care what she smelled. He was just glad she was on board. "Good. I am glad we understand each other, Narn. If you want to live, follow my lead."

The pretty, young human girl jumped when Trav called her name. "Asta, we're moving. You follow me too, do you understand?"

"Ye-yes, Lord!" she stammered.

"Okay good. How much time we do have left, Narn?"

"Probably only about ten minutes, slav—Trav."

"That means we really need to move. Don't bunch up. The light is dim down here, so leave space between us, but keep up. Narn, you bring up the rear. Let's go."

Trav turned and began moving as fast as he could down the tunnel. The time for caution had ended. He could only think of one way they might escape the mines now, and it probably wouldn't even work, but he'd be damned if he was just going to sit on his ass and let himself die.

There were still too many things to do. He refused to go down without a fight before he could even start the real battle, no, the war. The inhuman fuckers were going to pay for everything they'd done; they just didn't know it yet.

Chapter 4

Trav moved quickly but didn't need to consciously think about where to step. The trembles running through the ground from time to time meant he had to catch himself occasionally, but even that didn't take much active attention—he'd been down these tunnels often enough. Now the anger he had been running on wasn't at the forefront of his thoughts anymore. As he traveled, a piece of the wall just collapsed from all the stress the vibrations through the stone was putting on the tunnels. Trav barely even noticed, just hopping over the loose rock and new dust.

Now that he was alone with his thoughts, he realized how lucky he had been not to have been seriously injured from the explosion outside or the collapse of the tunnel earlier. It could have been Trav's imagination that the rumbling from the battle outside intensified as he led his two unlikely companions deeper into the tunnel.

In Asta's case, this was not the first time a human woman had been this deep in the mines, but over the last few years, every one of them had died. Women didn't work in the mines unless they had a death wish, and without fail, the emberstone and working conditions had always given them what they'd wanted.

Narnaste's presence wasn't unusual either; Kin guards could be male or female and were equally as brutal. Trav had never seen any guard that looked like Narn before, though. The guards were usually huge, angry, and stupid. However, by her introduction, Trav had gathered that Narnaste was minor nobility or something.

Now that was interesting, he absently thought. The Kin bigwigs he'd met until now had been the most savage and merciless of the bunch. Narn was, at the very least, more even-keeled than other Kin he'd met, but it could just be a survival instinct due to the tunnel collapsing. In fact, maybe she knew Kraachias, Beth's murderer. Maybe she had even committed atrocities of her own.

Trav suppressed that line of thinking with a silent snarl. Now was the time for action, not stewing—his life depended on it. He continued leading his little group through the claustrophobic tunnels. When they passed the point when little winking points of emberstone glowed on the wall, he heard Narnaste growl. This was the part of the tunnels that the guards usually didn't venture past, so it wasn't surprising that the Kin woman was uncomfortable.

It was good to remember that Narnaste was not human. Trav felt dirty for admitting it to himself, but he really was attracted to her. Beth hadn't even been gone for a year, and his dick was already trying to think for him...about an inhuman monster, no less.

Tricky dick, he mentally berated himself. *What is wrong with me?*

At least he had impending death to focus on—it helped stave off unhinged thoughts, probably influenced by sexual frustration. Then again, he should feel lucky the issue was even a problem for him. The other slaves had definitely had...relations from time to time, but usually not for long after getting to the mining camp, and definitely not the slaves that worked in the mines. The hard labor wore everyone down, made them tired and caused their bodies to not work right.

Trav had been one of the only exceptions until he'd met Beth, then she'd gotten more resources so she could be healthy-ish too. The other slaves had tried to give them what happiness they could. It had been a way for them to show their thanks for everything Trav did to help them—at least that was what Beth had always said. Just thinking about it usually made Trav tear up a little bit. People, humans, were usually basically good, and when worn down to their basest parts, the true nature of a person always shined through.

Humans were not Kin.

Trav's stress-fueled thoughts were cut to a halt when he reached his destination. Disjointed thoughts about Kin atrocities and Narn's heart-shaped ass could no longer replace the horror and fear that had settled in with the cave-in and had only gotten stronger over time. However, like before, Trav replaced the fear with anger, drawing on all the hatred that he'd carried around the mines.

Centered and steeled again, he stared at the fissure in the wall. *This is really a long shot,* he thought. Then he turned and said, "Both of you, come here. This is the spot."

Asta meekly scurried over, not meeting his eyes. Then she stood placidly, no doubt waiting for more instructions. She'd accepted Trav as an authority figure and now obeyed immediately and without question. Being regarded and treated this way made Trav a bit uncomfortable. This close to the girl, he could see she was only a bit underfed. She must not have been in the slave camp for long—all the other places that slaves came from usually treated them better than the red ore mine, which said something.

Narnaste moved in a measured way, studying the crack in the wall and looking searchingly at Trav. She opened her mouth to say something, but shut it instead and stood with her hands on her hips.

If Trav's plan didn't work, they were all going to die in minutes. He could feel the stress too, and the intermittent rumbling didn't help. Trav was thankful that Narnaste had the presence of mind to keep her mouth shut. She was Kin, and Trav hated her on principle, at least what she represented, but he appreciated that she wasn't wasting their time.

With a bit of rage still simmering in his chest, what Trav said next probably sounded harsher than he'd intended. He looked Narnaste in the eyes and growled, "Show me your chest."

The canine Kin woman narrowed her eyes at him and said, "Even if there was time to mate, I would not sully myself with a slave, slave."

Trav snorted. "Don't flatter yourself, Clifford the Little Red Dog girl. I don't care about your tits; I need to see your chest—like I said."

"Why?"

"I am going to do magic."

"What kind?"

Trav scratched his head in annoyance. His appreciation for the monster woman's sense of urgency was evaporating, so he told the truth. What did he have to lose? "I'm going to attempt rune magic. I am going to carve a rune into your body and then into mine."

"What then?" The Kin woman's tone was cool.

"We are going to escape through this crack."

Narnaste lifted an eyebrow. "And you think this can save our lives."

"I think there is a good chance it will. Now if you want to live, take your fucking shirt off." Trav scowled at the woman. Her only reaction for five endless heartbeats was to stand very still and clench her jaw. Finally, without further expression, she shrugged out of her vest and lifted off her blouse.

Underneath her top, Narn had a linen undershirt with small straps that functioned like a bra. Trav began opening his mouth to tell her she could probably keep the bra on, but she took it off before he could say anything, and he shut his mouth with a click. It seemed wiser to hold his tongue now.

The Kin woman had amazing, shapely breasts. They were human in appearance. In fact, her entire torso was. Her surprisingly full breasts gently swayed as Trav watched. Each nipple was inverted but didn't detract from the overall fetching appearance. Narnaste growled, and Trav said, "Be quiet. I'm sorry this hurts your pride or your modesty, but we don't have much time, and I'm trying to figure out where to work." He briefly glanced up to meet her eyes—she glared at him but turned her head.

Trav moved closer and said, "I need to touch you, and I need to hurt you, not bad, though. Stay still."

"This is necessary?"

"Yes."

"Be quick."

Trav nodded and touched the inhuman woman on her stomach, then he activated his emberstone eye. He wasn't sure what he was looking for, but he hoped he'd find it quickly. It could have been his imagination that the glyphs on the walls had started to flicker—he hoped so.

As he tracked a line of Narn's natural magical power over her stomach, she shivered and seemed to catch herself, putting her arms behind her back and turning her head even more. Trav didn't bother keeping his makeshift rock weapon at hand. If Narnaste attacked now, they were all dead anyway. The constant, low level of anger he held helped him stay focused on the task at hand.

Normally, seeing a woman naked would not be enough to make Trav lose his cool, especially while the seconds were ticking toward certain death. On top of that, he'd been enslaved on a hell world for years and married before. But something about Narnaste was magnetic, like a song he couldn't get out of his head.

Trav traced the lines of magical power across the Kin woman's torso, lost in the wonder of what he could see with his emberstone eye. A spiderweb of blue lines showed him the power thrumming through the woman's body. It was beautiful.

Asta gasped from where she crouched on the floor. Trav's glance showed the girl was wide-eyed, staring. When Trav turned back he could figure out why—he'd been tracing the lines over Narnaste's breasts, and even across her throat and down to the top of her shorts. The Kin woman quivered, her teeth bared, and Trav had been completely oblivious. After noticing, he mentally shrugged. She would either endure, or they would all die. There was no longer enough time to kill her and try this magic with her corpse.

Finally, Trav found what he was looking for. He pushed in on Narnaste's skin to hold the point and said, "Here. I found it!" Then he drew the shiv from his pocket that he'd taken earlier, and gently touched it to the point he'd found under Narn's left breast. "I am going to cut you," he said.

"Hurry!" hissed Narn. She briefly swiveled her eyes to meet his before angrily turning away again. "I do not wish to die."

"Alright," muttered Trav, trying to sound confident. The anger wasn't helping much anymore. It was one thing to stew on dark memories, but quite another to attempt new, unfamiliar magic on an angry Kin woman while facing impending death.

Trav was nervous, but he couldn't help but be a bit excited. This would be the first actual rune he'd ever drawn. He moved in with his crude shiv, but paused, suddenly realizing that he'd almost missed something crucial. "Shit," he hissed. "Narn, put your finger where mine is and hold it there. I need to take my hand off you."

The canine woman did as she was told, and Trav lifted the rags that formed his shirt. Asta stared, her jaw dropping, and Trav understood why. The other slave men were skinny, emaciated, but

Trav looked healthier than he ever had in his life before coming to Asgard.

He found the right place on his body much faster than he had on Narnaste—he knew what to look for now. This part was crucial to the magic. Trav was afraid to ask how long they had left before the mines blew; the Kin woman might just be guessing anyway. The fact they were running out of time was obvious.

Finally, he lowered the shiv and began making quick, shallow cuts. The blade was dull, and he had to drag the point through his skin more than actually cut himself, but it worked.

By the time he finished, his stomach was a bloody mess, and his handiwork stood red and sullen above the general location of his heart. He hadn't just drawn a rune; he'd made a rune equation—a three leaf clover symbol stood above a large "T" for his name. Then the downward chevron at the bottom of the rune, part of the T extended upwards to connect with the clover symbol. A triangle closed off the whole design.

The cuts and scrapes stung, but Trav breathed a sigh of relief. If he'd forgotten to do this part first and this crazy idea had otherwise worked, he might have killed Narnaste, or himself, or both. The symbol he'd just drawn was a way of establishing his mystical identity and preparing himself to receive power...he hoped.

"Okay, now you," he muttered. Trav moved forward and grabbed the Kin woman's bare hip to steady her body, but he soon realized that wouldn't work. "Put your back against the wall," he commanded.

Narnaste drew in air so loudly it almost sounded like a rattle or a wheeze. Maybe she growled too, but a sudden rumble through the stone surrounding them drowned it out. She moved back and hissed, "Hurry."

"Yeah, yeah, I know." Trav moved his hand up, pressing under the woman's opposite breast to steady her against the stone wall, then began carving like he had on himself. He hadn't even had time to clean the blade first.

Narnaste winced a few times while he worked but held still. Trav was lost in the process, watching everything he did through his emberstone eye. Working on another like this, he could actually see the magical power in the inhuman woman's body reacting to the lines he drew—his magic, such as it was, flowing down his arm and shiv to fill the shallow scrapes. Finally, he was done.

"Good girl," he said absently, patted Narnaste's shoulder, and surveyed his handiwork. The rune equation was simpler than his own but obviously related. A three leaf clover-looking rune stood over a "T", and a few lines around it formed almost a pyramid over the whole thing. Trav made a face, then gasped as his body grew hot. The rune equation on his chest and on the Kin woman flared crimson and burned. As he watched through his emberstone eyes, lines of force, power, or magic jumped off Narnaste and latched onto the runes over Trav's heart. He quivered from the force of it; the sensation was like drinking ten cups of coffee all at once.

This is how Kin feel all the time? he wondered. No, as he watched, he realized that this was just a fraction of the power Narnaste held. A minor noblewoman... Trav shook his head. No wonder the lowest-level Kin could tear a human to pieces.

Narnaste turned and studied him warily, touching the healed scars of her rune branding. "It is done? Can you save us? We are truly about to die, human. Perhaps I was foolish to hope."

"It's done," Trav said, and Narnaste began dressing again. A sense of wonder that the magic had worked threatened to replace his anger, but he focused on the task at hand. Bloody shiv in hand, he approached the wall with the crevice and made quick, economical lines, building a sigil surrounded by glyphs, but this time, he also drew a rune, the same rune he'd used for his own identity. The rune equation was complex, and it basically meant, "widening," and "stairway."

As power began flowing out of him, leaving him cold, Trav focused his will and instructed the energy on what he wanted to accomplish. He wasn't sure how he did it, but he strangely felt like he'd done this sort of thing many times before. The red lines on the wall glowed brighter before the solid rock wall flowed like water. Trav stumbled, his head spinning as the world took on a hazy look. Asta's scream seemed to come from far away, but Trav realized the magic must be terrifying her.

When the hole widened enough, Trav mechanically followed the two women as they fled down the magic-formed tunnel, shaking his head and trying to remember what they'd been doing.

He found a thin thread of anger he still held and pulled on it, dragging himself back into full awareness. The rune spell had taken a lot out of him, almost everything he had had. He carefully held the wall while descending the steps he'd formed from solid rock. Above, the rumbling intensified and began to mix with cracking noises.

"Hurry!" he yelled, and fled with the two women, moving deeper into the unknown dark.

Chapter 5

The rumbling and noise above turned to deep cracking, and Trav wondered if instead of dying in the mine, he just would end up crushed to death in this smaller, darker tunnel. At least he'd been able to use rune magic before his end; the thought was cold comfort but genuine.

Luckily, the escape tunnel opened up into a larger chamber. *There really was a cave or something down here!* Trav's thought was interrupted as he stumbled and fell to the rocky ground below, hissing as the unyielding stone bruised him all over. From above, the bedlam became a deep crashing, almost like explosions, and the world felt like it was being shaken by a giant. Sounds like pebbles rattling around the bottom of a bathtub made Trav's heart drop. He yelled, "Get away from the tunnel!" and followed his own advice, scurrying to the side as best he could in the complete darkness.

From the noise, Trav would have guessed that the entirety of the destroyed mine above was pouring through the little tunnel he'd created. He felt tiny as he huddled in the dark, hoping he wouldn't be crushed or killed by stray stones. Finally, the rumbling from above stopped, but earth fell, and stones bounced for quite a while. Trav stayed still, holding down the ground in his spot and protecting himself with an imaginary, invisible barrier. The fantasy protection was useless but made him feel better.

Finally, Trav cautiously stood. He slowly checked his body for serious injuries, afraid of what he'd find, but breathed a sigh of relief—he was bruised, but whole. Now that he had somehow escaped the mine collapsing, he needed to think of his next steps.

First things first, he needed light. Narnaste had to be somewhere close in the darkness, if she was still alive, and he wasn't sure what she would do now. As Kin, she would be physically superior to humans in every way, and if she decided to tear him apart, Trav would like to at least see her coming. His emberstone eye could help him see in low light, but wherever he was standing at that moment was pitch black.

He felt around blindly, trying to be as quiet as he could. Finally, he managed to locate a wall. There would be no helping the brilliant red lines he was about to draw. At least he could use magic in the first place, otherwise, his options would be bleak, probably ending up trapped in the unknown darkness forever.

Trav fingered his shiv in the dark, thinking of the irony of the murder tool being so useful for magic. He drew a couple burning red lines on the wall. As he worked, a little puddle of light sprang up around him, and a muttered, "What are you doing, human?" almost made him jump out of his skin.

Narnaste stood directly behind him, holding aloft something glowing. Upon further inspection, he realized she had keys in her hand, and the glowing thing was...a key fob with a glyph on it. Trav wheezed a little chuckle at that. She almost looked like a human girl using a flashlight keychain or a cellphone as a flashlight.

"What are you doing?" the Kin woman repeated.

Trav briefly considered being evasive, but he'd realized by now that Narnaste could probably sense lies. He replied honestly, "I am drawing glyphs for light."

The inhuman woman slightly narrowed her eyes at him, and her damaged ear twitched, but she nodded and turned. She held her little light higher, examining the stretch of wall nearby. Trav breathed a sigh of relief and got back to work.

Now that he was less worried about getting attacked in the dark by an angry Kin woman, Trav decided to take a little more time getting fancy with his runework. Instead of a single light equation, he would try making a tool. He'd gotten the idea ages ago from the glyph stampers used in the mines. Of course, he hadn't known before that it was even possible the slaves could have also been planting explosives. He was curious about experimenting with this new information, but it would have to wait. Now was the time to use the hard-won knowledge he'd scraped together over the last couple years while alone in the mines.

The light-casting glyphs in the collapsed mine above had used the nearby emberstone as their energy source. The glyphs had not been directly linked, but the red ore was so mystically potent that it leaked power like radiation. In fact, Trav had always figured this was what made humans sick around it.

Trav wasn't sure how far below the old mines they were now, but the little tunnel he'd made had descended quite a ways. In any event, there was no emberstone on the walls of the cave they were in now. Luckily, even with no emberstone nearby, Trav knew how to use the rock itself as an energy source.

Everything had magical energy—some just had more, and some materials were easier to work with than others. The Kin sigilcrafters did crude work, but Trav was a runecrafter, with endless knowledge inexplicably locked in his head. Frowning in concentration, he drew a complex pattern of glyphs, three circles of them with four glyphs each, all of them sharing one central glyph. Then he drew sigils inside each ring of glyphs, being extremely careful not to touch his lines or ruin the design.

After the last line was drawn, he could feel the sigils begin connecting with the stone it was inscribed on. *Can't have that*, he thought. Now that he finally had a tiny bit of power of his own, he stopped the glyphs' power flow and redirected it. Then he reversed the shiv and used the butt of the crude weapon to painstakingly trace over each line again, nudging the power from the stone to flow through the weapon into the red lines on the wall.

The shiv grew warm for a second as the glyphs and sigils flared to life before casting light like a 60-watt lamp. The light was still tinged a little red, but clear enough to see by.

Trav grinned. Now the shiv could quickly be used to make more light equations using only a simple shape and a minor effort of will. The actual energy powering the equation was coming from the stone. Each equation would only cast light for about an hour, but it sure beat fumbling around in the dark.

Trav had been so engrossed in his work, he'd temporarily forgotten pretty much everything else. He'd let go of the anger he had been running on, so when he turned to see the looks of astonishment on Asta and Narnaste's faces, the events of the last few minutes came rushing back, making him feel shaky. He'd almost died and had rune-branded a Kin woman...that he was trapped in a cave with.

This was not good. Trav desperately reached for a thread of anger, grabbing hold of memories, remembering all the injustices he'd endured during his years of freedom. Hopefully, the slaves hadn't died in all the fighting above and would get a break now that the mines were destroyed.

The slaves. Remembering the guards' cruelty and the way the Kin's battle with the unknown fighters had hurt the humans, ruined their homes, such as they were, rekindled Trav's anger. The feeling was a little artificial, but the frustration at its core was real.

Trav managed to mentally center himself over the span of a second, before Narnaste asked, "That is high-level sigil magic, and you just did it on a cave wall with a rusty knife. Who are you really?" The Kin woman rubbed her blouse over the area where Trav had marked her. Her ears flicked back and forth, and one eye twitched. Trav was not exactly an expert on canine Kin mannerisms, but even he could tell Narnaste would probably be unpredictable and dangerous right now.

Well, Kin were always unpredictable and dangerous, so that assumption was a safe bet.

Instinct instructed Trav to act natural, unafraid. The battered man listened to his gut—it had saved his life many times over the last few years. He mostly ignored both women and walked to the opposite wall of the cave. Now he could see they were actually standing in a wide chamber, part of a tunnel or a long cave. At the new wall, he tapped with the butt of his shiv, projecting just enough force through the tool that it made a smaller, but identical copy of his spell equation on the other side. That done, he framed the whole thing in a glowing red triangle, and sealed the new equation with a minor flex of will, attaching the whole design to the natural power of the stone it was written on.

The faint lines began to grow brighter, and Trav averted his eyes before the whole design came to life with light. It was good that these light equations required so little energy to set up. Whatever he'd gotten from his pact with Narnaste was mostly gone. Creating the escape tunnel had taken a lot out of him, even though the majority of the mojo had come from the rock itself. He was exhausted, and the fall to the cave floor hadn't helped matters.

Trav turned and beheld dust still swirling through the stale air, illuminated by his runecraft. The scene was strangely beautiful for a moment, almost surreal, and even more so when Trav witnessed a huge, green hand appear out of the darkness behind Asta.

An overwhelming sense of danger settled on Trav's nerves, his instincts yelling at him to freeze as Asta was taken. The young woman screamed as she was lifted into the air, then her sounds of distress became muffled. A second later, Trav heard sick crunching. Asta's screams stopped and her legs kicked even harder for a few seconds until they rested, hanging limply.

Back when Trav had been on Earth, it might have taken him some time to recover from the shock of something so unexpected and horrible happening, but after a few years on Asgard, things had changed. He took a step back and instructed his emberstone eye to help him see past the gloom at the edge of the light circle. Then after what he saw, he almost wished he hadn't.

A huge, misshapen creature stood crouched, but would easily be twice the size of a man at its full, hunchbacked height. Its pebbled, cracked hide had a rubbery texture, and bits of moss were actually growing on portions of its body. The creature wore a crude loincloth tied with rope.

Trav's eyes traveled up past its crooked, knobby toes, over its grotesque belly, and witnessed it...eating Asta. The creature's head was too big for its body and bobbed like a bird's as it feasted on the slave woman. Huge, blocky teeth were stained with blood as they ripped and tore at the body in its hands. Asta's dead limbs twitched with nerves, grotesquely making it seem she still struggled while being eaten alive. That couldn't be the case, though—her head was missing. The creature's big, watery eyes were half-lidded in pleasure, and its disgusting, bulbous nose twitched.

Asta still in its mouth, it suddenly turned to stare at Trav and growled, taking a step closer. Now within the light of Trav's glyph equations, he could see how its misshapen body rippled with hidden muscle.

The moment lengthened as they all stared at each other until Narnaste sucked in a breath and yelled, "Troll! Run!"

She didn't need to tell Trav twice.

Chapter 6

It didn't take long for Trav to realize the problem with headlong flight; he was already running out of light. The Kin woman was fast and had almost reached the edge of the light circle. Thinking quickly, Trav decided to lean on Narnaste's truth-reading ability he was almost sure she had. "Keep that thing busy, or we are going to die!" he bellowed.

"What!?"

Their tunnel was definitely too small to really fight or even evade the beast, so Trav yelled back, "You need to slow it down somehow. Let it try to get you, then dodge. I don't know! Just don't die either! If either of us dies now, we're both screwed!"

The strange woman's ears twitched, and she spun. As Trav ran past, she said, "It's too fast. I won't be able to slow it long."

"Just do your best!" Trav dashed forward, risking a glance back to see Narnaste pick up a massive stone, rear back, and hurl it at the charging troll. The beast didn't seem hurt, but it did get knocked back by the impact, slowing so it wouldn't fall. *Good*, thought Trav, they had a chance. He got the feeling that the huge creature was slow to accelerate but could probably move at terrifying speeds if it were able to pick up steam.

After running as fast as he could to the edge of the light, Trav had to slow down so he wouldn't break a limb or kill himself. He made some distance from the lighted cave that Narnaste still fought in, and found a good patch of wall. Then he inscribed a new light equation as fast as he could. With his shiv acting as a pre-set rune-tool, the complex glyph and sigil drawings luckily didn't take him long to draw. He was able to run, stop, and inscribe, and run again at a breakneck pace.

Trav didn't have much of a plan other than making more light so the huge, disgusting, terrifying monster wouldn't catch them in the dark. Poor Asta hadn't even had a chance. Hopefully, there would be an opening in the tunnel ahead so he and Narnaste could go back the way they'd come. After that, he hoped they could figure out a way to escape or hide.

Finally, he reached the end of the tunnel, or rather, it expanded to enormous size. Even after placing a light equation on the nearest wall, he couldn't see to the other side. The troll bellowed somewhere behind, and Trav's guts quivered as he fought primal dread. *What can anyone do against that thing?* he thought. He'd heard about trolls before. They were one type of feral monster on Asgard, or as the Kin called them, Wild Ones.

The Kin guards had sometimes told each other stories of troll sightings when not busy beating slaves or sleeping. Trav had largely ignored them, but after a few years in the mines, he'd picked up a few random bits of knowledge concerning the outside world. As a result, he knew that trolls were strong, fast, ate just about anything, lived for hundreds of years, and were notoriously hard to kill. Even higher-level Kin could have problems killing them since trolls had a nasty habit of healing themselves, and could tear just about anything apart given the opportunity.

By the time Narnaste emerged from the smaller tunnel with the troll hot on her heels, Trav had lined an entire wall of the huge, open cave with light glyphs. As he watched, Narnaste threw stones with superhuman strength, some hitting with devastating power, but the troll was still only slowed, not noticeably damaged. Then as it got close, the Kin woman stood her ground, waiting for the last second to dodge backwards, causing the troll to slow down, but end up holding nothing.

The creature screamed in frustration and held up a misshapen hand to shield its eyes from the new light. That's when it saw Trav.

With a terrifying bellow, the troll turned its bulk, ignoring Narnaste's stones, and oriented on Trav. "Shit," the tall man muttered. There was no way he could escape the troll now, except...yes. An extra dark shadow played against one wall and looked a lot like hope. It was his only chance.

Trav took off running, the light allowing him to move much more sure-footedly than before. He could practically feel the troll's hot breath on his back as he ran. After getting closer to the distant cave wall, he verified that there was a crack, one he might be able to fit in. With renewed vigor, he put on a desperate burst of speed. Even with his headlong flight and the short distance to possible safety, the troll still almost caught him. He reached the crack right before the creature's huge hand could close around him.

The troll shrieked as it crashed into the wall, and Trav scrambled to climb deeper into his dubious shelter. The distant light glyphs on one side of the huge cave filled his little hiding place with deep shadows and gave the terrifying situation a nightmarish, surreal feel. Light from the mouth of Trav's crack disappeared as the troll reached inside, its long, terrible claws scraping on the stone.

After reaching the end of the crack, Trav scrunched himself into it as tightly as he could, desperately avoiding the troll's searching hand. The beast's rancid breath filled the tight space and the man from Earth tried not to gag.

Trav could hear the creature straining, trying to get closer, and was reminded that the thing could see in the dark. The troll might actually be able to see him even as it cut off all the light. *That's cheery*, Trav thought, pushing himself harder into the jagged rock. He couldn't see anything, and the air grew more rank every second. Growls filled his little prison, growing louder every second. Trav's spine tightened in fear, sure that any moment a clawed hand would snag hold of his limb or clothing.

He wasn't sure how much time passed, but it felt like an eternity. The very tip of one claw touched the back of Trav's shabby trousers, and he shuddered. Suddenly, a muffled thump sounded through

Trav's claustrophobic hell, and the creature hissed in pain. Another thump and muted light filled the crevice as the creature turned. After the pitch black, Trav's eyes drank in the illumination, and he could see what had happened.

Narnaste stood with her feet planted, picking up large stones to hurl, much bigger than she'd been throwing earlier. She must have gathered a number of them while the troll had been occupied. Familiar with the Kin, Trav could figure out what had happened. Narnaste had realized that after the troll had killed its new prey, she'd be the only one left...and she couldn't make light. She'd be trapped, so she'd decided to stand and fight, attempting to take advantage of the creature's distracted state.

The plan hadn't been bad. Unfortunately, even from within his safety crack, Trav could tell the attempt had been a failure. The troll snuffled and growled as another huge stone bounced off of its head. Narnaste's aim was good, and she was probably chucking twenty-pound rocks like softballs, but the troll was just too tough.

As the creature began moving towards the Kin woman, Trav thought he saw a look of resignation cross her face. She'd played her best hand, and it hadn't been effective. The reality for Trav was if she died, he really had no hope—he was in the same predicament she was. Now it was his turn to act.

The troll closed with the Kin woman and bellowed, rapidly gaining speed. It slowed to grab at her, and Narnaste dodged like she had before, but this time the creature had feinted. The beast had been waiting for Narnaste's escape, and jumped, propelling its considerable bulk with powerful muscle. With the small bit of extra speed and distance it had gained with the jump, the disgusting creature managed to grab one of the Kin woman's ankles.

Growling in triumph, the troll hoisted Narnaste into the air, a huge grin slowly taking shape across its mouth, stretching cracked lips. Narnaste yowled and tried to claw at the hand holding her, but it was no use. Trav tried to move as quietly as he could while the troll gloated, moving closer. When the Kin woman finally saw him over the monster's shoulder, the huge creature noticed his captive's change of expression and turned to look, but it was already too late.

Trav clambered up the troll's back, adrenaline giving him a huge burst of energy as he practically sprang straight upwards. The troll screeched and turned, trying to reach the human man with its open hand. Trav had already reached the creature's back. He ducked the monster's clumsy grab and yelled, "Die, you ugly motherfucker!" in English. Mentally, he hoped his plan would work, his thoughts manic from a combination of fury, fear, and desperation.

With all his strength, he slammed his shiv into the troll's pebbled skin between two tufts of hair, barely managing to penetrate the thick hide. Trav levered his blade sideways to open the wound. Pulling the blade out might have let it close immediately, and that would simply not do. Then before the troll could shake him off, even as it began bellowing in pain, Trav rammed the emberstone-laced shard of rock from his pocket into the open puncture.

The enormous creature gasped. Trav climbed higher up its back while it stiffened and kicked the stone in as hard as he could before falling to the ground, painfully twisting his ankle in the process. He spun, ready for anything, resigned to probably die.

Instead, the creature stood still for another moment before screeching, every muscle in its body seizing. The troll crashed to the ground and began convulsing, thrashing in the throes of agony. Its skin actually glowed for a moment before the entire creature breathed one last fetid sigh and was still.

The troll twitched in death but didn't make any more noise. The surrounding cave grew painfully quiet other than the sound of labored breathing. Shock from having survived made Trav feel woozy for a moment, and he staggered over to the lighted portion of the cave. Finally he sat, his back against the wall, closed his eyes, and began chuckling.

His mind went blank, restarting as his limbs jittered from the aftereffects of the enormous adrenaline dump he'd experienced. *I'm alive*, he thought in wonder. His tired thoughts became interrupted a moment later by a soft sensation on his lip. Trav's eyes flew open, and he stared into Narnaste's half-lidded gaze. The Kin was kissing him, a thought that took a while to really land.

The inhuman woman growled deep in her chest and pushed Trav down. Now that he was touching her, her incredible strength could actually be felt. But inexplicably, his own ardor suddenly rose, and he half surprised himself by kissing her back.

A tiny portion of his body that was still capable of conscious thought noted that he'd just survived a life and death situation, two actually, and he'd rune-bonded the Kin female. Then the last of his conscious thought was completely muted as he ran his hand through Narn's hair, pausing to touch her animal-like ears. His caress passed over her back, to the swell of her ass, and he grabbed it while kissing her more deeply.

Narnaste responded by whining and panting with need, practically ripping her clothes off. The light glyphs on the walls cast harsh shadows, but the Kin woman's body was beautiful, the glow somehow accentuating her savage appeal. After that, Narnaste nuzzled Trav's neck, and her hands began clumsily working to take his pants off. Her damaged ear tickled Trav's chin, and his hands ran up the front of her body until he gently cupped her breasts.

The tiny, thinking portion of his mind asserted itself again, asking about Beth's memory, about the slaves, and the fact that Narnaste was Kin.

Trav snarled, letting the heat from his blood travel to his eyes. "Fuck it," he panted. "I'm alive." With that, he wrapped a hand in the canine Kin woman's hair and jerked her head back. Despite her much greater strength, she let him arch her body backwards as his mouth went for her throat to nibble at her collarbone and lick her jawline.

The Kin woman moaned, her tail wrapping around Trav as he embraced her on the stony ground. After that, the small, rational part of his mind stayed mute, and the man from Earth fully lost himself in pleasure, celebrating having cheated death yet again.

Chapter 7

Trav awoke with a gasp in complete darkness, trying to figure out where he was. Then he felt something soft next to him, and Narnaste grunted in her sleep. Everything that had happened before came back in a rush, and he realized several things at once.

First, he'd just been with a Kin woman, and she was still next to him, gently snoring. Now that he was awake and his mind was clear, he could actually sense her general direction, too. The bond he'd originally created between them had strengthened, and now...he was full of magical power! Trav's eyes widened as he closed his eyes and tried to sense the edges of the new magical energy inside of him. It was so vast, huge compared to the amount he'd used to burrow through rock before—why was he not being burned to cinders?

With an unsteady hand, Trav drew small glyphs on the cave floor. Using his finger, not a tool, was harder and usually took more energy, but he felt like he had enough raw power filling him now to power a sun. Once the modest light equation had been finalized, a soft glow sprang up from the white lines on the ground.

Trav sucked in a breath, startled by a distant shadow, but he quickly realized it was just the corpse of the troll he'd killed. Wow. He'd had sex with a Kin woman on the stony ground with a dead monster a stone's throw away...*What is wrong with me?* he wondered.

A wave of guilt threatened to descend, but he angrily pushed it away. Beth had been dead for over half a year now. On top of that, even before they'd been married, she'd told him that he was not allowed to mope around the rest of his life if anything ever happened to her. She'd known him too well. She'd also made it very clear that she wouldn't give up on life if Trav died, either.

Beth had just been that kind of woman. As slaves, they had never taken life for granted, and out of necessity had had a few very frank conversations. Trav would never stop loving her, he'd always remember Beth, but he'd understood his wife well enough to know she'd fiercely approve of his desire to avenge her murder...but also wouldn't want him to beat himself up for still having a pulse.

He hadn't done anything wrong, but on the other hand, he hated the Kin, and Kraachias most of all. Granted, Narnaste had probably saved his life a few times and was incredibly attractive...He idly reached behind him and stroked her leg before gently squeezing her shapely ass. The inhuman woman muttered in her sleep, and her tail wagged. Her hand came up and brushed Trav's before she settled back to sleep.

The tall man had never been more confused in his life—- not least of which because when the beautiful, scarred Kin woman finally woke up, she could probably still easily kill him. They were enemies, and he was a slave, after all.

Suddenly, he heard a voice in his head—weak, but definitely there. With a slight echo, it said,

Use the tree.

Trav frowned but immediately began searching his vast, alien knowledge for a tree, whatever that meant. The cryptic voice had made him doubt his sanity more than once in the past, but it had never been wrong, and its advice or hints were always helpful, even if sometimes Trav didn't understand what it had said until it was too late to use the information.

He kept searching, and finally sucked in a breath. The muscular man had finally figured out what the voice had meant. Some of the knowledge in his head still didn't make sense, but a chunk of it had turned decipherable. He had a much better understanding of runes now that he'd actually used them...and the power filling him gave a new perspective on...well, everything.

Trav's jaw dropped as he realized what had been locked away in his mind. Based on what he knew now, as best he could tell, he had enough power to craft one permanent rune equation. In fact, he'd even have a little bit of power left over!

Permanent rune equations!?

He delved deep into his artificial memories, figuring out exactly what this meant. As he did so, he thought about the voice, how it had popped into his head shortly after he'd found himself in Asgard. Just moments before that, he'd been on Earth, on his father's research ship with the rest of his family, then...darkness, a storm, a lot of confusion...and a forest. Of course, he'd been caught soon after that, captured and humiliated, but he didn't want to think about that.

The voice had appeared a couple days later and immediately began dropping cryptic hints about his new world or mumbling about rune magic. About that same time, Trav had gained access to the disjointed, foreign memories, most of which hadn't made sense, and over time, a staggering amount of other knowledge. Most of the knowledge hadn't made sense either, but he'd been able to figure out a lot of what he "knew" now about sigils, glyphs, and runes gradually, via trial and error.

He'd obviously still been missing a lot.

In Trav's mind's eye, he could see a large number of rune equations spread out, then two to four runes above each, with even more runes spread about above each of those. When he examined one of them more closely, he thought he knew what they were for. Each rune equation created permanent power within any object he installed them on. Some notes in his head explained the process of creating a nigh-invincible suit of armor that had both offensive and defensive capabilities built in.

"Wow," Trav breathed. This usage of runes appeared scary-powerful but also would require a massive amount of magic to achieve. The suit of armor example had a rune chain so long Trav couldn't bear to look at it. Some of the effects were truly jaw-dropping, though...like flight, and the ability to block all damage. With unlimited power, someone with rune knowledge could make a weapon that could crush mountains.

The rangy man looked up at the shadowed ceiling of the cave, crevices like black veins in the dim light. He needed to think. Narnaste's soft snoring actually had a calming effect, which was strange. He still wasn't sure that he trusted her—she was Kin after all—but other than Beth, she had probably been his greatest ally for the last three years. Their bond was weird. If his instincts were right, she would have a more magical power than before now, and it was because of her bond with Trav. She might sense that if she killed him, she might lose her new power.

Trav hated the Kin, hated them with a passion. They'd brought nothing but misery and heartache to his life for the last three years. Narnaste was just as alien as the rest of them, but...he'd fought with her, and she owed him as much as he owed her. The troll would have killed either of them if they'd been alone.

The link he'd placed on her moved energy mostly in one direction, the power flowing one way. He examined the bond again, his fingers tracing the lines on his chest. Something was weird; he'd been right before. He felt some sort of resonance, and Narnaste's power definitely felt greater than it had been.

Actually, that thought led to the troubling implications he'd been avoiding for a long time but really needed to think about now. Why could he even sense magic or do magic in the first place? The answer was both obvious and meaningless: the Voice.

All the uncertainty about everything—being transported to Asgard, sensing magic, understanding runes, and hearing the Voice—

all of it still had no answers, but he knew the Voice had to be involved. For a while, he'd worried the Voice was a Kin, or an evil alien or spirit, but over the years, it really had proved itself an ally of sorts.

At first, he'd thought the Voice might have actually transported him to Asgard or been responsible for it, but while it never seemed to give straight answers, he'd heard enough over time that he did not believe that anymore.

Some of the first nonsensical ramblings by the Voice Trav had ever heard were actually starting to make sense now. Rebirth had been mentioned at one point. Trav was scared to admit it, but he knew he hadn't just picked up all of his knowledge and power from the ground. The Voice was riding shotgun in his head, and merging with him.

He, or it, the Voice had given Trav both knowledge and power. The man from Earth had just begun to understand how powerful whatever the Voice must have been before it had wound up muttering about forbidden lore in his head at random times over the years.

Trav understood the rune tree now, but for anyone or anything to use it to its full potential would require a massive amount of power. Each permanent rune would need a constant investment of magic to keep running. Before bonding with Narnaste, Trav would have never been able to make any of it work.

Even beyond the power, his new bond with Narnaste worried him. Trav had slept with her, which he refused to beat himself up over, but his willingness to even do so in the first place had been strange. Sure, he found her attractive, well, smoking hot in a punk-rock-chick-with-a-tail sort of way. He also liked that thing she did with her—he shook his head. No, he had to think. Why had he just gone with the flow?

He'd been high on adrenaline before, but that still didn't really explain why he'd banged a monster girl in a cave. He'd just felt...drawn to her in a way he could admit now, but still didn't understand.

The odd, growing connection between them was undeniable, and Trav didn't really want to acknowledge any of it, but this wouldn't be the first time he'd had to stare harsh reality in the face.

With slight apprehension, he dove back into his alien knowledge, examining the rune equation he'd used on Narn and pondering its creation with the benefit of his newfound magical enlightenment. Then his eyes widened. His understanding of the bond before had been incomplete. "I get it now," he whispered.

The rune equation he'd placed on Narn had been a bond of master and servant. It worked mainly as a self-sustaining tracking link, to either find a servant or allow a servant to also feel their master's presence. The transference of power would be minor at this stage, but if the servant performed an act of fealty with the master of the bond, choosing to deepen it...

"How much power do the Kin have?" Trav marveled. *He'd opened the escape tunnel with a "minor" amount of power?*

So now he knew where his new power came from, but he still didn't know what to do with it. One thing was for sure—he needed to act, not sit around getting lost in memories. Even though he was fairly certain now that Narnaste wouldn't turn on him, at least not immediately, there could be another troll around...or worse.

The only weapon Trav possessed was the crude shiv, and he'd already turned it into a sigil tool. It was too small to really do anything else with, and he couldn't imagine investing so much power into such a crappy weapon anyway. No, he needed something better to enchant.

He didn't have anything else, though.

Trav sat on the stony ground, brainstorming what to do. With just the dim light on the floor that he'd made, the dark seemed to press in closer every minute that went by. Finally, when he happened on a solution, he quickly went through his rune knowledge and skimmed it to see if his idea was even possible, but he found...nothing. There wasn't a single thing in his forbidden knowledge about his idea at all.

"Weird," he mumbled. Maybe his plan was impossible, or maybe it would kill him, but Trav had already decided in the mines earlier that now was the time to stop playing it safe. There were still a lot of things he wanted to do in life and one psychotic Kin in particular that he needed to kill. He wouldn't be alive to do any of it if the next troll to come by bit his head off like had happened to poor Asta.

His plan decided on, Trav just needed to choose the right rune. He delved into his encyclopedic knowledge, looking over each rune equation with a critical eye. The paths he could take to evolve the overall rune chain in the future would be critically important...if he managed to live that long. Finally, he settled on, "Overall Strength," a complex rune equation that offered a larger number of less powerful benefits than some of the others. It would be a good experiment, and would also allow for some really amazing future evolutions along its possible branches, whatever rune chain Trav created.

The man in tattered clothing gritted his teeth, located his shiv where it had fallen to the ground earlier, and lifted his shirt. He brushed the weapon off as best he could on his tattered clothing. Then, with more concentration than he'd ever spent on anything in his life, he used his makeshift knife to carve the rune equation into his body below the one over his heart.

The entire process took a great deal of time, but Trav didn't rush it. The burning lines on his skin actually felt cool, at odds with the heat of his shiv as it cut him. He knew that a single mistake could mean permanent disfigurement or worse. There was no guarantee that the rune equation would work in the first place—Trav's alien knowledge had been remarkably silent about permanent upgrades directly to a body.

He'd been shocked when he'd verified that earlier, especially since his trove of information included other ways to increase a fighter's strength, or even infect their blood, but he was sure of it. There was nothing about physical modification. Trav really hoped that his idea wouldn't kill him, but he'd run out of options. To survive, and perhaps to dig his way to safety, being the same as he had been a day ago would not cut it.

Sure, he could have used his new power to open a tunnel to the surface, but then what? There might be a way to use drawn rune equations to kill, or to protect himself, but during a fight? No way. Asgard was a dangerous world, and Trav refused to be a slave any longer.

Finally, he completed his work. After gently investing power into the new rune equation, which took a while because it required so much, he activated it and tied it to the line of magic flowing from Narnaste. Nothing happened for a few seconds, and the former handyman smiled grimly, accepting that the process had not worked. Then, suddenly, his entire body arched with suffering, filled with every pain he'd ever experienced, but all at once.

The feeling overwhelmed him, and he could not even open his mouth to scream. His body felt like it was on fire, like he'd just been skinned and thrown into a pile of salt. He couldn't breathe, only...exist, one agonizing second after another. Finally, it all became too much to bear, and he passed out.

When Trav awoke, he could taste blood in his mouth, and he definitely felt weird. He sat up, rubbing his head, and slowly turned to see a pair of luminous, glowing eyes staring at him from a few feet away in the dark.

Normally, he might have been alarmed, but too much had happened to him to react that way anymore, and he was feeling strange, so he just stared back. Eventually, Narnaste crossed her arms across her naked chest and bowed her head. She slowly moved to prostrate herself and bowed again. Her voice full of joy, she said, "I can feel it for sure, it's stronger now. The divine!" She moaned in happiness and looked up, her eyes full of an emotion that Trav couldn't place. "The High Masters have returned! The Faithful stand ready!"

Trav adjusted his sitting position off of a sore point and rested his hands behind him. He was still groggy from waking up and definitely felt odd. He frowned and blinked. "What?"

"My Lord, thank you for returning to us! Some of us, the Faithful, have prepared! We serve." Then Narnaste lowered her forehead to the floor, her arms extended.

Okay, that just happened, Trav thought. He had no idea what Narnaste meant but could figure out that she was not going to kill him. That was good. She seemed to have also accepted their master-servant bond. But in a really strange way. Honestly, her submission, her beauty, and the fact that he'd just had sex with her hours ago all combined to excite him again, but he ignored it. His brain was in charge, not his dick.

The unsteady man got up and began getting dressed. Narn still knelt, and after Trav was done, he shook his head at the kneeling wolf girl.

"What is going on?" he wondered out loud. Then he facepalmed, realizing the simple answer to his question. He could just ask.

Suddenly, a buzzing filled Trav's mind combined with a pulling sensation. Something was beckoning him, and it felt like it might be nearby. The Voice muttered,

Yes! Go!

Trav placed both hands on his face for a moment before sighing. Everything seemed to be happening all at once, but he was still alive and wanted to stay that way. The Voice hadn't steered him wrong before, so it'd be stupid to ignore it now. He definitely needed more information, though.

"Narnaste, I think we need to have a talk."

Chapter 8

Moving through the cave took time. Being ambushed by another troll would be bad, so Trav methodically drew light-casting glyph equations at regular intervals, even placing extra ones before bends. Narnaste followed without complaining, and every time he turned, he caught her studying him. If she'd been a human woman, the open staring might have been less unnerving.

As Trav drew yet another light sigil, he wondered if he should use some of his new power to make a sigil lantern. Before his...transformation, he hadn't had enough power to even try it. Now that he could, he'd been putting it off because such a thing would constantly draw magical energy while in use. The problem was, he wasn't sure if his new power would regenerate, or if he should save it all.

He studied the wall for a while before nodding. The future wouldn't matter if he died today, and they were moving way too slowly right now through the tunnel. He had chosen to move in the opposite direction that the troll had come from, hoping they'd find a way to escape the tunnel—the weird pull he'd felt ever since he'd rune-modified himself led this direction, too.

His decision made, Trav searched around for a flat stone about the size of his palm, then, after a moment's hesitation, he located another. Narnaste squatted and watched silently as Trav used his shiv to inscribe a variation of the light sigils he'd been drawing earlier. Once he got done with both, he said, "Give me a finger."

With a completely different attitude than when they'd first met, Narnaste made a face, shrugged, and offered her clawed hand. Trav channeled a tiny bit of energy through his blade while touching one rock before raising the shiv above the Kin woman's finger. She said, "Oh, blood," and pulled her hand away to nip her finger, then placed it back in Trav's hand.

The bearded man raised his eyebrows before shrugging and let a drop of the woman's blood fall on the shiv. Once the tip was wet, he used it to make one last line on the stone. "Done," he said. "If you will the stone to come alive, it will glow. It can be turned off the same way. You can will it to dim or brighten as long as it's close enough, but it will draw more power from you the brighter it shines."

Narnaste's expression seemed to be equal parts bemusement and awe before she held her stone and gently brought it to life. The flat rock acted like a powerful flashlight that she shined ahead, moving it from side to side. She turned her head, eyes wide, and whispered, "I have never seen such a thing. Even the sigil masters in the great cities can't do this." She bowed her head. "Divine, I apologize for doubting you. Please forgive me for my anger before, and my arrogance for plying you with this body."

Trav coughed and busied himself fixing his own glyph lantern. His shiv really needed a cleaning. It had been covered in troll blood, and God knew what else, but being a rune tool, at least it would be magically sterile. Trav raised a lip in distaste as he nicked himself to finish the sigil equation. Since he was expecting it, he felt the connection establish, then willed his lantern to cast a soft glow. The resulting energy loss would have been worrying the day before, but now he knew he could maintain the draw for a full day without a problem.

His lantern complete, Trav said, "Speaking of which, we still need to have our talk. I need to ask you some questions."

"I will answer."

Trav eyed the Kin woman, but she had already begun sweeping her light back and forth, leading the way but following his direction, somewhat like a guard dog. The dirty man shook his head. "Okay, before anything else, the most obvious question is why you are following me now. In the mine, you were ready to kill me. I am a slave, and you are Kin, and you're a noblewoman too, right? Please explain what changed, and be thorough. I will listen. Also, let's take a right at this fork up ahead." Trav let the phantom pulling sensation guide him. On his own, he probably would not have followed it, but he trusted the Voice.

Narnaste nodded, then said, "Yes, Lord, but if we are to talk, we should keep our voices down in case there are more Wild Ones nearby."

"Oh yeah, that makes sense," Trav said softly. He still wasn't sure why she was calling him Lord, but he would find out soon enough. With the sigil lanterns, moving was faster and safer now, so other than periodically sweeping his light to the rear, ensuring nothing could sneak up on them in the dark, he focused on Narnaste's explanation.

She said, "When we first met, I thought you were just a human. Unlike many other Kin, I do not hate humans; they are just not important to me. I do not believe that humans were responsible for the disappearance of the High Masters."

"High Masters?" Trav asked.

"You might call them gods. Members of The Faithful, like me, feel the concept is too limited."

Trav sighed. "This conversation is going to go nowhere fast if you keep using obviously capitalized names that I've never heard before. Just assume I know nothing and explain everything."

"How do you know nothing, Lord? You are a High Master. It's unmistakable. You are also a greater sigil crafter than the most talented line mages on Asgard. Are you teasing me?"

The tall, scruffy man eyed the Kin woman while deciding how to answer. Not for the first time, he felt thankful that he'd been able to learn the language of Asgard so quickly. What Narnaste had just said had been fairly complex in the Asgard language.

Trav had never been all that great with languages before, and he could only assume that the Voice had helped him learn. This theory was backed up by how at times he had randomly seemed to understand a word even if he hadn't heard it before. It also helped explain his quick realization that the Kin spoke differently than the slaves, using different words and grammar. Trav decided to switch to the more formal Kin way of speaking during this conversation and confirm a suspicion before continuing.

"Narnaste, can you sense whether someone is telling the truth when they speak?"

The beautiful, inhuman woman narrowed her eyes and glanced at him before searching the way ahead again. "Yes," she said.

So much for High Master or Lord, thought Trav with a hidden grin. It didn't take a genius to figure out the scarred Kin was still keeping secrets. *That's fine,* he thought. Out loud he said, "Asgard is not my homeworld. I came to this one about three years ago." He waited for the Kin woman to react, and when she didn't, he said, "You suspected?"

"I knew. If the Kin in charge of the slaves were not so stupid and blind, they could have figured it out too. You have a strange accent, stand differently, possess more self-confidence, speak more intelligently, and you have the aura of a High Master. I didn't know what it was when I first met you, but now it is obvious. Well, the feeling is still rather weak, but close to you, it is plain if I allow myself to search for it.

"Beyond that, the signs are all there for one who knows them. One prophecy of the High Masters is that upon their return, they will be changed, arriving from other worlds."

Trav frowned. "You can feel something from me? Are you

sensitive to this sort of thing?"

"Yes. Which is probably another reason you remained undiscovered for so long. If your captors had found out, the Dacith might have just torn you apart. At the very least, you would have been taken to the High Lords and given a trial."

"Then what?"

"You would have been executed."

That aligned with what Trav already knew. The Kin leaders would kill humans for just being in the wrong place at the wrong time—like had happened to Beth. High-level Kin did whatever they wanted—Trav had seen evidence of that. He felt the deep, ugly hatred well up inside and struggled to suppress it.

His new power responded to the dark emotion, swelling, growing. Trav felt a murderous desire to lash out, to manifest his anger on the world. Narnaste glanced at him warily, probably feeling at least something from him. The gesture helped Trav get himself back under control. This was not a game, his magic was real, and losing control would probably be a bad thing. He focused on breathing slowly, reminding himself that everything had its own time, even revenge.

Once his burst of rage had been quelled, and he was back under control, Trav asked, "Okay, fine, but what is all this 'Faithful' stuff?"

Narnaste shrugged uncomfortably, and Trav tried not to notice the interesting way it made her chest move—now was not the time for those sorts of thoughts, either. The Kin woman said, "I would never have revealed myself to you if you were not a High Master. The Faithful are not...popular now among the Kin. The popular thought among most Kin of Asgard is that the High Masters abandoned us or were killed somehow by human treachery. The Church of Self has more or less seized control of the three Kin countries. The Faithful exist in secret now, but we have known that, eventually, the High Masters would return."

Trav thought he understood—Narnaste was in some sort of fringe religion or at least adhered to an old, unpopular way of thinking. He said, "That makes sense, but now what? What do you want with me?"

"I cannot force you to do anything. I am just a woman, not a Crafter, but I am not ignorant. The bond between us is of master and servant, which I was at peace with even before discovering your true nature. However, I request you make your way to a hidden town of the Faithful. I can lead you there. Of course, I will follow and assist you. The Faithful will help you reclaim your rightful position."

Trav said, "What about the slaves? I have been helping them for years. Actually, wait." He thought about how the mine had been collapsed. Perhaps the Kin would even start a mine somewhere else. Actually, if he had to leave, this would be the perfect time to do it, at least from the perspective of not bringing more hardship on the other slaves.

As he thought through the last day or so, Trav actually realized something. Narnaste probably didn't actually know how he'd killed the troll. After they'd woken up and she'd announced he was a High Master, she'd been taking a lot of things on faith or just rolling with the punches, which seemed to fit the fact that she was having a religious moment.

Narnaste was keeping things to herself as well, so Trav decided not to tell her about his ability to touch emberstone. He decided to be honest about his motivation, though. "I want to kill one of your High Lords, I think. The Kin fucker that killed my wife."

"You had a wife, a slave?" The canine woman pursed her lips and said, "The High Lords are very, very powerful. Which one do you wish revenge on?" Trav told her, and Narnaste's face fell. "Yes, he is one of the cruelest, and also not to be trifled with. You are not ready to face him."

"I know that."

"Yes, I can tell," said Narnaste, nodding in approval. Trav didn't know what she'd meant at first until he remembered her truth-sensing ability. She said, "Now, Lord, I must ask, do you know where we are going?"

"Not really, but I've been following a pull. I think this is the right way to go."

"Ah, I see." Narnaste focused on lighting the way and didn't say more. Trav could tell she didn't understand and wondered how often in her life she had just had to trust that others could see or hear things she couldn't. A normal Kin person's life must be very strange at times.

Trav shook his head. No, he refused to think of Kin as people. They were monsters, all of them. Narnaste was an ally, and Trav would think of her as such unless she turned on him, but it would be wise not to forget what she was. Now that he was changed, he didn't feel physically outclassed anymore. Of course, the muscular man couldn't know for certain how much more powerful he was now, but he could sense that the change had been significant.

The pulling sensation grew stronger as he walked with Narnaste in silence. He activated his emberstone eye a few times, but the glyph lamps were so good, he couldn't really see that much better with the eye, and so he just turned it off. There was no reason to risk tipping off Narnaste to the eye if he didn't have to.

The pulling sensation got even stronger as the tunnel widened into what seemed to be a large cave. Suddenly, lights flared all around, and Trav partially shielded his eyes, ready for an attack. Narnaste growled next to him, probably doing the same. An attack never came. Trav strained his ears, listening for any signs of danger. After his eyes adjusted, he breathed out in wonder.

"Wow." Trav hadn't been sure where the pulling would lead him, but he definitely hadn't been expecting this—a temple of sorts.

Narnaste gasped. "A memory shrine!" she exclaimed. "I've never even seen one before in person! I can't believe we found one!"

"A what?"

"Come see!" said the Kin woman, bounding forward.

Trav suspiciously glanced around first, but then he shrugged, following the shapely Kin woman forward. Despite his recent changes, he assumed that Narnaste still had better senses than he did. But just in case she wasn't paying attention, he gripped the shiv in his pocket tightly and warily walked towards the old, stone building in the middle of the subterranean cavern.

Chapter 9

The temple was not large, but the closer he got, Trav had to privately admit that it was impressive. Each pillar had been carved with such detail; he could see individual facial features on each fighter in large, disturbing battle scenes. Men, Kin, unidentifiable things, and huge nightmarish creatures all fought each other to the death on a field under a lightning sky.

"I bet that wouldn't be fun," he muttered.

After he climbed up the steps and entered the open area inside, Trav stopped and looked around. The memory shrine was definitely not what he'd been expecting. The inside was all one bare room except for a pedestal with a dark, almost black sphere in the center. The globe had at least some translucency, weirdly distorting the light passing through it.

Four large doors led inside, and Trav had a feeling based on the knowledge in his head that they probably corresponded to the four cardinal directions on Asgard. In fact, as he took another hesitant step inside and noticed that the walls were made of what looked like white marble with gold crown molding, something triggered his alien memories and rune knowledge. Narnaste slowly walked forward near the center of the room and the pedestal, almost in a trance.

Trav felt a burst of adrenaline and a sense of dread. "Get back here," he whispered as loudly as he could. Narnaste kept moving forward, her hand extended. "You stupid Kin! No! Stop that, you idiot!" Trav pulled his hair and shifted weight, from foot to foot, trying to decide whether to run or dash forward.

Every instinct he had screamed at him.

Narnaste touched the sphere.

Instantly, the room lit up like a department store back on Earth, all white, sterile light. "Oh shit!" muttered Trav, and took a step back, but the area behind him, filling the doorway, was now hazy and as solid as concrete.

A pulse of lavender light shot around the circumference of the room before doing a spiral along the floor, even passing under Trav's feet before eventually running up the pillar, making the globe glow. Narnaste jerked her hand as if it had been burned, jumping back to land in a crouch, issuing a feral growl.

The atmosphere of the room grew more dangerous as Narnaste turned, her unfocused eyes landing on Trav. Lips pulled back, the Kin woman bared her teeth. Lithe, powerful muscles in her limbs tensed.

Something inside Trav snapped into place. Even after being a slave to inhuman monsters for three years, the only day worse than this one had been when his wife had been murdered. This day, well, maybe two days, had been a really shitty day among an endless parade of really shitty days. On top of everything that had happened, even witnessing poor Asta get eaten alive by a troll, now the Kin woman he'd just slept with was looking like she might attack him? *Oh hell no,* he thought.

"Stand down, woman!" Trav heard his own voice crack out with such authority, he almost didn't recognize himself. As soon as he'd spoken, all of the tension in Narnaste's limbs vanished, and she blinked owlishly. She glanced back in confusion, then terror, and scrambled over to Trav, hiding behind him. "What were you thinking?" Trav hissed.

"Something—something is making thinking hard. The power, it's too much!" she muttered, her voice slurred. Up close, now Trav could see how dilated her pupils were. The Kin woman was sweating bullets.

In the center of the room, the globe pulsed, its lavender light growing brighter. Thinking fast, Trav drew his shiv and tried scribing a quick glyph equation that would erode a hole in the wall, but as he drew, no lines appeared. "What the—" he muttered. The light in the globe grew brighter and all around the room, runes began to flash.

Despite himself, Trav took a step back. He turned to the distressed Kin woman next to him, and asked, "What did you call this? A memory shrine?"

Narnaste seemed to have regained more of her senses. She nodded. "What is it for?"

"I don't exactly know, I just know they are sacred. Relics of the High Masters. Nobody I know has ever seen one in person. Only one or two have been found, but they are said to be very powerful. I've only seen drawings, and that was only when I was with other Faithful. They are holy places. I don't know what is happening!"

"Oh great," said Trav. "Just wonderful." He turned to fully face the center of the room, watching all the runes appear, running in rings around the walls. He was only half surprised that he could actually understand what they meant, and what was happening.

"Oh wow," he breathed. Whoever had set this building up, had really known what they were doing.

After another few breaths, the entire building flashed with runes from top to bottom, and the crystal globe in the center of the room exploded in light. Trav shielded his eyes while Narnaste cried out in terror. Without thinking, Trav dropped a hand, resting it reassuringly on the crouching Kin's head.

When the light faded, Trav exhaled in startlement. A woman stood before him, armored from head to toe, her fierce, inhuman gaze directed fully at him. Every bit of her body glowed lavender, and she seemed somewhat translucent, almost like a hologram. She wore a round shield on one arm and held a spear in her other hand, butt on the ground like she was about to give judgement.

Red sigils glowed at each corner of the temple. The room pulsed with runes and lavender light as the armored woman spoke. "Announcement: Name Amain. Returning directive, prime function. State passkey or be eradicated."

The world seemed to shrink for Trav and then turn sideways. The next thing he knew, he was standing in a featureless void, facing an old, scarred, one-eyed man. When the man spoke, Trav immediately recognized his voice. All the sourceless mutterings in his head for the last three years, the Voice...how could he mistake it for anything else?

"We finally meet, boy."

"Boy?" Despite the strangeness of the situation, Trav refused to be talked down to. Not now, not after surviving the mines as a slave. Now that he was free, he wasn't taking anyone's shit ever again.

The stranger smiled, showing his teeth, the expression right between friendly and predatory. "Save the fire, boy. I'm here to help you. In fact, I have spent a great deal of time and effort to be here."

Trav decided not to play coy. "When you spoke before, I could barely understand you most of the time. Why are you suddenly not only actually understandable, but also appearing to me like this, and stopping time or something? I really doubt that our little conversation here is real. Out there, or wherever I actually am, I was in a bad situation."

The bearded, weathered old man, dressed in furs, reached up under his eye patch to scratch his socket. "You wandered into enough energy for me to steal some, and get some of my mind back. Besides, what's real, boy? If information, if knowledge is accurate, does it matter how you get it? What is real to one person may not be real to another. All that should matter to you is the truth. Barring that, all you should care about is the truth you can impose with your will."

After thinking about what he'd just heard, blinking, Trav scoffed, "That was some obvious bullshit dressed up like sage wisdom. Who the hell are you?"

The man laughed, a real belly laugh this time, and his single eye twinkled. "That's perfect! I don't generally make mistakes, but it is still good to see proof that I chose well."

By this point, Trav had a good idea what had happened. Talking to Narnaste earlier had given him the last few pieces of the puzzle. "So you are a god, right?"

"Correct."

"Who are you? Why are you in my head?"

"I have had many names, boy. And—"

Trav held up a hand. "That's evasive. Name."

The god's eye narrowed and his mouth firmed. "I can tolerate a bit of cheek, but you should still offer some respect."

"Bullshit. I just spent three years as a fucking slave and got to watch my wife die while I was powerless to do anything. The best I've been able to do is bust my ass working so other people wouldn't die doing the same thing. All this knowledge, probably your knowledge, has been in my head but I haven't been able to use most of it. Heck, I haven't even seen most of it. My life has been hell. For you to be in my head in the first place, you need me, and last I checked, I'm a freed slave with a half-crazy, horny Kin woman. I am wearing rags, armed with a shitty knife, and about to be destroyed by some glowing armored woman. I don't exactly have a lot to lose."

"That is fair, and not incorrect. However, you don't know the full scope of—"

"Name," growled Trav. "Start. With. Your. Fucking. Name."

"So stubborn," sighed the old god. "I hope it serves you better than it did Loki. Fine, I have truly been known by many names and titles, but as you have pointed out, the last of my consciousness has been sustained by you. I know you far better than you know me at this point. The name you would best know me by is Odin."

"I see." Trav hadn't exactly been a scholar back on Earth, but he had a good memory. It wasn't like the name of the father of the Norse gods had been obscure. In fact, now he felt stupid. He'd literally lived on Asgard for years now as a slave but had never recognized the name of the world he'd been imprisoned on until now.

Odin nodded. "Yes, I see that you do. Time is short. I need to make this quick, and I have much to say. This will probably be the last time I am ever able to speak to you like this."

"Why?"

"Because I'm dead, or at least, about to be! All things come to an end, boy. The fact I was able to make it this far to pass on my knowledge to you was only through great sacrifices and a bit of luck on my part."

"What happened?" asked Trav.

"Second Ragnarok."

The chill that Trav got was more due to echoes from his borrowed memories and second-hand knowledge than any half-remembered mythology from Earth. He got the point, though. "All right. Talk."

"Good. You are my adopted son in every way that matters. I will die, but I have chosen you to carry on my legacy."

"Why me?" Trav crossed his arms.

"I thought you were going to let me talk."

"Sure, sure."

Odin harrumphed and continued, "I chose you because there was nobody else. Or at least, my auguries told me that you were the best option for my goals. Reaching you would be risky, but traveling to a specific time and place would allow me to find the best candidate to accept this birthright—you! Before you ask, I will answer—I did not bring you to this world, and I had nothing to do with that. Instead, I took advantage of your transition as a doorway, using the last of my energy to attach my spirit to your soul."

Trav thought that sounded fairly disturbing, but realized he could sense Odin's sincerity. He also reasoned that their link probably went both ways, so Odin would likely be aware of what other things Trav would want to know. He kept his mouth shut and listened.

Odin gave him a look of approval and said, "Fire is good, but is vastly better when tempered by wisdom and action. You truly were the best choice. I am content with this."

The old god slowly shook his head. "Endings are strange, even to one such as I who will never truly, completely die. At least I am able to pass on my knowledge. You are my adopted son, family in every way that matters. You did not choose this burden, but now that we can properly have this talk, and before we can continue, you must make your choice.

"If you choose my mantle, you will face great hardship and danger. You will inherit old enemies and make new ones simply due to who you are.

"If you reject this burden, I will simply die, or at least fade away.

The knowledge that I built over a thousand lifetimes will vanish with me, and the world will be both lighter and darker for it. Don't be mistaken, boy. I value power, knowledge, not good or evil. If you choose to follow my path, you will know terrible things, and will learn more of the same."

Without being told anything further, Trav understood. He truly grasped what was happening, that this was a test of sorts too. This was a choice between living or dying. Back on Earth, before Trav had been a slave, it wouldn't have seemed like much of a choice at all, but now, he knew there were worse things than death. While he thought, he met Odin's single eye with his own, and saw past the old god's persona, recognizing the ancient, inhuman being that truly stood before him.

Did he really want to accept Odin's legacy? There were sure to be strings attached. He didn't want to die either, that was for certain. If he rejected Odin and returned to his body from wherever he was now, he and Narnaste would still be in immediate danger.

Despite knowing what a serious burden it would probably be, Trav thought about the other aspects of accepting Odin's offer. The Kin monster that killed Beth still definitely needed to be put into the ground. Trav had to admit that the rune knowledge in his head was interesting, and he sensed that the wanderlust and curiosity that he'd felt his entire life was resonating with the presence of the god standing before him.

Finally, he asked, "I'm going to stay me, right? Like, I'm not going to just become you?"

Odin made another of his smiles with no humor. "If I could, I would take your life in a heartbeat, boy. I like you, son, but I want to live too. Luckily for you, I do not have that power—but then again, if I did, we would not be talking like this in the first place. The best I can do for you and for me is to attach pieces of myself to your soul to give brief guidance from time to time."

Trav frowned. "Then why do we even need to have this conversation?" He almost asked how he could trust anything Odin said, but then remembered their link. There would be no lies in this conversation.

"You may have been born only human, but you have a sharp mind, lad. The crux of it comes down to my blessing. Just like how you claimed your pet, but only her choice truly bonded her to you, I marked you, but you must choose to accept my legacy."

It took Trav a second to figure out that Odin had meant Narnaste when he'd said, "pet." That single throwaway comment also helped him realize what had truly happened between himself and the beautiful, scarred Kin woman. "So what about my lack of power?"

"You are not a god, well, not yet. It is your responsibility to discover how you will grow my legacy—if you accept it."

"No more freebies, huh?" muttered Trav. He thought about it some more. "What is the price? There is always a price."

"Indeed there is, and you have just proven yourself worthy of hearing it."

Trav frowned. "What does that mean? This part was a test too?"

"You know it was a test. We are inside your head, so I can see you thinking. You have merely proven yourself capable of shouldering my mantle."

"What does that mean?"

"Think about it. You will figure it out over time, I am sure. The price for my legacy is to carry on my work. You already have a spirit, a soul that corresponds to mine or we would not be speaking   none of this would have been possible. But if you accept this birthright, as I already said, you will inherit allies and enemies, and all of my knowledge, but also my drive—to learn, to rule, and to transcend!" The old man growled the last word.

"Transcend?" asked Trav.

"Yes. To become more. To see the other side. To know the unknowable. To collect the greatest secrets of the universe! Boy, you have already begun! You bear an emberstone eye!" Odin lifted his eyepatch and showed what was underneath. Resting in the eye socket was a glinting silver object, and Trav recognized it was very similar to the red emberstone eye he'd placed in his own head.

"Emberstone? You too?"

Odin chuckled. "Boy, the depth of your ignorance still prevents you from knowing how truly ignorant you are. Emberstone is the lifeblood of Asgard, a tool of the gods. You will know more in time, but emberstone is tied to the Veil Gates and the rest of the Continuum! Only the gods or those touched by the gods can tolerate emberstone. The eye that I helped you fashion is a tool that can shake the heavens. You do not even know what rests in your head!"

Trav's eyebrows came together. "Well, that's because this is the first time in three years that you have spoken in full sentences!" he snapped. "I'm not an idiot. The fact that emberstone powers glyphs and magic just by being near is a big clue—that and only I could touch it." He sensed the darkness around them growing thin. "I can figure all this shit out later, though. What else did you have to tell me?"

Odin frowned and said, "Yes, yes, I am not great at maintaining a mortal perception of time. The price for my mantle is portions of your personality becoming stronger over time, more in line with the aspects of my divinity. You must accept this before we continue."

"A hard sell," growled Trav. He really gave the matter some thought, trying to remember everything he could about the myths of Odin from Earth. The king of the Norse gods had been sort of mysterious, right? Always wandering, pursuing his own, secret affairs. It wasn't a lot to go on. But ultimately, Trav needed to avenge Beth and to do that he needed to stay alive and seize every bit of power that he could.

Finally, he grated, "I accept."

"Good. Then I can burden you with truth that I have not told another soul. Asgard is in danger. Actually, all of the Continuum is."

"What?" Trav wasn't sure how to even start processing that.

"Asgard and the other realms connected to the World Tree already have their fair share of dangers. The Veil itself can destroy worlds. But, boy, the force that we met during Second Ragnarok, it is not dead. And over time, it will find its way here."

"What does that even mean?"

"With what I have told you, I have unlocked seals on my memory.

As you grow in power, you will understand further. Some of my memories must be relayed in their raw form, and you are not yet complex or strong enough to withstand them yet. Learning everything I know all at once will kill you.

You will receive pieces of my knowledge as you grow." Odin looked slightly apologetic. "This is a great deal to burden one such as you, one completely new to real power, but there is no choice. They come, and there will be no stopping them unless you tread my path and walk it well."

"Well, that is some unclear, cryptic-ass bullshit. Why not just say, 'The here is now, and now is here?'"

Odin grinned. "That is actually quite good! You should remember that one to tell mortals if you survive to live as long as I have."

Trav could tell the old god was needling him at this point. He could feel the darkness around them shrinking, and could sense that their time to talk was coming to a close. There were many more things he wanted to ask Odin, but holding all the god's important memories meant he would probably know everything in time—if he survived that long.

Odin smiled genuinely. "See, that is why I'm glad I was able to choose you. It would have been a shame for you to die on this world after only a few months, as was your original destiny. You have potential. I will help you activate the memory shrine that you found— that knowledge is at the front of your mind now. My parting advice is to search for more memory shrines. This one feels somewhat poor, but they will all offer assistance. I was one of my kind to prepare for this day."

"What exactly am I even supposed to be doing?"

"What do you want to do? This life, my drive, it is yours now, and your burden to bear!" Odin laughed. "Give them hell, boy! You now have my mark, and ownership of my darkest knowledge. Make sure to ask the shrine guardian for a signet ring, and use it on your little pet.

"That Kin woman, she would have gladly killed you before, but now she will gut your enemies instead. Treat your pet Kin, those loyal to you well, lad. We did them a great disservice, possibly greater than was done to your kind."

Odin began to fade, and Trav grunted in frustration. "I have more questions than answers now!"

"Life is hard, son. Fight!" Odin thundered.

The darkness around them turned upside down, and Trav suddenly found himself back in the temple, facing a glowing, angry, see-through, armored woman. Now he knew what the apparition was, though everything had changed. Trav was still himself, but he felt a depth that hadn't been there before.

He needed a plan, but first, he needed to give the scary armored lady the passkey she'd asked for so he and Narnaste wouldn't get fried.

Chapter 10

Trav fixed the armored woman with a steely glare. "You said your name was Amain, right?"

"Correct. This site is the domain of Vanir. Provide valid passcode or be eradicated."

Strange knowledge bubbled at the forefront of Trav's mind, and in a different language, he rattled off:

"Over hills and mountains distant, I seek the knowledge of a star.
If you stand before my way, I will destroy your body and soul.
Move aside or face the wrath of heaven, forked spears of light to burn you to ash.
The might of stars at my disposal, destruction is a truth of life, move aside."

In the language he'd spoken, the words he'd said rhymed and had flowed almost like a poem. Beside him, Narnaste gasped. Trav ignored her.

After standing still for a couple seconds, the lavender apparition seemed visibly shocked, taking a step back and briefly bowing. "Greetings, Lord. I have run additional tests based on your answer and verified your identity—apologies for my rudeness. Over the ages, this site has been attacked many times despite its remote location. Recently, one of the large local fauna—a troll—has assaulted this site multiple times with large stones after I eradicated one of its kin."

The information about the troll was interesting. "Do you know if there are any more trolls down here?"

"I do not have the capability of scanning the area, but I have only had encounters with one specimen over the last standard year."

"Oh, okay, I think I killed that one."

"Acknowledged, Lord."

Now Trav knew the purpose of the memory shrines—caches of the gods. This one was not directly affiliated with Odin, but the wily old man had hedged his bets, placing his mark on every temple in Asgard. It was time to find out what secrets this building held—Trav's knowledge still had gaping holes, and he wasn't sure how directly helpful this location would be. "What assistance can you offer?" he asked.

The construct, Amain, knocked her spear against the floor, and a wave of lighted runes spread out until they hit the wall. She stood still and said, "Processing." Then she answered, "Power and raw material are low, but I can offer several basic items at your request. I can also give you appropriate clothing for the era, surrounding culture and climate, and a basic-level Aesir weapon."

"Basic level?"

"Yes, Lord. This memory shrine is remote and was not intended specifically for your use. I was placed at this location due to the nearby emberstone. It was unlikely but possible that the Aesir or Vanir might happen by. If you request emberstone, I apologize, but I do not have much to spare."

"That's fine, just give me what you have. In fact, I'd like to take everything I can. For basic items, I need a pack, basic traveling gear, a change of clothes or two, a change of clothes for the Kin woman here, and anything else I can get for a long journey."

The woman paused, thinking, and with his unlocked knowledge, Trav knew she was accessing her memory banks, doing calculations. The glowing woman was an admin spirit, like the magical version of an artificial intelligence. Memory shrines were like rune-driven computers created by the gods, failsafes in case of Ragnarok, the end of the world. The gods had probably never suspected that they would have two Ragnarok events, both far off-world.

The AI, Amain, finally looked up and said, "I can do that for you, Lord. Is there anything else? If not, I will need to power down to conserve energy."

"Why? Isn't there emberstone nearby?"

"Yes, but generating resources is very energy-intensive, and I will need to recharge my reserves."

"I understand," said Trav. "What about a weapon for my companion here?" He pointed at the wide-eyed Narnaste. "Something simple would be fine."

"Would a steel seax suffice?"

"Yes. Oh, and I need a signet ring and a medallion too. What they are made of doesn't matter."

"Sized for your wear?" asked Amain.

"Yes."

"So be it."

The entire room flashed brilliant white, and Trav covered his eyes with an arm. After a few moments, the room was mostly dark again like it had been before, except for a single, glowing rune in the corner, providing a bit of light.

"Thank you, Amain," he said. The light seemed to flicker in response. Trav walked to another corner of the room where a pile of items had appeared. On the way, he heard a thump and turned to see that Narnaste had fallen to her knees. "What are you doing?"

Narnaste slowly lifted her head and said, "You have truly returned. One of the High Masters has come back to us. Thank you. I believed, or at least I tried to, but I never—" She trailed off.

Trav didn't know how to respond to that, so he gruffly said, "Get up and come over here. Let's get geared up. I need to ask you some more questions—I think I might have a plan."

"Anything, Lord."

"Don't call me that. Call me Trav."

"Anything you say, Lord Trav."

The dirty man sighed and said, "Just tell me more about this hidden town of the Faithful you mentioned before. Also, where is the other memory shrine that you know of."

Trav used his sigil lantern for more light and began examining the loot that Amain had left for him. He almost wept when he saw the new clothes. Rustic or not—clothes!

He changed, listening carefully to Narnaste, and a detailed plan began to grow in his head.

***

The mental pull from the memory shrine had disappeared. Newly dressed and armored, Trav looked down at himself as he left the temple behind. Now he wore rough but serviceable clothing, looking somewhat like the best-dressed humans on Asgard he'd ever seen. A thin, chainmail vest provided some protection on top of his plain tunic. He'd received a cloak and a shirt that could go over the armor too, but he didn't need them now and had stored them in his new pack.

The pack itself looked like leather from the outside, but it was not an ordinary tool. It could easily expand to fit more inside. Narnaste had insisted on carrying it. At her side, she carried her new weapon, a steel seax, the blade's straight blade safely held in a thick leather sheath.

Trav had a new spear. The weapon looked like a finely crafted steel weapon, but he knew better. Even a basic weapon of the gods would be extraordinary by mortal standards.

The tired man walked silently for some time, lost in thought, and Narnaste left him alone. Now that his mind had expanded, he could use his emberstone eye to see telltale marks in the cave wall, noting an exit. The eye itself felt stranger now too. Hot. Trav could tell that things were changing within him. It wasn't like he could do anything about it now, though.

Instead, he contemplated his new signet ring. The unidentified silver metal was blank, just like the new necklace he wore, but Trav knew he could touch it with his imprinted shiv to burn his mark into it, leaving a tiny bit of his newfound power inside. If he did so, he'd be able to use the ring for mystical things, like further binding Narnaste—but he wasn't in a hurry.

Going that route would require fully embracing his role as...whatever he was. Now that he was past the heat of the moment, and had had some time to think about his meeting with Odin, Trav felt a little overwhelmed. The implications of what he'd been told were staggering.

Luckily, at least he had a plan now. He turned to Narnaste and said, "How far away is this Faithful village again?"

"Bruman is about two weeks away, Great One."

"Don't call me that or Lord."

"Yes, Holy One."

Trav gritted his teeth and spun, grabbing Narnaste by the shoulder. He moved her to fully face him and his single, uncovered eye blazed as he grated, "You are following the letter, but not the spirit of my request. Scratch that, it's not a request, that was an order."

The Kin woman's eyes widened, and her bottom lip trembled. She seemed torn between anger and fear. Her natural unease at taking orders from a human was probably warring with her religious convictions and the connection that she had with Trav now. A hand began drifting down to her side, toward her seax, but the tall, bearded man from Earth searched his borrowed memories and snarled, "You will follow, little wolf. This situation was as much your choice as mine. I can compel you using our bond, but that would ruin you. However, if you will not even follow my wishes about this, I have zero reason to believe you will listen to me about anything else."

"I don't want to cause any offense or disrespect," said Narnaste. Her damaged ear quivered.

Trav thought back to how Kin he'd watched before had always required their human slaves to address them. "Fine," he said. "You will call me Master, or Master Trav, then."

The bestial woman's mouth gaped open for a second, showing her fangs, but she closed it with a snap. She was silent for a moment, before quietly replying, "Yes, Master."

"How disgraceful," said a new voice from the darkness. Trav and Narnaste both spun, and the Kin woman began growling deep in her throat. From beyond the pool of light cast by the glyph torches, four Kin walked forward.

Two in the back were Dacith, chittering to each other and staring hungrily at Trav. Their rat-like faces bunched up, showing sharp front teeth, and their beady eyes glittered. One of the two Kin in front looked like a huge, muscled man with a goat head. He wore armor and was practically covered in weapons.

The last Kin, also male, had three yellow eyes, a too-large mouth with pointed teeth, and a forked tongue. He stared at the canine Kin at Trav's side and said, "Narnaste, we meet again. If I had not witnessed that little scene, I would have never believed that you would ever turn traitor...but here we are. As you probably know, you have to die now. Obviously, if I didn't already hate you, I'd probably take a payment, perhaps even your body, but that path is closed. This is actually great luck. I can take care of you; I'm sure I'll be praised, maybe even given a promotion!"

The four new Kin moved forward, and Trav gripped his spear.

Chapter 11

Before he'd been a slave, prior to all the painful, terrible lessons he'd endured, Trav might have taken a step back. However, he was different now, free. More importantly, his body still burned with magic power, and he currently held a real weapon for the first time on Asgard. "Who are these chucklefucks?" he asked Narnaste, the last word in English.

"The one with three eyes is Fodrik Prirbani. He tried to wed me; his family has money, but no legitimacy. Luckily, my family is not useless and cruel like the Prirbanis, so my father actually consulted with me and refused. Fodrik did not want to take no for an answer and tried to kidnap me. After I fought him off and left him with three black eyes, he made himself scarce for a while. It's safe to say he's hated me ever since then."

The three-eyed Kin man bared his sharp teeth and hissed, "That was years ago. You may find that things have changed now, bragging, human-loving whore." The insult had been in the Asgard language, and Trav narrowed his eyes at how harsh the words had come. There was definitely no love lost between these two.

Narnaste ignored the slur but didn't take her eyes off of the advancing Kin. She continued sideways to Trav. "Quite a few have wondered how his family has stayed in power—Fodrik in particular. Some Kin that opposed this piece of dung over the last few years have disappeared. I guess we just stumbled upon how that has happened. Murderer," she spat directly at her old foe.

Fodrik narrowed all three of his eyes. "After the attack, when the order came last night for our generation to take Dacith and round up lost human slaves, I'd taken it as an opportunity to check my caves here. Who would have known that I would have received such a blessing from the Dead Masters!"

"High Masters," corrected Narnaste, showing her fangs.

As the menacing group prowled closer, the Dacith moved up front, their eyes boring holes into Trav. The horrible, vermin-like creatures trembled in excitement, their hand-paws making grasping motions.

Behind them, Fodrik chuckled and said, "I always suspected you were one of the Faithful, Narnaste, but even I would never have guessed you were a traitor. On top of that, addressing one of these Midgard creatures as 'master?' Letting one talk to you like that? I thought I was a deviant for some of the things I've done in these caves to humans, or with the lower caste, but you definitely win in this regard. Even after the attack by the Cultists, and the damage they did to one of my businesses, I have to admit this might end up being one of the best days of my life!"

Trav frowned and tried to think of the best insults in the Asgard language that he knew. This Fodrik Kin bastard seemed to be everything that Trav hated about their kind. "Hey, freak, you ugly fuckstick. How about you stop taking joy in what a cowardly, womanly, weak-armed moron you are, and focus on how you are hiding behind Dacith while bullying a human and a female. Coward."

Narnaste turned in surprise, eyes wide, before warily watching their advancing enemies again, but Trav had caught a slight smile. Fodrik, on the other hand, let out an explosive breath, almost like he'd been gut punched. When he finally spoke, his voice came out as a near whisper, like he still couldn't believe how Trav had spoken to him. "Who do you think you are, slave? Some nobody Kin woman indulges in depravity with you, and you suddenly think you are my equal? You may be the stupidest, most arrogant creature of your kind I have ever seen. Who knows, maybe some of the human women I brought down here to ravish also thought they were above their station after I was done with them, but most were too busy wailing to talk before I cut their throats. I guess we will never know."

Trav snarled, "That doesn't surprise me, goat-fornicator. Actually, I see you have a goat friend right here. Do you ravish him too? But yes, it is not surprising that you must force yourself on human slaves for pleasure. Any Kin woman would be strong enough to get away from the awkward advances of your misshapen little worm." The insults were definitely not like any that Trav had used before on Earth, so for good measure, in English, he said, "Get fucked, you creepy, something-under-the-bed-looking, stereotypical villain with an inferiority complex, momma's boy rapist." Trav let every bit of hate and scorn that he held for Fodrik and everything he represented fill his voice.

"Goats?" asked the three-eyed Kin softly. "Goats? Beornik is one of my family's faithful servants, but even he is too good to kill something as useless and unimportant as you." Mottled white and red rage filled the ugly Kin's face as he visibly struggled with his temper, but he ultimately lost, screaming, "Dacith, kill him!"

After that, all hell broke loose. Narnaste moved as if to protect Trav, but the two Kin men went straight for her. The Dacith drew a large sword, and Beornik, the goat man, produced daggers in both hands.

A darting Dacith hissed in pleasure as it clawed for Trav's throat. The tall human man darted back, moving much faster than he could have a couple days earlier, and the attacking creature seemed utterly stunned as it looked down at Trav's spear in its stomach.

There was no time to check on Narnaste as Trav fought with the Dacith. The disgusting creature he'd spitted was slower now, and bled like a stuck pig, but it wasn't down yet. Of course, Kin resilience was one of the many reasons why any human that fought fairly with them would almost always lose.

As Trav dodged deadly claws and gnashing teeth, he remembered whispered stories told by slaves in the mines, tales of humans killing Kin. It was said that the only time Kin could reliably be killed was through strength of numbers, or massed fire, or surprise, or some combination. But even those advantages didn't always work for more powerful Kin...or at least, so the stories went. Luckily, Dacith were some of the least powerful Kin on Asgard, and Trav was...greater now.

Although he was no master with a spear, Trav's checkered past on Earth had involved more scuffles than he cared to admit. He'd also known some martial arts even before his cousin Ash had become the family's little crown jewel, a martial arts genius. Before their relationship had turned sour, Ash had taught Trav some of what he knew. Old resentments burned even as Trav fought nightmare creatures on a different world.

The heavily wounded Dacith held back, letting the other, fresher one take the lead. Trav had still gotten some hits in, though—the lead monster still bore a few cuts and stabs. The human man was having a hard time landing a good hit, though. Kin were so fast, almost as soon as Trav managed to draw any blood, the damned things were already springing back off the point!

Despite being armed, and the Dacith being unarmed except for natural weapons, Trav had a hard time just staying alive. Every time he thrust with his spear, the second murderous Kin would dart forward, trying to end his life and usually almost succeeding. The amount of power the small, rat-like creatures had was unreal. Trav outweighed them by probably almost double, but before his rune-driven transformation, either of the creatures could have easily overpowered him.

Now he was definitely stronger, and probably even technically faster than they were and armed to boot, but the Dacith had had a lifetime of experience with their natural strength, while Trav had had less than a day.

As he fought, dodging another set of sharp, snapping teeth, Trav heard some worrying sounds coming from Narnaste's fight and gritted his teeth. He realized that he was too new to his newfound power and didn't know how to really use it yet. In the middle of a fight like this, he couldn't exactly take a break to start drawing runes, either.

He needed a plan. Trav had a feeling that Narnaste wouldn't last much longer two versus one.

After a half step back, the bearded man felt a rock on the ground behind him and ignoring the danger, took a chance. Feigning a stumble, Trav fell back. Almost immediately, the lead Dacith leaped forward, clawed hands grasping. But instead of pliant human flesh, all the creature found was a sharp spear point through the roof of its mouth. Trav had braced the butt end of his weapon against the ground to be sure of a killing strike.

Unfortunately, the other monster was still free to act.

The second Kin, the one Trav had first wounded, sprang on top of him, pinning one of his arms. The muscular, scarred human man managed to grip the top of the Dacith's snout, keeping its teeth away, but the creature's claws flashed forward, ripping and tearing. Trav's armor was not made of ordinary steel, probably originally crafted for a hero or a noble. Otherwise, it would not have withstood the Dacith's ferocity. Although the armor stayed whole, the creature still managed to fit the tips of its sharp claws through the metal rings, painfully scoring Trav's side, turning that half of his clothing into a bloody mess.

With a grunt of effort, Trav kneed the thing as hard as he could, creating enough room to free his pinned hand. The creature was almost immediately on top of him again, and Trav snarled, feeling himself reflexively activate his emberstone eye. After a curious whimper, the Dacith recoiled, and Trav drew his magicked shiv, planting the crude weapon through the Kin creature's eye socket. Its horrible mouth opened impossibly wide, displaying its terrifying yellow teeth, and it thrashed back. Trav freed both his weapons, pocketed the shiv and turned to help Narnaste.

The first thing he noticed was another lantern of sorts, one he had never seen before. The light device looked very complex at first, but Trav eventually realized it must house emberstone inside as a power source. Fodrik or his friend must have dropped it to create more light.

The bearded human man grinned viciously as he saw the dead or dying goat man on the ground, terrible wounds visible on his head, neck, and shoulder. But then Trav looked further down the tunnel and sprinted forward with a curse. Narnaste was on the ground, Fodrik standing over her.

On his way past the downed goat man—Trav had already forgotten his name—he scooped up a dagger from the ground and hurled it at the leering, three-eyed Kin. Through more luck than skill, the weapon flew true but hit the Kin-man with the butt end, not the blade. The energy of the impact still spun Fodrik around, making him grunt in pain. His trio of eyes widened, and he barely managed to get his longsword up in time to block the charging Trav's spear.

Trav struck again, forcing the Kin man back, farther away from Narnaste. He didn't know if she was still alive, but the way the disgusting, evil, frog-faced monster had been about to stab her was hopefully a good sign. Trav planted himself in front of Narnaste, glaring at Fodrik over the tip of his spear.

"Try me, fugly," he growled.

The Kin man's eyes widened in outrage, and he screeched, flashing all his sharp teeth and a thick, slimy tongue. The scream echoed down the tunnel, and Trav wished he had another set of hands to cover his ears. Then Fodrik attacked, and there was no more time to think about anything other than staying alive.

Even in the tunnel, where Trav had a huge advantage with his spear over the evil Kin's longsword, and despite technically being a little bit stronger and faster than the monster he fought, it was all Trav could do to hold his ground. Even so, it surprised the hell out of Fodrik.

"What are you?" he growled.

Trav didn't answer; he just felt a sinking feeling. He was breathing so hard he couldn't even spit any more insults. If things kept going this way, he was going to die for sure. After three years in the mine, escaping the collapse, after learning magic and taking control of his destiny, it would be brutally tragic if he perished like this.

He held on longer, desperately thrusting with the spear, kicking, using every trick in the book to keep the deadly longsword blade away. Trav truly began to despair, ironically remembering poor Asta when he saw a chance approaching. Like with the Dacith earlier, this opportunity would come at great risk, but Trav didn't know what other option he had.

As he used his carved eye to see better in the dark, keeping his face under control was difficult, and grew harder as the seconds passed. Finally, the perfect moment arrived, and Trav put everything he had into a series of lightning-fast stabs, the explosive attacks forcing his skilled opponent backwards...into the claws of a troll.

Fodrik screamed as he was pulled into the darkness, and Trav didn't wait around to watch what happened next. He bent down to retrieve his enemy's fallen longsword before turning and running to Narnaste. When he saw her condition, he hissed, but her chest still rose and fell. She was alive.

Trav dropped both weapons he carried before lifting the unconscious, heavily bleeding Kin woman into a fireman's carry. She still wore the pack from earlier—getting her up was a bit awkward, but fear gave Trav energy like nothing else ever could. His back felt cold, imagining the troll's huge hand coming out of the dark for him.

After the Kin woman's weight had been settled, he bent at the knees to grab his spear, Narnaste's fallen seax, and the longsword before running for his life. Behind him, he could hear snarls and howls, but he didn't take any time to look, he just mentally turned off both glyph lanterns on the ground using his failsafe switch and kept his emberstone eye activated to see in the dark. It was noticeably more powerful now.

Everything ran together through time, just a series of different aches, pains, and fears all congealing as Trav escaped through the dark tunnel. In the back of his mind, he considered dropping Narnaste but decided not to for multiple reasons. Kin or not, it wasn't right—she was at least a firm ally by now, and even three years as a slave couldn't change the core of who Trav was. His heart rebelled against thinking of Kin as people, and part of him deeply distrusted the lupine woman, but another part of him had ached to see the horrific combat injuries that had been inflicted on Narnaste's beautiful body.

Trav had no idea how to help the Kin woman. He'd seen the wounds after all, and he had some basic first aid items in the pack, but nothing like the minimum required to save Narnaste's life.

With his mystic night sight, Trav noticed skeletons against the walls, some old, some new. He wondered how many of them were human and Kin that Fodrik had brought down here to kill...or worse. Trav smiled grimly as he raced through the tunnels, following the mystic signs toward the exit. He wasn't a fan of trolls, but they had to eat too, and he was glad the one he'd just encountered had been able to meet that three-eyed asshole. Hopefully, they killed each other.

Narnaste continued to bleed out as Trav huffed, his muscles cramping, limbs burning, but he didn't dare to stop, not even to shift his burdens. He'd made the decision not to leave Narnaste behind; now he just had to endure the pain, much like he had before in the mines.

Chapter 12

There was no mistaking the situation—Narnaste was dying. Trav crouched next to the wounded Kin woman lying on the forest floor. He wasn't sure where they were and didn't know if it had been safe to stop, but he'd run a good distance away from the mouth of the cave he'd burst out of. Continuing had seemed risky since the lupine woman had lost so much blood.

The tall man felt exhausted, and Narnaste obviously didn't have much time left. Trav had a decision to make.

He twisted the heavy ring around on his finger, breathing heavily, running through what he knew...and what he didn't. If Narnaste was anything like a human physically, normal medical supplies probably wouldn't save her at this point. She'd been stabbed at least twice and had bled out quite a bit. Luckily, she'd managed to clamp a hand over the wound in her side at some point before, but she was only half conscious at this point, and the only thing that had kept her alive had been clotted blood in her clothing.

Trav didn't have any serious medical supplies to begin with, so mundane medical action was not a real possibility.

The only other options he had were mystical, and there was only one thing he knew he could do. If Trav put his brand on the Kin, a divine mark, it would form the last of three seals that he'd begun with his initial rune equations binding them together. However, to accomplish this, he would need to imbue his blank ring with a divine rune, one he would need to create and claim for himself. This would require completely accepting Odin's legacy, and going all-in as a demigod, or god-hopeful, or whatever he would be.

Trav didn't have many logical reasons to hesitate—Odin's help had been the only reason he'd realistically survived until now. However, deep down, he felt like if he accepted the mantle of power, it would be like accepting Asgard, and the fact that he would probably never get to see Earth again. His slavery was something he would never be inclined to forget—or forgive.

Of course, he could just let her die too, but that didn't seem right. As Trav watched the Kin woman bleed out and suffer, he kicked himself, angry that he was letting emotion get in the way of what he knew he should do.

Narnaste may be Kin, and Trav may not entirely trust her, but she had been wounded while fighting at his side, and that mattered to him. He went back and forth with himself several times, but ultimately, the urgency of the situation coupled with his frustration with himself finally led him to grumble a few curses and act.

He drew his crude shiv and paused, frowning. There was definitely a new current of magic in it, something he didn't feel was dangerous, but he couldn't quite put his finger on. He shrugged, dismissing it. If he sat around all day staring at his shoddy dagger, Narnaste was going to die. Staying distracted for too long so close to the Kin mines like this, he might also get ambushed by a troll or finished off by some new patrol.

Trav took off his ring and centered himself, emptying his mind of anything else. Then he thought of his life, running through everything he'd done before his captivity on Asgard, and then everything he'd done as a slave. He remembered Beth's smile. Holding everything that made him who he was firmly in his mind, he also thought about what he believed, what mattered to him. With every bit of concentration he had focused on his self-identity, he touched the tip of his shiv to the ring. After he'd made contact, he ran a bit of his energy through the tool he'd created, having already imbued it with some of his essence. Then after a deep breath, he willed himself into the ring.

A bright but small light flashed at the contact point, and Trav quickly buried the ring in the dirt with at least a hand of soil on top of it.

He hoped the insulation of the soil would help mask the mystical mojo of what was happening. Kin probably couldn't feel anything, but any Restless out there would probably be able to sense it like a signal flare. The man from Earth frowned at that thought. Odin had obviously been extremely paranoid, but in general, Trav approved of cautiousness—it was the unfamiliar name that had made him pause.

The Restless, a name Odin had given the gods, encompassed more than just the Aesir and Vanir pantheons. The Kin called them High Masters, but Trav felt glimpses of new, related, hidden knowledge at the edge of his mind. All he really knew right now was that there was a lot more to the Restless that he didn't know yet, and maybe he'd be able to understand later.

Right now he had a dying Kin woman to save.

Trav stared at the spot of ground where he'd buried the ring and eventually shook his head, digging it up. Soil could cover some mystic power, but what had just happened with the ring was like the magical equivalent of a nuclear blast with resulting supernatural fallout. Any Restless in the galaxy had probably felt it, so a little bit of dirt wasn't going to do much. Trav's divine senses were crude, much weaker than he knew they could probably get in time, but the energy and buzzing coming from the ring made his teeth vibrate.

He gingerly reached down to pick up the ring and whistled soundlessly as he turned it over to see what the magic had done. The entire band had been deeply etched with complex runes, and on the front, a stylized wolf stood flanked with two arcane symbols, interlocking runes formed of tiny glyphs.

A wolf huh? Trav wondered. With a bit of nervousness, he placed the ring onto his finger and lights exploded behind his eyes. He let out a grunt, feeling like he'd just been kicked in the gut, but he endured it, and slowly, awkwardly invested a small bit of his magic power into the ring. As soon as he had, the power bounced back into his body, and he became fully connected with the completed ring. Now the pieces of metal formed a physical representation of his power and authority, such as they were.

The creation of the ring hadn't really been something he'd done, more like something he'd let happen. Symbols of authority were a birthright of the Restless, something they knew instinctively how to create and would be imbued with their unique essence to enact very unique, dangerous magic.

And now Trav was one of them.

Oh joy, he thought—the implications of becoming a god, or Restless, or magical alien, or whatever he was now definitely compelled a mind fuck that would keep him awake at night. He vowed not to let it go to his head, though. All of Odin's power hadn't prevented the wily old god from dying. Remembering that fact would always be sobering.

Finally, the huge, ridiculous, flashing neon sign of what he'd done began to fade from the ether, and Trav breathed a sigh of relief. If anyone had been paying attention or was even half asleep, they'd probably just seen it.

Trav bent down to Narnaste and felt her forehead, clucking his tongue. What he was about to do was going to hurt both of them—a lot. He hoped she stayed alive, or he'd be risking a lot for nothing.

One of the Kin woman's wounds opened again, sluggishly soaking the area around it with blood as Trav turned her over. He winced in sympathy, but he had already chosen where the mark had to go. Besides, Narnaste was going to die anyway. What he was doing would give her a chance to live, but he didn't have a lot of time, so he couldn't afford to be delicate.

Finally, he got the firm-bodied Kin female on her stomach, and pulled her clothing aside, baring her lower back. Her bloody tail kept getting in the way, so he eventually just moved it under one of her legs. "Stay," he said gruffly.

Then he winced and gingerly lowered his god ring to touch Narnaste's lower back. "This is going to be a tramp stamp from hell," he muttered. He sucked in his teeth, counting down from three before channeling power and some of his essence through the ring.

Trav had known that creating the mark would be dangerous—he was too new to his power. Having more magical power would have shielded him from the backlash, but the actual energy powering that he was trying to do went deeper, down to his purview, where his authority would come from if he were a full-blown god. Even though he didn't have access to that well of energy yet, he was still connected to it through Odin's mantle. The memories in his head had let him know to expect indescribable pain, so that part wasn't surprising—but the sheer amount of it was almost too much to tolerate.

Stealth be damned, Trav screamed as every nerve in his body lit up in agony. His bones felt like they were breaking, and his eyes like they were boiling out of his head. Trav tasted blood in his mouth.

Through his haze of pain, he held onto consciousness just long enough to continue channeling the divine power running through his body. He thought he saw Narnaste stir as the world faded into darkness.

***

When Trav woke, he was in a shelter of some kind; a thin

membrane stretched overhead. He surprisingly felt fine but had a feeling that a few days ago, what he'd just been through would have killed him. After studying his surroundings, he realized that his spear and shiv had been laid on the ground next to him, both blades covered in rags to keep them safe.

Now that Trav was conscious and rested, he cast about with his senses and didn't notice anything amiss. The logical thing to do would be to exit the tent he was in—now he recognized it as part of the travel kit he'd gotten from the memory shrine—but the shiv drew his attention.

He touched it and felt the strange current of magic in it again, one he hadn't ever placed there. The tall man frowned as he tried to figure out what it meant, but the front of the tent suddenly split, opened by Narnaste.

She wore a thin towel and nothing else. Clean again since the first time Trav had seen her, he admired her as she bent her way into the tent. Her imperfections and scars all accentuated her inhuman beauty. Trav still felt a bit strange about his attraction to her—most Kin had repelled him in the past—but he accepted it. After discovering a new kink or turn on, beating himself up about it wouldn't change the attraction.

Narnaste fully entered the tent and closed the flap, then she turned and fidgeted. Her damp hair hung around her shoulders and made it obvious she'd just bathed. Now that Trav thought about it, he realized he'd been cleaned too. *Interesting.*

"Where are we?" Trav asked.

"Far away from the caves...far away," said Narnaste.

"How did we get here? You were almost dead last I remember."

"Yes, you healed me and changed me. You blessed me. I don't know how to thank you. With my new power, I carried you all this distance, and I have been making camp ever since, cleaning us and washing our bloody clothes."

Trav glanced under his thin blanket and verified he was, in fact, naked, which made sense. He lay back down and stared at the roof of the tent. His choice to place a divine mark had already been made, but now he was worried about what he'd done. If any Restless had been nearby, they would have felt it. Hopefully, if they had been on other planets, they wouldn't be able to pinpoint the source right away. Actually, hopefully they were all dead. That would definitely make matters simpler. Trav felt somewhat amused to know that Odin would have thought exactly the same thing.

Narnaste began fidgeting more, and her gaze went to his face before darting back down. Trav frowned and reached up and touched his cheek, his eyebrows going up at what he felt. "You trimmed my beard," he said, stating it as a fact.

"Yes, Master," said Narnaste. "You are a High Master; you should look as impressive as you are. If you must punish me for my arrogance, I am prepared to accept it."

Trav's eye twitched, and he wondered, *What kind of fucked up culture do these people have? No, not people. Kin. Monsters. That's right.* Then he amended his thoughts, reminding himself of human history and various religions. Actually, Narnaste's reaction made sense—Trav was the strange one on Asgard. He decided to ignore the beard for now—after all, he would have fixed it given a chance anyway; he just didn't know how he felt about Narnaste messing with his face while he slept. Instead, he asked, "Are you washing our clothes?"

"Yes, my soiled set was also almost ruined when I was changed. I will need to mend them."

"When you what?"

"You saved me and changed me. I—I—" Narnaste's voice broke, and she flung herself forward, prostrating herself. The towel she wore slipped off, and Trav got a good look at the mark he'd placed on her—a black wolf flanked by sigils on her lower back. The view was nice, but he still had some thinking to do, and the Kin woman's figure was making his head fuzzy.

He looked up again and thought about the mark, and about what he'd actually done. Some of his knowledge was still hidden, but he'd effectively claimed Narnaste, made her part of his...people. Odin had probably been capable of creating dozens of divine marks like the one above Narnaste's ass. However, Trav sensed he was only capable of making between five to ten, and each one would be riskier than the last. Each mark, each claiming, drew on his soul. If he ever failed, it would destroy him.

Fun.

"How long was I out?" asked Trav.

"About half a day. It is currently morning," mumbled the Kin woman. Her tail swished, and Trav scratched his head before he could help himself and grinned. Kin or not, Narnaste could be very sexy.

Her fierce appearance and attitude seemed deeply at odds with how she acted when her guard was down.

"Stop cowering, Narnaste. Raise your head."

"Yes, Master." The wolf woman slowly rose, the towel falling off the rest of the way. Her shy demeanor slowly faded as she raised her eyes and her face lost all emotion. Trav still noticed her ear and tail twitching, though. Her tone formal, she said, "Master, you saved me. Even if I didn't bear your energy now, even if you were not a High Master, I would be compelled to follow you through honor. I am yours to command."

"I accept that," said Trav slowly. He didn't know what to make of the woman's sudden proclamation, and her nudity was making him wonder where to look. Finally, he just decided to be frank and looked her up and down in appreciation.

"Master, I wish to serve you," said Narnaste and bit her lower lip.

"You what?" Trav blinked. "What do you mean?"

The Kin woman moved forward on her hands and knees, eyes full of heat, and her tail wagging faster. Trav quickly learned what had been on the wolf woman's mind, and how she'd wanted to serve him.

Chapter 13

"This is probably going to be a good day for traveling," said Trav.

"I agree, Master." Narnaste placed the last few items from last night's camp in their special pack.

"How much longer do we have to travel to this village of yours?"

"Before, it would be two weeks, maybe three depending on weather and speed of travel. Now, I have no idea."

"That's fair," said Trav as he checked his weapons. It wasn't like they had to walk now after all, or at least he didn't. The previous day of travel had been eye-opening.

He turned just in time to see Narnaste transform, and it still made his scalp prickle. As the Kin woman began to glow, Trav wondered if he would ever get used to this new ability. They hadn't talked much the day before, mainly focusing on getting the hell away from the mines, but the divine mark that Trav had placed on her had made Narnaste stronger, faster, and more resilient.

She'd acquired some instinctive insights into Trav's power, like the fact that she would get stronger as he did now.

And lastly, she could get huge.

The transformation complete, Trav looked up into the yellow eyes of a giant, red-furred, eight-legged wolf. "Are you ready, Master?" asked the creature, and Trav mutely nodded.

He asked, "Where do the pack and your clothes and stuff go?"

"I don't know, Master. I can still sense them, sort of. They are here but not here."

"Oh, alright. That makes everything extremely clear."

"Good. Would you like to mount me, Master?"

Trav decided not to explain his sarcasm, nor acknowledge the double entendre. It wasn't wise to anger a wolf with the jaws of a T-Rex, nor rile up a Kin woman who seemed likely to jump him any time she could.

He was beginning to understand Narnaste better now. She had lived a very regimented, romance-free life before meeting him. Now that she'd found a real High Master, her situation, religion, and honor were all giving her the go-ahead to be as uninhibited as she wanted. The fact that she legitimately seemed to like and respect him and the fact that he didn't quite smell human anymore hadn't hurt anything.

With a bemused shake of the head, Trav grabbed big handfuls of fur and hauled himself up the side of the massive wolf. He had talked a little bit with her about her transformation already, and its somewhat mind-bending implications. They both agreed that Trav's power truly was connected to Odin's mantle, at least the things he did that directly drew from it. There was no other explanation for Narnaste's new form. Trav had reasoned that Odin had probably marked animals first in his life, not Kin, hence his animal companions in legends.

However, the mark also could create Odin's personal warriors, Valkyries. The old god had never created anything like Narnaste before, Trav was sure. Her new form was strange enough that if any Restless came chasing the giant, magical signal Trav had created, they might be able to follow easier now. The thought was worrying.

But now Narnaste was effectively Trav's mount and his first bonded warrior. She was truly a part of his new journey now, body and soul. If her transformation hadn't saved her life, and she hadn't been enthusiastic about the whole thing, Trav might have felt a little guilty. But now as she began loping along, taking joy in her huge body and easy movement, he just smiled.

Maybe becoming a god wouldn't be so bad after all.

Riding on the giant wolf's back like this, communication had turned out surprisingly easy. The day before, after his initial shock at her form had faded, they'd experimented with communication. Luckily, Narnaste had been able to easily hear the man on her back. She was so big, Trav had no problem hearing her either.

As she loped along, Narnaste suddenly spoke. "Master, we talked about my life yesterday, but what about your life?"

The question caught Trav off guard. Among the slaves, asking anyone about their past had been taboo. The last person he'd ever really talked to about the subject had been Beth. He cleared his throat and said, "What do you want to know?"

"How about you tell me about the world you come from. Also

about the wife you had." She paused. "And what happened to her."

Trav felt like he'd been punched in the gut and sucked in a breath. He thought for a while, and Narnaste patiently waited for him to respond. On the one hand, he didn't really want to talk about his past, but as he pondered the subject, he decided that maybe it would do some good. He wasn't a slave anymore, and it was time to start dealing with his issues. Learning to trust again would be nice too. Granted, he trusted Narnaste—he effectively owned her now. But for him, relying on someone for his life was a lot easier than trusting them with his feelings...and secrets.

The tall, muscular man grinned without humor at that thought. He knew that back home on Earth, lots of people would probably cringe and call him all kind of names if they knew he owned a woman, despite the fact that she'd chosen the situation. They'd probably think plenty of things about Narnaste too. Well, they could all go fuck themselves, living their safe lives without constant mortal danger. If any of those people could survive for three years as a slave in the mines on Asgard, with the constant threat of being killed or eaten or worse by inhuman monsters, maybe he'd give a damn about their opinions.

The reality of his existence would probably be unimaginable to a normal person where he came from, even to himself in the past. Trav had taken a step into godhood on an alien hell world full of psychotic monsters. He currently rode Cliffordess the huge red wolf, and would probably ride her at night in the tent. Actually, Narnaste was still pretty strong, and he wasn't sure she'd take no for an answer. That uncomfortable thought didn't make him feel very masculine or in control of his life anymore so he quickly moved on, deciding to speak.

"I am from Earth. Specifically, Oregon state in the United States, a large country."

"What's a state?"

"Like a territory...or a smaller area in the country."

"Ah, I see."

Trav continued, "My world has no magic. Well, not like you think of it. What we do have is technology."

"Technology?" Narnaste's lupine jaws mangled the unfamiliar word.

"Mechanical know-how like bows and wheels, but much more complex."

"That sounds weak. Your kind are already weak. Well, not you, Master. How does your world survive?"

"You don't understand," said Trav. He racked his brain, trying to find a way to explain tech to a magical wolf girl on another world. "Technology creates light with no heat, allows people to talk face to face at long distances, and can help people live healthier, easier lives."

"So can magic."

Trav thought of another example. "Technology can also allow an average person, a human, to travel faster in a warship through the sky than sound can move, or transport hundreds of other people in less than a day using airplanes that would otherwise take months or even years with boats and horses."

Narnaste said, "Because of the magic called technology, yes?"

"Yeah," said Trav slowly, trying to imagine how to explain atomic weapons to his giant, talking wolf girlfriend. "Like magic that anyone can use."

"Normal people can fly those 'airplanes?'"

"Well, yes and no. Some technology still needs skill to use, but anyone born on my world can operate it. It isn't hereditary like magic power on Asgard."

"Not all power is hereditary. In fact, sigilcrafting is not."

"You know what I mean," sighed Trav.

"It still sounds like technology is weak compared to magic."

Trav narrowed his eyes. "Technology can split the atom, the smallest piece of a thing. With a single weapon, a human being can destroy an entire city, and can do so from halfway around the world, a longer distance than a person can travel on foot in one hundred days. Technology can create diseases that will spread for days before killing people, and kill millions of people, maybe more. Technology can be terrifying. The most powerful Kin I've seen might even have a tough time against regular human armies armed with the right kinds of technology."

There was a moment of heavy silence. "I can't imagine such a thing," rumbled Narnaste. "What does your world look like?"

Trav honestly didn't know where to start. "Imagine the tallest building you have ever seen, but ten times that height, made of steel and glass. Now imagine an entire city like that. A large city."

"I would like to see this if I could. How did you come to be in this world?"

Trav hadn't told this story for a long time. He cleared his throat.

"I was on a research vessel with my father—"

"A what?"

He realized that he'd used English and searched for how to convey his thoughts using the local language. "A big boat."

"Ah."

"My father decided that we would all go out on the boat in order to celebrate my mother's birthday. I hadn't been home for a while, and it was a good opportunity to see the family. My mom asked that I go as a favor to her, too. I'd been avoiding everyone for a while."

"Why?"

Trav made a face. "Ashley would be there, or Ash as everyone calls him. In hindsight everything seems small now, but at the time, my relationship with the kid was tense, and my parents would take his side every time, so I just stopped coming around as often.

"Ashley was my cousin, but more like my brother. His father, my Uncle Josh, is kind of a piece of shit and was always into and out of trouble. Ash came to live with my family when he was young, and ever since then, he was like the son my parents never had. I'd always been a disappointment." Trav's fist clenched. Even after all this time, after everything he'd endured, the old frustrations were still real.

"I think I understand," said Narnaste. "My friend Tala-tala had a similar situation, I think. She had always been interested in a warrior path, but some in her family wanted her to embrace disciplines she just…never did. It created a strain."

"Yes, my situation was something like that. My parents wanted me to be a scientist like my father. When I pointed out that most scientists on my world don't make good money unless they get lucky, at least compared to the time and cost of the education they need, my family decided I should be a doctor or something. But I didn't want to spend another decade in school."

Narnaste's ears quirked. "I believe I understand this as well. On Asgard, Kin do not become civil servants for wealth, but for power."

"Well, that's not exactly what I was talking about, but I didn't want lots of money, or power, or a title. I wanted to see the world. So instead of finishing school, I flew to Alaska and worked on a crab boat."

"I do not know what this means."

Trav thought for a minute. "I traveled a long distance when I was young to do a dangerous job that paid a lot instead of continuing my education."

"Oh, I see. And do you regret it or not?"

"No, not at all. I learned a lot about myself, learned some of my limits, and it started a decade of wandering where I got to meet a lot of people and see much of my old world. My parents weren't happy, but I'd never been really exceptional at anything, so I got good at lots of things instead."

"And your cousin Ashley was different?"

"Yes. Ash didn't seem to think things through sometimes, but he was naturally gifted at the handful of things he really cared about. For one thing, people just...seemed to like him. He never had a problem with women, and more importantly, he was a real genius at martial arts. Both kata and sparring, he was good at all of it. In fact, I think he learned a handful of obscure martial arts for fun. He was even good at school. So for my soccer mom, book club mother and my fussy, scientist father, Ash was like...a kid they could be proud of—not like me."

"They weren't proud of you?"

"Well, I think they were relieved more than proud, happy that I had never gotten in any serious trouble. I mean, they didn't really understand me for most of my life. When I worked as a DJ, my parents couldn't even grasp how I made money." When Narnaste moved like she was going to speak, Trav interrupted her, "It's not important what a DJ is. The point is that my parents and I never saw eye to eye. They always said I didn't focus on anything enough and never reached my true potential with anything I did."

"Were they right?"

The question seemed to weigh Trav down, and he was quiet for a while, thinking about it. A few years before, maybe even three years before, he might have reflexively answered no, but now, after Beth was gone, things were different. Finally, he said, "They probably were right. That is a bitter pill to swallow, but Ash taught me martial arts before, and I was able to hang with him on the same level for a while. I think it actually motivated him to start trying for once. Maybe if I'd tried at a few things, spent more time on them, I might have found a place for myself too."

"So you were a wanderer?"

"Sort of, yes." Narnaste couldn't see him, but Trav shrugged.

"I am sorry for all of my questions. How did you come to Asgard?"

"As I said, I was on this boat with my parents and Ash. We were in the Bermuda Triangle—a place in the ocean on my world where strange things happen, and ships used to disappear. That night, my father had just gotten done studying a fish or something, whatever it was he did. I was watching a movie with my mom, and Ash was practicing martial arts with sticks somewhere else when I felt something weird. We all saw a bright light, and I felt weightless. Sounds disappeared, and the world flashed. Next thing I knew, I was sitting on the ground in the middle of nowhere in Asgard."

Narnaste turned her massive head and fixed Trav with one huge, golden eye. "It sounds like you were in the middle of a new Veil."

"A what?"

"It was already fairly obvious that your world is not familiar with Veils, yes?"

"Well, yeah."

Narnaste turned forward again as she loped along and said, "Veils are the doorways between words. Shimmering portals. A few are permanent, but most last a short time, and some only exist for a few seconds. The cultists that attacked before we met came through one."

"I see." Now that he thought about it, Trav had overheard something similar among the human slaves before, but never in this much detail. "There has to be more to it than that."

"Yes, true. If any Kin crosses a Veil, we slowly lose our power over time, the vitality that allows us to use magic or our natural abilities just...fades. I believe the same is true for the cultists or any other warriors from other veil worlds."

"I can imagine how that could really make invasions more difficult."

"Yes, and there's more," rumbled Narnaste. "The more powerful a warrior is, the faster they lose their vitality, their mana, or whatever it is they use as a power source. Kin both hate and fear the cultists because they seem to enjoy bringing us back to their world to serve as slaves. Over there, we are helpless."

"And you know this, how?" asked Trav.

"Sometimes, slaves escape."

Trav felt strange as he mulled over the answer. The thought of Kin being slaves like he had been, held against their will by people who at least looked human should have filled him with savage glee. However, the more he thought about it, he just felt sadness.

He decided to change the subject. "Alright, so I think I have a pretty good idea of where we're going, and we talked about that a bit yesterday, but what kind of land are we traveling through? Will it be dangerous?"

"Life is dangerous, Master, but yes, there will probably be trials. Other than the great cities of Asgard, settlements tend to move, and the Wild Ones establish new territories, so I cannot accurately answer your question."

"I see." Trav rubbed his chin. "I wish we could find some other memory shrines or other ways to add to our security."

"Won't you be using your magic for that?" Narnaste's ears twitched as she asked the question.

"Yes, but the power I can use is limited. It comes back every day, but I need to stay at maximum power while we travel in case we're attacked, and I'll need to create glyph wards around our camp every night. Even then, it'd be a good idea to keep at least a small reserve. Some of the things I want to experiment with will need a few days of runework anyway, so while I do have plans, they will take time. My limited power makes that time even longer right now."

"I understand, Master. What sorts of things do you want to work on?"

"Well, for the time being, some protection for both of us is a priority. I also want to create a few weapons, and utility items—more permanent than those rocks I made back in the cave."

"That sounds like a good plan, Master."

Trav idly scratched his arm and watched the scenery pass for a few minutes before asking, "You are part of a noble family, right? Are you fairly well-educated and connected?"

"I believe so, yes."

The tall, muscular man slowly nodded to himself. "Ordinarily, this situation would be different—well, not that there is any ordinary on this world—and it would not be appropriate to share so much. But we are bound together now. I am going to fill you in on some of my plans later tonight." Trav didn't have any logical reason not to treat Narnaste as a full-fledged ally, Kin monster or not.

"Later tonight? Will this be before or after I please you, Master?"

Trav's eye twitched. Narnaste's version of pleasing him was less servitude and more hyper-horny, female monster in heat, but he had a feeling that trying to rebuff her attentions would hurt her feelings and be a bad move in general. Instead, he curtly said, "Before."

"Understood, Master." The giant red wolf's tail began to wag.

Trav nervously wet his lips but ignored the god-marked Kin's excitement. "As for right now, I want you to tell me more about the noble families on Asgard and about the major cities. I want to know about the different types of Kin, too."

"That will take a lot of time, Master," muttered Narnaste.

"Yes, I figured." Trav adjusted his spear where it was stowed. "But the more I talk to you, the more I realize that there are a lot of things I need to know as soon as possible. And at least right now, we have the time, so we should use it."

"I understand." Narnaste's ears flicked wildly for a few seconds before she hesitantly asked, "Will you teach me how to craft any glyphs or sigils one day, Master?"

Trav blinked. "I don't see why not, especially something like light. Do a good job with teaching me everything I want to know, and I will teach you in return."

"Thank you, Master!" Narnaste's step seemed to get an extra bit of bounce, and the giant wolf cleared her throat before beginning to lecture. "Nobody knows for sure how large Asgard is—"

At first, Trav focused on the Kin woman's words with the assumption that the information would be dry and boring, but over time, he became completely enthralled by everything Narnaste said. Despite hating the Kin on Asgard, he soaked up information about their culture and world like a sponge.

Perhaps being stuck in the mines, surviving as a slave for so long had left his mind starving for exercise, but the hours seemed to fly by as Narnaste gave Trav a crash course on Asgard geography and politics. By the time they'd settled down to make camp for the night, Trav was more than happy to give Narnaste a quick lesson on the basics of glyphcrafting and the building blocks of knowledge that could lead to sigilcrafting, eventually maybe even runecrafting.

Then later that night when the Kin woman surged into his bed like a force of nature, Trav felt much less conflicted about it. His wolf girl was silly and savage, but he realized that he was glad that he had an ally. He wasn't alone anymore. And as a traveling companion, he could do a lot worse than an attractive woman with a sharp mind, strong spirit, and a curious nature.

Maybe in another life, another world, Narnaste and Beth could have met. He had a feeling they might have been friends.

Chapter 14

From his vantage point of his branch, high above the top of a hill, the surrounding wilderness spread out in every direction. Trav climbed most of the way down from his tree and regarded Narnaste where she crouched on the forest floor. "I saw smoke in the distance," he said, his voice soft.

"And you are sure you sense something down there?"

"Yes. I can feel it tugging now. It's different than a memory shrine, but definitely, something tied to the Restless."

"You mean the High Masters?"

"Sure. Whatever."

Trav climbed down the rest of the way, hopped to the ground, and dusted himself off before turning. "The smoke seems contained. It isn't natural."

The surrounding forest was thick in this area, so Narnaste was currently in her woman form. Her huge wolf body would have had problems moving without knocking over trees. "I could smell it before," said the Kin woman. "It didn't smell like a brush fire. We are quickly approaching winter too, so it's too late for something like that. It could be other Kin, or maybe it's a human settlement."

"I thought all humans on Asgard were slaves." Trav frowned.

She shook her head. "No. I think I have said this before. Some humans live in the wilderness and in hidden places, places that Kin won't look or have no reason to go. The frontier areas of Asgard are not exactly of interest to the cities. Some Kin believe that all humans should be enslaved, but most of us won't go out of our way to make that happen, especially if we already have enough slaves. If a big project comes along or a sickness kills a large number of Midgardians, humans, that can change."

Trav slowly turned to look the wolf woman in the eyes, but she didn't flinch. *Why should she?* he thought. From her perspective, she hadn't said anything wrong. Narnaste had never been brutal to slaves and found the whole establishment distasteful, but she was still Kin. This exchange had been a good reminder.

Trav said, "Alright, so what I'm sensing is probably in the human settlement, or whatever it is?"

"I suppose."

"Then I guess we need to check out what I'm sensing. I need every edge I can get. There is no guarantee that there is even anything there for me at the Faithful town you are taking me to."

"There are no guarantees in life, yes, but I don't like this," said the wolf woman. "Kin will kill you, but I am almost sure a settlement this far out in the middle of nowhere will be human. A human settlement will probably check to make sure you are not Kin, so I cannot come with you if you must go."

Trav raised an eyebrow. "Since when are you worried about humans? You could handle Dacith even before I marked you. Why do you care if they know you're Kin?"

Narnaste's ears twitched. "You were human, so I assumed you would order me not to fight them."

"Not necessarily. My goals are more about survival and revenge right now. I'm not exactly in the mood for charity or brotherhood."

"Even so, we must be cautious."

Trav rubbed his chin. "Still, you can turn into a wolf the size of a house. What is the problem?"

Narnaste's expression turned shifty. She paused before responding and said, "Wild humans can be dangerous."

"Oh?"

The Kin woman grew noticeably uncomfortable. "Natural Kin abilities and runecrafting are the only pure magic that is stable and will not alter the user or the environment on Asgard. There are other kinds of magic, though. Dark magic, twisted power does exist, and some humans have recently been seeking out some of the lost secrets that should have stayed buried. Witchcraft is almost always evil or at least harmful to the user. Plus, there is only one of me; they will outnumber us for sure." She shrugged. "Even if I survive, if you were to die, I will have failed—both as Faithful and as your vassal."

That bit about witchcraft made Trav pause. He briefly wondered whether he could trust Narnaste's information due to her Kin perspective, but he decided that caution was wise. At the very least, he could ask more questions. "What do you mean they alter themselves? Witches, right?"

"Human mages who practice witchcraft eventually show marks of their deals with spirits, and they will almost always give in to the temptation for more power through evil means. When humans kill each other, the Kin do not care, but sometimes they even try to trap Kin."

Trav briefly thought it was a little ironic for a Kin to talk about anyone else being evil, but avoided quirking an eyebrow. "They trap Kin?"

"Yes. And sacrifice them."

"And they can actually do that?" Trav asked, thinking about the massive difference between the Kin and human slaves back at the mines.

"Sometimes, yes. Human witches make pacts with things from beyond the Veils that should be left alone. And a truly powerful witch can even sometimes attract worse things."

"Like what?"

"I don't actually know for certain. They have not been seen in many years, but there are legends and histories that describe them. In fact, it is part of why most Kin believe that the High Masters are dead."

Trav checked the time by the sun in the sky and sucked his teeth. The current subject of conversation fascinated him and wasn't triggering any of his foreign memories yet. He wanted to keep pumping Narnaste for information, but time wouldn't stand still if he did, and he wanted to get moving. He wasn't sure where his sense of urgency was coming from, but it was real nonetheless. "We will talk about this later. For now, I think I will go visit the village alone. Will I stand out with what I'm wearing?"

"A bit, but they will probably assume you are a human frontier mercenary or some other sort of fighting man." Narnaste didn't look happy.

"What about my story that I am an escaped slave?"

"The humans in the wilds and the frontiers don't exactly love the Kin. They will probably not question it."

Trav stood still for a moment, thinking. He agreed that the beacon was probably at a village. Going by himself was potentially dangerous, but he was not a normal human anymore. The forest was so thick that horses would need to stick to roads, and Trav was really, really fast these days. He'd been running down game over the last couple days without many problems. Ultimately, he wanted—no—needed more power, and it was time to get some revenge. None of his plans would be possible if he was not willing to take some risks along the way.

The Kin woman flinched as Trav began talking, obviously having predicted his next few words. He said, "Narnaste, I want you to stay here and wait for me. I am going to head into the village alone. If there are any problems, I will come back here right away."

"May I move closer?"

"Only if you feel it's truly necessary."

"Fine." Narnaste folded her arms. "I will obey, Master, but please do not be reckless. If you give a signal, I will come."

Trav merely nodded, not sure what else to say. The power dynamic he had with the Kin woman could be confusing at times. He cleared his throat, secured his gear, and began heading toward where he'd seen the smoke.

***

On his way through the forest, Trav idly practiced summoning his shiv, something he could do now that the weapon was soul-bound to him.

When he'd first realized that the process had begun, he hadn't exactly been happy. He had a few memories of Odin's soul-bound Gungnir, a mighty spear worthy of a god. As far as Trav knew, the soul-binding phenomenon was unique to the Restless, and there were so many variables that it couldn't be forced. Not all of the Restless had ever even managed it. Weapons, armor, or tools, anything could be soul-bound. The effect on each item varied as well, but the strange magic imparted was almost always useful.

Odin's powerful spear had been terrifying. Meanwhile, Trav had gotten lucky enough to soul-bind with a tool, but it had happened so soon after receiving Odin's mantle that he hadn't even had any possessions worthy of it. If the wild magic had bound his new spear, it wouldn't have been so bad, but instead, his crude shiv was now a part of him...forever.

Trav stared glumly at the blade in his hand, remembering how he'd acquired it in the first place. The weapon wasn't much more than a piece of sharpened steel with a dirty leather grip. It was ugly and would remind Trav of his days as a slave for the rest of his life, but at least he could imprint it with new rune equations now.

As far as Trav knew from Odin's memory, this ability was completely unique for a soulbound weapon—it had never manifested before. He was just happy for small favors. His shiv wasn't the greatest weapon in the world, but being able to store and quickly scribe rune equations was actually handy, even though he still needed to spend his own energy to make the magic actually work in most circumstances.

After climbing a tree again, he verified that he was getting closer to the village. It was time for a quick break, an opportunity to scribe a few more rune equations to save with the shiv, coaxing the tool to remember the complex spell formations.

As a soul-bound weapon, he could feel the thing pulling on him, almost demanding a name. The sensation was strange, and Trav didn't really want to name the ugly knife in the first place. He could put it off for now, but he knew he'd eventually have to deal with it.

For now, he concentrated on loading a couple more rune equations that didn't require too much energy to activate, as well as a few basic glyphs, sigils, and basic runes. He'd been training the shiv every few hours ever since he had discovered its nature, and had quite a few rune equations to call upon now. It was difficult to know what he might run into now that he was free in Asgard, but he had no desire to die any time soon, nor be recaptured.

Trav snarled as he thought about the smug Kin. Some of them would get the surprise of their lives when Trav eventually came calling, armed with the power of Odin. Of course, he needed to survive to that point and keep growing in power first...somehow.

With that cheery thought, Trav began moving again. He was getting close enough to the village now that he could actually smell it. Smoke and other smells of primitive civilization assailed his nostrils.

After walking farther, he stepped out of the trees and found himself on a bare earth path with wheel ruts worn on both sides. The little road was crude, and Trav noticed how the surrounding vegetation hadn't been cleared very far from the edges. He didn't know what it meant.

The wary man began moving in the direction of the settlement, ready to run away as fast as he could if he actually ran into any Kin. With nerves vibrating like piano wire, he rounded a bend and got his first good look at the village.

The first thing he noticed was that the heavy open gate had burning torches atop it, even during the day. The gates and surrounding walls were made of rough logs. A few children were playing outside the entrance. As soon as they saw Trav, one screamed, and all three of them ran inside the gate.

A few moments later, a couple roughly dressed men in furs hurried out, bows in hand, arrows on strings. They stared at Trav, eyes moving from his armor and clothing to his spear, sizing him up. "Who are you?" one asked.

Trav relaxed a bit now that he knew he was truly dealing with other people but didn't let the reaction touch his bearing. "I am just a traveler," he lied. "What is the name of this place?"

The man on the right ordered, "Don't come any closer." His

fingers on his bowstring twitched, and a piece of food in his beard fell to the ground. The two men must have been eating. "What is your name?"

"Trav. Who are you?"

"It doesn't matter right now. These are dark times. What is your business here?" Behind the men, Trav could see a few more men gathering, probably ready to shut the gates. Movement at the walls suggested at least one archer was taking position, ready to pop up if things got ugly.

Trav thought fast. "You are right; these are dark times. Traveling alone has been dangerous. I seek food and shelter."

"Can you pay?"

"I can pay in trade." Trav carefully reached back and raised the wrapped longsword where it has been secured to his pack, the weapon he'd acquired during the fight with the Kin several days earlier. "I have a Kin longsword. It has been marked with a sigil and will not dull."

The two men with bows slightly lowered their weapons. The one on the left who looked a bit smarter asked, "Truly? How did you get such a thing?"

Thinking fast again, Trav said, "They kill each other, and someone lucky or patient enough—" He let his voice trail off.

From behind the two men, another man walked out of the gates. He was large, his arms burly. One side of his rough clothing seemed to be stained. The new man shifted the baldric he wore with an axe and pouches attached, then he planted his fists on his hips and spat. "Let him in. We haven't had as many come by lately for trade."

"You just want to examine the sword," said the guard on the right, sullen. The other guard shot him a look.

"Yes, well, I'm the blacksmith, and the headman will hear me on this. Do you want to argue, Harl?"

The guard looked like he might say something in response, but eventually he just shook his head. Still, Trav didn't move until the burly man beckoned. "My name is Feth, and I do most of the ironwork in these parts. Come take your entry to Wall Home and let's take a look at that blade, eh?"

Trav had to think for a second about what guard had meant, the wording had been strange. He slowly walked forward, trying to appear calm and confident, but he still didn't feel safe. If anything, the atmosphere felt tenser than before. He didn't miss how people kept eyeing his spear, either.

Chapter 15

Trav's rickety chair creaked. He sat in a crude room he had paid for, resting his chin on his hand, thinking. The faint light cast from the room's little oil lamp was not a problem since his emberstone eye allowed Trav to see just fine. In the back of his mind, his strange new senses buzzed, telling him that what he sought was nearby. Now that he was closer, he was even more sure it was not a memory shrine like before.

Something was wrong with Wall Home, the village.

He still couldn't quite put his finger on what the problem was, but his instincts had been jangling, demanding his attention.

Over the last few hours, he'd conducted trade and seen most of the village. He'd received barter for the longsword, amounting to a handful of jewelry, all of varying value. The weapon had been worth far more than that, enchanted as it had been, but Trav hadn't made a fuss.

Around the village, only a handful of people looked happy, vibrant, and healthy. The majority of the villagers were malnourished and seemed terrified.

As a smiling old woman had led him around, Trav had paid careful attention to his surroundings. He'd eventually determined where the strange, tugging sensation had to be coming from—straight from the only guarded area in the village other than the walls.

The village had been built at the base of a cliff, with the high, rough-hewn walls actually attached to surrounding trees as well as buried at the base for strength. A section of the cliff had been fenced off, and no-nonsense guards stood outside. The always-smiling blacksmith, Feth, and Grood, the settlement's headman, had explained that the area was where the settlement's mine was located.

Now that he was back in his room and thinking, Trav slowly shook his head. He'd kept an eye on the mine the rest of the day and hadn't seen anyone heading in or out of it. If it'd been a real mine, shouldn't someone be bringing out ore, or at least doing something other than just standing guard outside?

The small plate of food in his room was still warm—a slice of bread, some vegetables, and what looked like mutton. Trav hadn't touched any of it, nor the water skin he'd been provided with. He'd paid for them along with the room for the night, but he still had plenty of money left over after selling the Kin longsword. He'd been eating well while traveling with Narnaste. The Kin woman had made hunting easy, and luckily, Trav didn't really feel very hungry.

His nerves grew more agitated by the minute, and now that he had memories of an eons-old god locked away in his head somewhere,

Trav decided that listening to his instincts was a good idea. It was time to check out that mine, hopefully get what he came for, and get the hell out.

Trav held out a hand to summon his shiv—every bit of practice with his new abilities was probably wise. As the weapon appeared in his hand, he frowned. He really did need to name the damn thing, but it could wait.

He quickly grabbed some of the salt from the table. Apparently, salt on Asgard was easier to find than in medieval Earth. This would make his job easier.

With a few economical motions, Trav made a circle with the salt. If he grew more powerful in the future, a salt circle wouldn't be necessary for the types of rune equations he was about to do, but now it was.

Inside the circle, he placed some power in the salt, purifying the area he was in. Then he lightly scratched the rune equation he had in mind on his own skin, making sure to press down deeper on the last line. A drop of blood welled up, and Trav carefully tipped his arm over the salt circle. The blood fell, landing wetly, and Trav expended a whisper of magical power.

He felt the working take hold and glanced down, verifying that his body had gone misty. He'd be harder to see now.

That done, he activated his emberstone eye, allowing him to easily see in the dark. Then he created one last rune equation, this one on his stomach. When it was finished, his footsteps grew quiet, magically muffled.

There wouldn't be a better time to leave than now. Trav gave one last look at his spear, wishing he could bring it, but knowing it would be too great of a risk. He stealthily left his boarding room and the building serving as the makeshift inn. This late at night, the village was dark, a few houses lit with tapers, and quiet. For the most part, even the farm animals stayed silent.

Trav slowly crept through the village, taking his time. Villagers passed at least twice, but he was taking no chances, and it must have paid off. Nobody noticed him. The fact that so many villagers were still walking around seemed strange in itself, though. Trav had always thought that in low-technology societies, people went to sleep and woke up early. Of course, this was Asgard, so he wasn't sure what normal was for this world.

After arriving at the mine, Trav crouched behind a tree, watching the entrance. He felt fairly optimistic about sneaking in undetected, and he hadn't used much of his magic on his stealth buffs. Now that he was getting used to his new life, he'd decided to use some gamer terminology from Earth to keep all of his powers straight.

His cousin Ash had gotten him into a few video games in the past. Trav would never be a gamer, but he had enjoyed some of the open world role-playing games that he'd played. In fact, some of those games that had included old Viking mythology were how he knew more than the average person about old Odin myths to begin with.

Funny how life could turn out.

Trav grabbed a rock and threw it as hard as he could, away from the entrance to the mine. The stone bounced off something in the distance, making enough sound to draw away the guards.

Trav made his way to the door as quickly and stealthily as he could. Luckily, the door didn't squeak as he opened it and stepped inside.

The interior of the mine was not like he'd expected. Instead of a small, cramped tunnel, a clean stone hallway led deeper into the earth. Trav blinked. *Right. This is totally a mine,* he thought. There were no torches. Instead, the walls had strange glowing bundles hanging from hooks. Trav looked closer and realized that they were bones, feathers, and hair tied together in a very specific manner. The entire bundle emitted an otherworldly green glow.

He had a hunch what they could be, and Odin's memories confirmed his suspicions. *Witchcraft fetishes,* he thought. A few steps into the mine, two skulls stood on sticks, decorated with woven bones underneath, like shawls. Lines of symbols, similar to runes but not the same, spiraled up the wood of both totems, glowing with an otherworldly light.

Wards.

Trav almost turned back. This was more than he'd bargained for in this little human village in the middle of nowhere. He was brand new to his power, surrounded, and hadn't even had his freedom for a full week. But as he turned, he felt the strange pulling sensation, even stronger now that he was closer. Something was ahead, something important, and he knew he'd never be able to find any new power without taking risks.

His goals were too difficult, too huge to back away from

challenges. Before accepting Odin's mantle, he'd just wanted to get revenge for Beth's murder, but the reality was that he probably would have just died trying. Now he had a real chance to bring justice to a world of chaos. And maybe it was Odin's influence or his own renewed relationship with freedom, but he had been starting to ponder what his new status actually meant. Maybe if he couldn't bring peace to Asgard, he could give it one hell of a war.

Someone had to rule, why not him?

But that line of thinking was all pointless if he was not willing to brave danger, especially on a world like Asgard. Trav nervously scratched his beard for a minute and even briefly glanced at the door behind him before slightly nodding. He'd made up his mind.

With careful steps, he walked forward until he was directly in front of the wards. His emberstone eye allowed him to see the patterns of magic, and even moving trails of energy across the tunnel. Trav didn't know much about witchcraft, but Odin had—the half-remembered knowledge felt somewhat old, though. Trav drew his soul-bound shiv and severed a few lines of magic across the empty air in front of him. The careful cuts didn't collapse the entire web, but now he could walk past without triggering whatever traps or alarms the wards had created.

Trav continued down the tunnel and encountered a couple more ward barriers. His nervousness grew as he continued, but so did the tugging from whatever was down here, continuing to pull him along.

After descending for some time, Trav climbed stairs cut in the solid stone and found himself at an entrance to a side tunnel. The homing sensation pulled him down the main tunnel instead, so after one quick glance to the side, he continued on. A ways farther, and he discovered a couple other side tunnels. *Just how big is this place?* he wondered. The village outside hadn't seemed all that large.

His first clue to the true nature of the tunnel complex came when he noticed a bit of dust by the wall, far too thick to have happened naturally with regular foot traffic. With that, he reasoned that the tunnels might have existed before the village had, or maybe the village had even been built after the tunnels had been discovered. He didn't have much to base this assumption on, but it felt right in his gut.

Finally, he came to a portion of the tunnel that began to grow wider. More unnatural witchcraft lamps began filling the walls, creating criss-crossing shadows. A new room had an altar at one side, made of dark stone. The altar had rivulets of fresh-looking dried blood at the base. Two side doors stood open, and Trav caught a glimmer through one.

"What the," he muttered, and barely caught the slight sound of scuffing on the stone behind him. He began to turn, but something crashed into his head.

Trav saw stars, and the world went black.

Chapter 16

The next thing Trav knew, he was bound, being carried through a tunnel he hadn't been through before. His head hurt like hell, and it took his eyes a few minutes to focus. Something must have rung his bell pretty badly. He had a feeling that if he'd still been a normal man, he would have been out for longer, if not dead.

Knocking someone out wasn't easy in reality, unlike the movies. Something had hit him really, really hard. When he slowly turned, trying to disguise his movements, he was able to see who.

A short, powerfully built man with a long beard and a bald head strode forward with an air of authority. His dark robes were embroidered with white, mystic symbols, and he carried a staff with deep carving and decorations. A heavy chain woven with bones, hair, and sinew hung around his neck.

The man was probably a witch since he wore fetishes similar to the ones on the cave walls, but Trav activated his emberstone eye just to be sure. As soon as his mystical sight was in effect, he closed his good eye, hoping that nobody had seen him wake up. As usual, he could see just fine right through his eyepatch with the arcane prosthetic.

The first thing he verified was the robed man was indeed a male witch, a warlock. Trav was no expert, but based on what the emberstone was telling him, the man was powerful. A few villagers walked with the warlock, and Trav recognized a couple of them. Their veneer of happiness and friendliness had vanished, and now he mostly saw naked fear or greed.

Lovely.

"Let us hurry," ordered the warlock, his voice high, reedy. "We must dispose of this one."

One of the men from town argued, "But, Your Holiness, we took all his weapons away. He is just a man."

The warlock shook his head. "Something about this man makes the air move. The spirits are restless. We must dispose of him."

A voice that Trav recognized spoke—one of the men who'd been guarding the village gate. "Why don't we just kill him then?" After the question was voiced, Trav mentally nodded. He was glad to be alive but had been wondering the same thing.

"That is one option, but it would be a waste," said their leader. "The sacrifice needs to eat. Our ceremony is not for another couple days."

"Wouldn't a goat or a pig work for that?"

"No. It will be a more powerful sacrifice if it has as much power as possible, and it will get more of it if we offer it a man." Trav could hear the smile in the warlock's voice.

The answer seemed to satisfy the others, because they walked in silence after that, clip-clopping on the solid stone floor. Trav tried to test his bonds without giving away that he was awake but quickly gave up. He was surrounded, and the warlock made him wary. It would probably be smarter to wait until this little group of psychos took him wherever they were going before he made a move. Otherwise, if they knocked him out again, he might be fed to whatever they'd been talking about while being unconscious. That would be bad.

He knew they'd reached their destination when he felt a chill that had nothing to do with the cool air of the tunnels. A powerful magical barrier made his skin crawl, so potent that even without being targeted by it, it still made his cells feel like they wanted to come apart. Unless the villagers all had superhuman endurance, the field hadn't seemed to affect them as they carried Trav like a rag doll.

The moment he had passed through the powerful wall of magic, Trav's emberstone eye seemed to get heavy static, making it hard to see. It'd never done that before.

Trav was carried forward another ten yards or so, and a door opened on squeaky hinges. A low growl, like one from an animal, buzzed from wherever the warlock was taking him. Interference in his emberstone eye made it hard to see, but the door seemed to be set at the end of the tunnel.

Then Trav was tossed forward like a rag doll. As he passed through the door, he felt another barrier, somehow even stronger than the first one as it crawled over his skin. He landed on the stone floor in a heap—somehow holding in a pained grunt and landing like he was still unconscious—and felt the magical wall snap shut behind him, becoming an invisible prison that was stronger than steel.

The door slammed shut behind him, meaning he could stop pretending to be out cold. He rolled over, and even through the thick wood, he heard one of the villagers chuckle darkly. Trav thought fast and summoned his shiv into his hand. The strange magical barriers were so strong they practically made his teeth buzz, but luckily they didn't seem to affect his soul-bound connection. The moment his weapon was in hand, Trav sawed at the rope binding on his wrists and kept constant pressure on his arms. The rope snapped before it'd been fully cut.

He rolled to his feet and opened his good eye, helping his fuzzy emberstone eye to take in the dimly lit room, a row of glowing fungus near the ceiling. A creature was almost on top of him, its eyes wild.

Trav growled and held his shiv out in a menacing way before chambering the weapon at his hip to use defensively. The approaching monster got the hint and stopped. After it came to a halt, Trav realized that it was a she and Kin.

In the dim light, Trav couldn't make out too many details, but what he did see made him pause. She was half-naked, wearing small but luxurious clothing with elaborate needlework that looked easy to move in, sort of like a belly dancer. Her inhuman legs ended in talons, and her fingers had large claws. Feathers covered her arms, and a small crest of feathers on her head framed her inhuman face. High cheekbones gave her fierce eyes an upward slant.

The Kin growled deep in her chest, her sharp teeth on display, and

Trav got the uncomfortable feeling that he was being sized up like a piece of meat. She swayed back and forth for a while, and Trav began to relax, hoping the dagger would hold her off. Then she suddenly sprang forward, attacking. Her first swipe was lightning-fast, and Trav barely evaded it. If he'd been a normal man, it might have taken his hand off at the wrist. The room was small, but he darted back, cursing.

With a curious, bird-like hop, the Kin woman panted and moved forward, heat in her eyes. Trav dodged a grab and slashed with his shiv, but the Kin woman was fast, avoiding the attack and backhanding his arm out of the way. The force of the blow knocked the blade out of Trav's hand, and it skittered to the other side of the room.

Then she was all over him. Trav knew he was going to die as he was tackled to the ground, both of his arms being held over his head in one powerful, clawed hand. The Kin was strong, stronger than Narnaste. He fought, refusing to give up, wincing as he imagined getting his throat torn out. Chin down to protect his neck, Trav kept struggling, warily watching the Kin's other hand. Her claws flashed for his stomach, and Trav managed to free one hand to grab her wrist, holding her natural weapons away from his vulnerable middle.

He strained with all of his enhanced strength, but it wasn't enough. The hand inched closer. Trav tried to headbutt her in the face, but when she dodged back, she used both their motion to force her hand to his stomach—and began unbuckling his belt.

Trav blinked as the Kin woman fumbled at his waist for a few seconds, growling. Her growls changed, sounding frustrated, and one claw slipped down, ready to tear at his clothes. The cobwebs filling Trav's mind finally faded and he was able to think clearly, intuiting the situation. He was in great danger, but he might still be able to save himself.

When he dropped his hand to start undoing his own clothing, the feathered Kin woman panted with need. Trav moved his head forward, and she hissed, so he leaned back, trying not to flinch. His pants came off, and when she moved forward again, he managed to kiss the side of her neck. She didn't snap at him or bite, and only focused on his shirt. Trav mentally breathed a sigh of relief, painfully aware now that she was stronger than him and covered with weapons.

Playing along was probably currently saving his life. Actually, he was sure of it—half-remembered, borrowed memories confirmed his hunch. He would still die if he couldn't save himself, though—and he didn't have much time.

His clothes off, Trav tried to ignore what the Kin woman was doing, which was easier said than done. He stared at the ceiling and tried to move his arms. His plan hinged on sneakiness. While he kept his mind somewhere else other than what was happening to him, waiting for a chance to act, he examined the room he was in.

When his emberstone eye gradually became less scrambled, he realized the truth of his situation. The magic barrier at the door was incredibly strong, and the entire room was lined with its energy. He guessed that the spell walls had been placed long ago—they had the feel of ancient magic.

In his current state, even if he killed the attacking Kin woman, he would not be able to escape. He didn't need to try consulting with Odin's memories to figure out this would be bad. No, his escape plan would need to be altered.

On top of him, the Kin woman writhed and bit his shoulder. Trav winced but remained focused. The situation was dire and distressing, but Trav was tough, and surviving in the mines hadn't broken him— it'd just made him stronger...and more ruthless.

Finally, a minute or two later, a chance presented itself. The feathered Kin, a harpy, was completely absorbed in what she was doing, which meant Trav could call the shiv into his hand again without it being seen. He was tempted to plant the weapon into her back, even as she used his body, but he couldn't do that, at least not yet. He wouldn't exactly feel bad for her if things worked out in his favor, though.

The things the harpy was doing were getting more difficult to ignore and were already fuzzing Trav's muddled mind. He quickly used the shiv's memorization function, instantly scribing a number of glyph equations on the stony floor. Then he burned a very specific sigil underneath each of them.

The harpy still hadn't noticed what he was doing, which was good. He needed to work fast. She would be sure to kill him after she was done with her carnal attack, and probably if she found out what he was doing. This next part would be tricky.

Feigning enthusiasm, Trav dragged his nails down the harpy's back to disguise any other pains, and before she pushed him back down, he managed to touch the tip of his shiv to her skin, burning a glyph there. The glyph equations he'd placed on the floor would work without it, but now they'd be fully locked on.

Then everything was ready, and just in time. The Kin woman's eyes suddenly narrowed, even through her mania, and she turned her head. Trav kicked out with all his might, rolling away and the harpy hissed, probably seeing his shiv. She was probably wondering how he'd gotten ahold of it again, and the split second of hesitation let Trav get far enough away to activate the glyph equations.

Magic surged out of Trav, supplemented by the meager energy of the stone in the floor. Luckily, the room's barrier didn't interfere.

The moss in the ceiling writhed, snapping down and shooting across the walls, instantly growing to reach the Kin woman. Glowing vegetation, strengthened with magic, wrapped around the harpy's wrists and ankles, then began forcing her down.

Trav cautiously backed up while in a crouch, watching as the harpy was fully bound. The moss manacles held her fingers back and her arms to the ground so she couldn't use her natural weapons to break free. Her talons scraped on the floor, but she was helpless, pinned. She writhed, her naked, feathered body straining against her bonds.

After slowly standing, Trav reversed his shiv, holding it against his wrist, and dropped into a squat. He watched his captive and spat a bit of blood out of his mouth, touching his swollen lip. "My, how the tables have turned," he said, voice dark.

The Kin woman froze, and turned her head, eyes clearing. She breathed heavily and showed her sharp teeth. Just to be safe, Trav drew a few more glyph equations with his shiv in case the harpy's bonds broke, then he examined his new jail cell more carefully.

After a few minutes, he shook his head. The situation was grim, but he was still fairly confident of his plan. His issue now was moral, pondering where his ended and Odin's lack began. This was further complicated by wondering how many of his own were left after years of slavery.

Trav narrowed his eyes at the helpless harpy and rested his chin on one palm, studying her. At first, she looked away, but then she turned to meet his gaze, staring directly into his eyes. "What are you going to do with me?" she asked. Her voice sounded surprisingly cultured.

"That's what I'm trying to figure out. We both know that I should probably just kill you right now, but that would probably be bad for both of us. We need to talk."

Chapter 17

"What is your name?" asked Trav.

The trapped harpy wet her lips and stared before lunging forward...or tried to. The moss restraints held, and she growled in frustration before going limp. "This is not a good time." She flexed her claws as best she could, trying to reach the magic restraints that held her immobile.

"Tell me about it." Trav didn't bother trying to hide his sarcasm.

"Don't come any closer right now," she snarled. "Unless you want to be ripped apart, human."

"You don't worry about that. I'm not a fan of how we met."

The ferocious captive seemed to deflate a bit and hunched down. If Trav hadn't known better, he'd think she was embarrassed. "Yes, well..." She blew out a breath and shrugged. "You may not believe me, but I am not exactly in complete control of myself right now. You are a human man, so I doubt you will understand, but I am being starved, and my...sense is being overtaken."

Trav folded his arms and made a face, wondering if he might "know" anything about the Kin woman through his new memories. "You are a harpy?"

"Yes. A plains harpy."

That got Trav's attention, and he slowly nodded, information from his benefactor flooding his mind, like something he'd always known but had just forgotten. He asked, "How many kinds of harpies are there?"

"Plains, forests, coastal, and swamp. The plains harpies—"

"Pride themselves on knowledge and control," interrupted Trav, nodding. He suddenly knew about harpies. And the way this one was talking to him, strange situation notwithstanding, was very different to how Kin had acted when he'd been a slave. He wondered if the rune magic he'd demonstrated had something to do with it. ...Or maybe, it was just because Trav currently had the upper hand. The cynical thought twisted his lips.

"Yes, but—"

Trav held up a finger. "But you are still Kin. If you are starved, your mystical life force begins to wane along with your body, and you lose your reason. And you are a harpy, so you will attempt to steal the life force of a male through sex before killing and eating them. It's instinct."

"Be that as—" The harpy gave a calculating look. "Who are you? How can you do this?" She nodded at the moss restraints and the glyphs on the floor.

"You first. What is your name."

"So you are not with those darkness feeders?" She spat the words. Trav didn't know what it meant but figured she was referring to the warlock.

"No. I didn't know this village existed until earlier today." He let his eyes narrow and gestured with the shiv. "Name?"

"Yaakova."

"I'm Trav. So how did you get captured, Yaakova?" He paused. "I am assuming you are captured and are going to be used as a Kin sacrifice, but how did they even get you in the first place?"

The Kin woman eyed Trav warily for a moment but then looked at her restraints again and sighed. "I got careless."

"Explain."

Yaakova gestured at the glyphs on the floor with her chin. "You are obviously not a normal human, and can sense magic, so you probably felt the draw of this place, yes?"

Trav masked his expression and decided to give away as little as possible. "Explain it to me."

"Oh, Dead Masters, are you really playing games with me when we are both prisoners and I am in this state?" Suddenly, the harpy's eyes flashed, her expression turning bestial, and she lunged at Trav again. She struggled for a while but the restraints held, and she finally collapsed backward, panting. Her eyes cleared after a short struggle, but she didn't seem particularly sorry for losing control again. She stared at Trav in challenge.

"Fine. Yes, I felt something here. It's why I came." Trav didn't mention the divine nature of what had drawn him before. In fact, without the strange pull, he would have only otherwise felt the magic if he were nearly on top of the mine. The harpy woman must be more sensitive to magic than he was.

Yaakova nodded. "Among my tribal unit, I am a scholar of the old ways, ancestral spells mostly lost through time. I also study rune magic, though I am not as advanced as you are. In fact, I have never seen any rune crafter who could do what you just did. I would suspect you were a full rune lord, but they don't exist, and you are human—" Her voice trailed off before she started speaking again. "I came here seeking power or fortune, and I was not careful enough. I failed to notice a trap before it was too late, and now I am imprisoned, waiting to die. Simple."

Trav could relate to that. He blinked slowly as he thought about what to do. As he pondered, the harpy squirmed a bit, and the motion put her nudity and helplessness on full display. Trav might have been distracted if she hadn't been trying to have her way with him earlier before probably killing and eating him. She was a monster, and part of him still wanted to just kill her now and get it over with. She must have sensed what he was thinking, because she asked, "Why am I still alive? You are not a normal human, not at all."

"That is a good question," muttered Trav. "Can you see or sense the barrier around this room?"

"Yes, of course. I could not exactly leave before, after all."

"You know it is very strong?"

"Yes." The harpy woman answered slowly like it took effort to speak in a civil manner. Maybe it did.

Trav glanced around again, taking in the walls of his prison. Unwilling to completely give up the thought, he pondered killing Yaakova, letting righteous fury run through him one last time. Even beyond the fact that she was a violent monster, she'd made him feel weak again, even after taking his first step towards...whatever he was becoming. He'd just feared for his life, only moments ago, and had been attacked in a way that might have upset him more before he'd come to Asgard. His heart was growing hard as stone, and he wasn't sure he really liked it.

Yes, part of him wanted to kill her, to punish her, but he also needed her. "I can't get through these barriers on my own. I need more energy. That's where you come in."

When Yaakova stayed silent, Trav continued, "I can break the magic containment field."

"That's impossible! I can't even come within a finger-length of the door!"

"No, it's possible, it will just take a lot of power." Trav sighed and hefted the shiv in his hand.

"Are you going to kill me after all?" The Kin didn't seem scared, just disappointed.

"No. I'm going to mark you and make you my vassal."

Trav doubted there were many things he could have said that would have surprised the harpy woman any more than he just had. She cocked her head at him, a look of naked curiosity on her face. "Are you mad?"

"No. I'm desperate and don't have a lot of options." Trav gritted his teeth. He really didn't want to bond Yaakova, this...harpy. He was still coming to understand the ins and outs of his new, divine mantle, but he knew there were a limited number of times he could place his mark to create a vassal. This actual number was still unclear, but wasting any of them on a harpy who'd just tried to rage-mate with him before eating his face rubbed him the wrong way.

He moved closer to the Kin woman, examining her. Despite his strength, regardless of all the scraps he'd been in during his life and the small bit of martial knowledge he'd gotten from Odin's memories, even training he'd received from his cousin Ash, the harpy had beat him. When he came to a stop, the winged monster smiled, flashing her pointed teeth like she'd been thinking about the same thing. "I am going to mark you now," said Trav.

"So you lied, then. I see. Sacrifice. You are just a human after all."

In the past, in another lifetime, Trav might not have known how to deal with a psychotic monster woman with the strength of several men and claws long enough to take his head off. But things were different now. He stepped forward and punched her in the jaw with most of his strength. Her head snapped back and after a second to shake off her surprise, she lunged forward, snapping her teeth. Trav dodged, cocking his hand back again. Yaakova's eyes narrowed, and she slowly relaxed.

Trav shook his head. "That could have been my blade. Now shut up and listen. I don't like this situation either, but we both need each other. After I do what I'm about to do, you will not be starving anymore; your magic will be restored. You will have more power than you had before, and I will have the power to get us out of here."

"Lies. I have never heard of such a thing."

"Maybe. But look into my eyes."

The harpy laughed. "You must think I am truly gullible. Look into a 'crafter's eyes?'"

Trav firmed his lips. "If I wanted you dead, you would already be dead, Kin."

"There is that." She seemed to think for a while before announcing, "Fine."

As Yaakova met Trav's eyes, he willed his mantle to the surface, hoping that it wouldn't buzz too much, creating too many waves through the ether, but then realized it didn't matter. He was intending to shake things up, after all. He didn't have much of a choice.

The Kin woman suddenly recoiled and gasped. "What are you?"

Trav answered honestly. "The hope of a dead god. Something new."

"What are you planning to do?"

With a mental sigh, Trav relaxed. Now the harpy was listening—he had her full attention. "I need to place a mark on you. This will connect us. If I do this, I will receive power from you, but not much. I need to create this connection in order to permanently mark you as my servant. If I do that, it will permanently increase both our power."

The process would need to be different with Yaakova than it had been with Narnaste. After he'd met the wolf woman, and after he'd placed the rune equation of binding on her, they'd worked together, bonded, and he'd saved her life. She'd unwittingly sealed the bond herself, at least the first half of it.

But he had no such relationship with the dangerous, feathered Kin bound to the stony floor. No amount of sex with this monster would be enough to get the power he would need. His only choice would be to fully commit, create another divine vassal.

He hated it.

Yaakova blinked her inhuman eyes. "What you are claiming...It can't be."

"Well, it is, because I already have one Valkyrie running around, and I am beginning to seriously wish I had taken her with me."

"Why are you telling me all of this?" The harpy still had heat in her voice, but something had changed in her expression. A bit of respect moved across her face and some fear. Trav had a hard time telling due to the moss holding her, but it almost looked like she was trying to inch away.

"I am telling you for a simple reason." Now was time to get creative with the truth. Ever since Trav had met Narnaste, he'd decided to avoid lying whenever possible while dealing with Kin, just in case. He would always try to be honest. "If you enter into this pact willingly, the magic will be stronger, and so will the benefit to both of us."

"I see." Yaakova seemed to sag in her restraints. "This is—I am having trouble thinking, and this is not exactly something easily understood."

"Okay. I will draw the rune equation on you now, then. This will bind us together but is not the final step. I will get some energy from this, but not enough to break the barrier. But you will receive clarity, won't be starving anymore, so you'll be able to think better."

"Do as you will."

Trav moved forward with his shiv raised. The weapon seemed almost eager to carve flesh again, and the man from Oregon tried to pretend he was imagining things.

***

About ten minutes later, Trav stood tapping his foot. The binding rune equation had been successfully created without a hitch. Since he'd still been wary of the Kin woman, Trav had carved the lines and whorls into her back—in case she'd been able to break free of her imprisoning moss. He was beginning to worry that the human freaks in the tunnels might return before he could escape.

The Kin woman needed to make a choice now.

After marking the harpy's back, he'd explained what he planned to do to her in as much detail as possible, and Yaakova had seemed to take it with an air of fatality. She never apologized for what she tried to do to Trav, nor did she beg for her life or ask Trav to reconsider. On Asgard, power seemed to be everything, and the Kin didn't often ask for mercy—nor give any.

Trav made a face and frowned at the door. If a guard were outside, they still, hopefully, probably, hadn't heard anything. He believed the magic barrier probably blocked most sound, but the fact that he'd heard the warlock and his minions leaving was worrisome. He hoped it had just taken a while for the magic to completely take effect once they'd thrown the lock.

Finally, Yaakova stirred. "I have decided that I will do this."

"Oh?"

"Yes. Everything you have told me is ludicrous and unbelievable, but I don't have any way to disprove your words. You have demonstrated things I cannot explain, and nothing I know about magic, nor the Dead Masters, contradicts anything you've told me. Further, you are going to do what you want to me anyway. I should accept it to obtain the most benefit I can."

Trav just nodded. He was impressed with her reasoning but didn't say anything in return. If things had gone differently earlier, she might be snacking on his arm like a chicken wing right now. After stepping forward dispassionately, he held up his ring and asked, "Where would you like the mark? Any preference?"

"No."

"So be it." Trav moved behind the bound Kin again and focused on a portion of her lower back above her bare ass. Now that some time had passed since he'd fought for his life, he could admit that Yaakova had a very, very shapely ass.

Too bad it was attached to a crazy, clawed monster.

Trav warned, "Get ready. The last time I did this, the other person was unconscious, but it hurt me—a lot."

"Get on with it!" Yaakova snarled.

"Fine." He touched his ring to Yaakova's lower back and reached out to the strange well of power that still felt attached to him by little more than a string—Odin's mantle. Trav gritted his teeth and began channeling the essence of his purview through his body, through his ring, and into the harpy.

He wasn't sure who screamed first, him or his would-be murderer.

Chapter 18

This time, the pain hadn't been as great as the first time he'd bonded a vassal, mainly because he'd had more magic power to act as a buffer. As a result, Trav didn't—quite—lose consciousness.

He gasped, holding his chest, and curled up into a ball on the ground. In the clarity of blinding agony, he realized that this time, the divine broadcast of what he'd done would probably be fairly well blocked by being so far underground, but the warlock would have to be magically blind not to have felt something. There was no time to waste.

After painfully forcing his eyes open, Trav held in a startled oath and merely blinked instead. Yaakova's inhuman face was less than a foot away from his own, eyes dilated. The Kin's expression was strange. She breathed deeply, so hard it ruffled Trav's hair before standing to her full height. The moss restraints had been torn apart, and something had changed about the harpy woman, both physically and magically, but Trav couldn't quite put his finger on it.

"I am not sure I could even attack you if I wanted right now," she said absently, seemingly talking to herself. "It is a strange feeling. Actually, I think I could, but like biting my own arm, it would feel unnatural. But—" She held up a hand in wonder and focused on Trav again. "New power...you were not lying, Awakened One."

Trav worked on getting his breathing back under control and eyed her out the corner of his eye. He could feel his own strength growing too, but it would take some time before fully settling. The new increase in power would also need to finalize before he could choose any more permanent increases to his abilities or his body. If he never used another rune equation to modify himself, he'd just have more raw magic power to call on.

Trav's raw magic was currently expanding, but Yaakova would be growing in overall power. She was already physically stronger—the shredded moss was evidence of that.

The mark and the bond he'd placed on the Kin was obviously holding her at bay to some degree, but Trav needed to establish his leadership position. Escaping would be good too. He ordered, "Stand back; I'm going to break the magic barrier. We need to be quick. Someone must have felt what I just did."

Yaakova nodded and walked to the rear of the room, her movements a bit jerky, predatory. "I will take my clothes and get dressed then."

Trav nodded at the harpy's words but otherwise ignored her, trying not to show any weakness or hesitation. He focused on his task and opened his emberstone eye wide, cycling through the different ways he could see through it.

The prison had been constructed well and had been created with several layers of rune equations that could be easily activated by someone on the outside. Earlier, Trav had suspected that the system was old, and now he confirmed it. A normal rune mage would probably not be able to break a prison like this regardless of how much magic they could channel, but Trav was hardly normal.

He still had limits, though. His power would slowly grow for a while now, but he'd already gotten most of his increase in magical energy in one surge. *Interesting*. He'd received more from Yaakova than he had from Narnaste.

Trav began wrapping his head around the new energy he'd gotten, the raw power that could be used for magic and to upgrade his strength. After some thought, he decided to think of it in terms of bars or points. He pictured a spreadsheet in his head with boxes representing his power, stretched in a line.

After reviewing his knowledge of permanent rune equations, he had a good grasp of the minimum amount of power necessary for a personal upgrade and decided that this value would be one bar or point. With that in mind, he'd counted a total of three bars of power from Narnaste, and he had spent two of them on his first, general, permanent upgrade, leaving one bar in reserve.

Bonding with Yaakova had just given him four bars of magical power, so he currently had almost five bars available. Unfortunately, removing the powerful magic around his prison cell would require three bars. *Wow.* He'd need to succeed the first time. If his attempt fizzled, he'd only have two bars left for the day, and wouldn't have enough energy to try escaping again.

Trav slowly knelt and carefully began scribing rune equations directly into the stone. Faint light made each line glow. Linking the complex rune equations, he created joining systems with a series of glyphs supported by sigils. In the center of the complex rune working, he even used smaller rune equations as a more complex join, just to make sure everything would work correctly. Each rune equation was designed to fire off in sequence, like a firework with stages. If he was right, the large, intricate magical working should destroy the magic barriers.

Once he was finally done, Trav thought, *Wow. This really is going to take three bars. I'm glad the harpy decided to cooperate.* Then he cleared his mind, picturing what he wanted his power to do. That done, he took a deep breath to steady himself, gathered his magic, and shoved raw energy into the large rune working.

Points on each rune equation began to glow, getting brighter as the magic swirled and magnified itself. "What is happening?" asked Yaakova, her voice mostly steady. "What are you doing?"

Trav smiled grimly. "The barriers were made too well to break out of normally. So instead of attacking the lock, or even the rune working, I'm convincing it to destroy itself."

"I see." The floor began to rumble. "Is it going to work?"

"We will find out any second now." Trav didn't know what to expect, but about a minute later when the rumbling suddenly stopped, he blinked. *Is that it?* He hesitantly moved forward and touched the wooden door before grinning. "It's done!" The fact that he'd just used up most of his new magic power for the rest of the day gave him pause, but they were almost free! He began drawing on the locked door with his dagger.

"Step aside, Awakened One." Trav felt himself being gently pushed out of the way and watched in astonishment as Yaakova slashed forward with the flight feathers on her arms, demolishing the door. Trav was almost sure she hadn't been able to do that before.

"Wow." He exhaled.

The harpy nodded seriously but did not turn around. "This will not be my only new ability. Something inside me is growing...changing. I am glad I took a chance on this union. Humoring your plan instead of killing you has probably been one of the best decisions I have made in my life. This is," she muttered, "more than I had expected."

Trav wasn't sure what to say. "Well, good." The harpy's new attitude sure beat her homicidal tendencies and terrifying sexual advances. He was really getting tired of nearly being killed by thugs or eaten by monsters. If he lived through this situation, he vowed to put some serious thought into how to become stronger as quickly as possible.

Out in the hallway, he was pleased to find that the second barrier had already come down too. It must have been attached to the system that Trav had just destroyed. More glowing witch fetishes lined the walls of this tunnel, so it wasn't difficult to see, but the witchlight made everything appear ominous, surreal.

After following Yaakova a few more steps, Trav wondered how she knew she was heading the right direction, but then he remembered she could feel what he'd come for, too. He briefly considered whether he should just run away, let the Kin woman and the crazy warlock kill each other, but something was bothering him. Whatever was tickling his instincts had been near the altar he'd found before, but he couldn't nail down the exact reason. He decided it must be related to an Odin memory—one he wasn't able to access yet. *Great.*

All the runecrafting he'd just done must have created echoes and ripples in the ether. Trav kept waiting for an alarm, and his shoulders itched when it didn't come. The fact that there hadn't even been any guards outside the cell seemed super strange too.

His thoughts were disrupted by the appearance of two men ahead, perhaps new guards, or doing rounds through the tunnels. They walked normally, apparently not aware of the massive magical upheaval in the area. The short, bearded, dirty men were armed with blades at their waists, maybe heavy knives or langseax, and one held a small torch. Both groups saw each other at the same time, and Yaakova froze. The local men dropped their jaws in surprise, and one said, "Oh, s—"

The harpy sprang forward, on them like a flash, her claws and feathers ripping the two men apart in a shower of gore. Blood splashed against the walls, and a few drops hit a witchlight fetish, making it sizzle. The scene was horrific, but Trav had seen worse on Asgard. He made a face and held his breath, waiting again for an alarm...but none came.

Yaakova seemed to feel that something was off too. She stood motionless, dripping blood from her iron-hard feathers and breathing deeply. One of the dying men tried to scream, but it came out as a whispered wheeze. He feebly moved an arm as the Kin woman standing over him cocked her head, listening.

Trav waited what felt like an eternity before moving again. On the one hand, he was tired—physically and emotionally drained. It was likely he could be discovered or ambushed at any time. On the other hand, nobody was currently attacking, and what limited time he had was ticking away.

Should he escape? Isn't that why he broke out of the cell? He wondered if Yaakova would agree. The harpy unnerved him, but he'd bonded with her. If she died now before their bond was finalized, Trav might even suffer a backlash. In fact, if she died at all, he'd suffer a huge setback—like it or not, she was one of his Valkyries now, and he had used up one of his divine marks.

As Trav hugged a wall, he wished he'd brought his spear. His armor and gear he'd brought were still missing too, removed before he'd regained consciousness earlier. Since he wasn't being attacked and wasn't sure what he should do, he paused.

"What are you doing?" asked the harpy.

"I'm thinking. Be quiet."

Yaakova opened her mouth to speak, but Trav said, "You'd still be in the cell if not for me. Rushing forward is stupid. Be calm."

After an unreadable look, the Kin woman nodded and settled back against the wall, adjusting her feathers as if she weren't filthy and covered in blood. She said, "I will watch the tunnels and listen for attacks. Don't take too long...thinking. The warlock will probably not be idle during this time." Trav acknowledged her with a nod and absently picked up a few loose stones from the ground as he considered what to do.

Yaakova had a point about the warlock, but everything had happened so fast, Trav needed to get his bearings. He'd survived Asgard so far by trying to pause to think when he needed to. Of course, he hadn't ever exactly gotten many opportunities to do so.

It was clear that the smartest course of action would be to escape. However, he had a few other considerations. One, they'd taken his gear. In fact, they might have taken his spear from his room, too. Two, they'd tried to kill him. Three, something about the altar room and what he'd seen really bothered him. And lastly, he could still feel the pull of what he'd come here for to begin with.

Ultimately, he still couldn't identify the best course of action, but it was time to be decisive. He defaulted to the most practical course of action. "We are going to find my armor and leave."

Yaakova didn't look happy, but the apparent rush she'd gotten from escaping her cell seemed to be fading. "Fine. I am not a tree-dweller, but I am tired of existing underground like a mole."

Trav nodded, focused on the stones he'd picked up. With a relatively simple glyph equation, sped up with a few sigils and glyphs he'd loaded into his shiv, he created a tracking device with one stone. It would point to a unique, complex glyph chain that Trav had scribed on the inside of his armor. If he weren't so frazzled, he would have patted himself on the back for the forethought.

With another couple stones, Trav took a few minutes and a dismaying amount of magic power to create a couple fire flowers, a type of magical grenade. A lot of his remaining magic power had been spent, but he wished he had time to prep more. Unfortunately, most other magic weapons he could make, or items he could craft, would take far longer. No, this was the best he could do in the time he had.

"Okay let's go," he muttered. Trav moved quickly down the tunnels, following the direction of the heated rock in his hand. The half-naked harpy who had almost killed and eaten him an hour earlier followed close behind.

Asgard sucks.

Chapter 19

The former slave found his armor down the hallway in a hidden room, deep in the tunnels. The entrance had been built in such a way to take advantage of a natural outcropping, hidden from plain sight. Trav still hadn't seen any more guards, although he thought he heard chanting and stamping in the distance. Other, less easily identifiable noises raised his hackles, but he wondered if he was imagining things. In his situation, plenty of people might have already broken.

This was not a fun thought.

Trav practically threw on his gear and got a welcome surprise when he found his spear in the corner. He grinned nastily at that. Without the spear's anti-theft measures, he doubted it would have just been stashed away after being fetched from his room. He hoped someone had gotten burned badly while moving it.

Yaakova found a box full of jewelry that apparently belonged to her and began putting it on, clucking to herself in pleasure while she did so. A few pieces gave off an aura of magic and made Trav's eyebrows raise.

While the Kin woman finished getting situated, Trav noticed something strange out of his emberstone eye. One side of the room had disturbed flows of magic, and he could trace the shape of a rectangle. The wall itself didn't show any breaks at all, but after getting closer, he was able to confirm that it was a hidden door. The low power, self-sustaining glyph equations blocked sound and also provided a weak shield against magic.

After Trav knew the door was there, it was easy to find the hidden button to open it. The magic flows made it obvious. "Do you see this?" he asked Yaakova.

The harpy squinted her eyes and moved her head from side to side a few times before slowly saying, "I see something, but it is not clear."

"Got it. Well, I am curious now." Trav decided to trust the geas tied into the mark he'd placed on the harpy. "Guard the door to the room, please. I am going to check this out." Other than the two men that Yaakova had killed, the escape so far had been smooth—too smooth. Trav knew everything could go horribly wrong in an instant and vowed not to take long taking a look behind the door.

After hitting the button, and as the rock appeared to swing inward, he paced forward slowly, spearhead forward.

On the other side was a wrought iron gate with a lock on it, and a wooden door set in the opposite stone wall. Weird. Trav tapped the lock with his shiv, and the lock fell apart. The gate opened soundlessly, and he discovered the door behind it was locked too. After another tap with the shiv, he moved forward and frowned.

He could only imagine that he'd found the warlock's quarters. A big bed covered in filthy furs took up one corner. Storage chests and arcane-looking decorations filled much of the room. Two wooden doors stood closed. In the corner, a woman was chained to a ring in the wall and reclined on a stack of pillows. Her long dark hair was greasy but thick. Bushy eyebrows topped a couple of large brown eyes and a generous mouth. Her clothing was not much better than rags. She had a paper and pencil in her lap, and discarded doodles lay all over the floor. She wasn't drawing when Trav came in, just staring at the wall with a dead look in her eyes. As soon as she noticed him, she gasped and stood in a rush.

"Who are you? Toggit will kill you if he finds out you were here! Leave now!"

"Is Toggit the bald warlock? He might find I'm harder to deal with when I'm awake," growled Trav. The woman just opened and closed her mouth like a fish. Now that he got a better look, he realized she was young, but her age was hard to place. People on Asgard could age quickly. "What are you doing here?"

The girl's wonder turned to an ugly scowl. "I am Toggit's plaything—well until he needs another sacrifice. They took poor Lvinsi last week, so now only I am left. I guess now that the children are all gone, they need women."

"Sacrifices?"

"Yes. Toggit brags all the time. He wasn't happy with being a regular witch, so he formed a contract with something big and really evil. At first, he only sacrificed animals, but then he made a dark pact, lost his hair, and found this place." She seemed to crumple in on herself. "I hate it here. Please, free me! This place is not safe!"

"What do you mean? And what is your name?"

"I am called Halfa." Her eyes darted around nervously. "The big sacrifice is coming! Toggit and his disciples even found a Kin to help it along! They are working on the rituals right now. The dark, demon god that they serve wants to come through the veil."

"Dark god?" Something stirred deep inside Trav, from the new portion attached to him, his divine purview.

"Yes. Toggit is not the only follower of," she whispered, "Myalingra. He was shown the way by a priest somewhere to the east. He and his demon worshippers have some plan or other, and from what Toggit said, something is making the dark things stir. Witches all over Asgard are receiving more power and new orders." Halfa pointed at her chain. "Maybe you can find more in Toggit's study! Now please, let me go!"

Trav frowned but moved forward to free the captive. She'd just thrown a lot of information around in a short amount of time. She'd been drawing some really strange things full of symbols, too.

Up close, he could see that he'd actually been wrong about her age. Fine lines at the corners of her eyes gave away her years. She breathed out in wonder as he drew a sigil to break the chain she had been bound with. Trav had expected her to immediately either hide behind him or ask where the exit was after being freed, but instead, she took off like a bat out of hell.

The woman sprinted out of the hidden room, screaming at the top of her lungs. "Toggit! Anyone! Intruders! Heathens! They—"

A powerful clawed hand darted out, ripping the woman's throat out. She went down immediately, clawing at her ruined neck, and Yaakova carefully stepped around her. "She smells like dark magic. Why did you free her?"

Trav blinked as he realized he still had a lot to learn. The harpy didn't need to know this, though. "I was testing you," he said coldly. "You did well."

The Kin woman gave him an unreadable, inhuman look before merely nodding. "I am willing to follow you for now. My patience is waning, though. You should hurry." With that, she turned back to watching the exit.

Trav frowned and moved to examine the closed doors. He could hear Halfa's drumming feet slow, growing weaker as she died. He ignored it.

Asgard had made him tough.

The first door he opened with a bit of magic was a water closet, a fancy one too. It even had a shower. The warlock had even done something with a skull and some magic to create a faucet. The second door opened to an arcane office. A desk took up a corner, and shelves held labeled jars of strange substances.

Trav began to search the place but didn't need to look long to find something of interest. One wall of the room was covered with a painting. He couldn't make sense of it at first. Globes, or spheres full of runes, covered the walls, and labeled lines connected them. Many of the lines originated from one central sphere.

Trav realized he could read the runes, and grew more puzzled, trying to figure out what it all meant. However, once he realized that the center circle was Asgard, it all made sense.

The painting was an invasion plan. He stared in horror, realizing that one of the circles connected to Asgard with a line had runes for Earth.

With a sinking heart, Trav ransacked the room, ignoring written spells, random pieces of animals, and jars of things he didn't want to examine too closely. In a drawer of a desk, he found what he was searching for.

The little, locked journal was bound with thick leather. For Trav, removing its lock, and the attached curse, was easy. The pages were full of small, neat writing—the warlock had kept meticulous records. From Odin's memories, Trav knew this was usually the case with witches since their magic was so closely tied to ingredients and crafting.

In the journal, his fears were confirmed. The warlock had somehow been taught to rip open veil gates, although it required a lot of preparation and a ridiculous amount of power. Trav still wasn't clear on exactly what veil gates even were, but he knew that this was bad. As he skimmed the journal, he realized that he hadn't been entirely correct before about what the painting meant.

Apparently, the warlock's master, the demon god, was trying to come through to Asgard. Trav had no idea what a demon god was, and the name hadn't rung a bell, but Odin's memories let him know that everything about the plan was disturbing. Powerful entities usually couldn't even pass through a veil gate, much less keep their power. The only exception was usually the Restless. However, the demon worshippers had been working on this little scheme for a while now. The idea seemed to be that this Myalingra had been taking advantage of the gods' absence for a while, and he was about to succeed in spreading his influence to other veils.

Trav felt time ticking and turned the pages almost frantically. He was finally getting answers, but he hadn't even known some of the questions existed. His stomach roiled, and he felt sick. Part of him was horrified now. He found a section detailing the individually targeted worlds and learned that the veil gate to Earth, or Midgard, was usually closed, but Myalingra could open it from Asgard.

Another part of him, the new, divine part felt guilt. The Restless were supposed to prevent things like this.

He cursed and shoved the journal into a pocket. There would be time to read more later—now it was time to act. He checked his magic as he moved, noting how much he had left. As he stalked back through the little hallway to the next room, Yaakova cocked her head.

Trav tensed his jaw and said, "We are going to go kill the warlock. Let's go."

"It's about time." Yaakova shrugged and followed, but Trav saw the gleam in her eyes. The harpy may try to act casual, but she was Kin and had one hell of a grudge after being imprisoned.

Trav was more than willing to turn her loose; whatever the Myalingra followers were doing in the tunnels needed to be stopped. But while whatever Yaakova did would be helpful, Trav would need to finish the deed. Both parts of his soul, the man and the divine, were in agreement.

Earth hadn't treated Trav all that well, but Asgard was a hellhole, and he knew now that there were even worse places out there. He would eventually like to find a way to go back home to Earth, maybe if he survived killing Beth's murderer. But if this Myalingra thing got there first, Trav might not have anything to go back to.

And based on what Trav had read in the warlock's journal, the Kin on Asgard were friendly and thoughtful compared to Myalingra's children.

Chapter 20

As he moved through the eerily empty, witchlight-illuminated tunnels, Trav's unease grew. His mind kept returning to the information he'd gotten from the dead woman back in the warlock's quarters. The fact that she'd probably been more of an apprentice than a pleasure slave and had been in league with the demon worshippers made Trav suspicious of everything she'd said. The village outside the caves really hadn't had many children, though. *Actually, did it have any at all?* Trav couldn't completely remember, and the implications were disturbing.

He really didn't want to believe that the villagers had killed all the kids off to appease some dark god, or had let it happen. Then again, in hindsight, quite a few of them had come across as terrified. But if that was happening, if they were being pushed into it, why didn't they just leave, or go get help?

No, maybe it's not that simple. Get help from who? Leave to go where? Trav answered his own question, and part of him felt sick. He'd been a slave for years and had never given up on life, but he'd seen plenty who had.

Knowing that human beings were capable of such evil was one thing, but Trav had seen it firsthand. Part of him wanted to give the benefit of the doubt, but he feared the worst.

The noises up ahead were growing stronger. Since he was heading toward danger, Trav tried to think of a plan, but eventually he just accepted he didn't have enough information to form one. The two fire flower, magic-crafted stones in his pocket were comforting, as was the spear in his hand. If he had to fight it out, at least he had decent weapons and some magic left to call on.

Still, whether they were going to fight or not, he didn't want to just go running in like an idiot. In fact, doing so last time had gotten him knocked out to begin with. He glanced at the harpy and whispered, "Hey, we are going to take this slow, alright?"

"Of course. I will follow your lead. As long as we punish the warlock and settle my debt to these heathens, I will be content." The harpy's words held heat, but her mannerisms were distracted like she was focusing inward. Suddenly, she cocked her head and said, "I can transform now, I think."

Trav's eyes narrowed in confusion before he slowly nodded. "My other Valkyrie can too, so I guess this doesn't surprise me that much."

"Truly?" The Kin's usual aloof air had disappeared. In its place, her voice held a sense of wonder.

"Yes. What can you transform into?"

"I am not sure." She didn't say anything else.

Trav watched the harpy a moment longer before turning his eyes forward again. He could definitely hear chanting now and other strange noises.

Farther up the tunnel, retracing the path he had originally taken before being captured, he found out what all the demon followers had been doing. After waving Yaakova to stay still, he'd slowly poked his head around a bend in the tunnel. The chamber with the altar was visible, and a large number of people had gathered, wearing dark robes and chanting. The altar was covered in fresh blood, and a huge puddle of it had run all over the floor, flowing into a small gutter that led deeper into the room. The demon worshippers seemed to be in some state of euphoria and were waving their hands around as little green motes of magic floated through the fetish-lit cavern.

The warlock Toggit stood in front of the altar with his head uncovered, a knife held in his bloody hands. He chanted in a language that Trav didn't understand at first but placed as similar to Sumerian after his borrowed memories kicked in.

None of this made sense at first. *Why are they celebrating, or whatever it is they're doing?* The warlock had to know by now that Trav had escaped. Apparently, a lookout had been posted—one robed person stood to the rear. Luckily, they were facing the other direction at the moment.

Now that he was seeing the room again, and had a better view of the layout, Odin's knowledge helped Trav to understand what he was seeing. Cycling through the filters of his emberstone eye helped too. He gritted his teeth.

Through one arched doorway, he saw a veil door for the first time. The rift in time and space shimmered—its magical aura and flows were unique, interesting; it had been artificially stabilized. A large number of protective rune equations had been placed around it, both to stabilize the veil, and to keep it contained. The altar was magically attached to it somehow—the cultists had been offering prayers and power—and blood—to whatever was on the other side of the veil. Presumably, the humans didn't have the power to break the rune equations binding the veil, but maybe something on the other side could.

Now that his magical senses were turned to the maximum, he felt something terrible, something cold from the other side. Half-remembered fringes of Odin's memories made Trav's hands shake. What he was feeling had something to do with how Odin had died.

Coming here to put an end to this madness had been the right decision. Trav wasn't a fan of Asgard, but whatever was on the other side of the veil gate was pure evil. He didn't like the look of the strange, wispy, fog-looking things coming out of the veil-gate, either. Another powerful, different sense of dread washed through him when he'd noticed them.

Due to the angle he was watching from, Trav could also see into the second doorway from the altar room. His eyebrows climbed up when he saw it was a doorway to a natural tunnel, covered floor to ceiling in emberstone. At this point, he also realized that the pulling he'd felt before came from this area.

He was about to turn away when he heard a faint voice. At first, he almost dismissed it, but then he remembered he was on another world. He focused, ignoring his ears, and trying to listen with his magic senses.

The voice whispered, *Help me. I can't last much longer. You, I can see you. I can feel you. Whoever you are, save me, and I will serve you forever.*

Oh, Erinyes, it has been so long…

I have asked so many times, and nobody hears me, but you are different. Ah, yes, you hear me! I swear upon the night and the day that you will not regret it!

Take me, free me, and I will be your sword!

The voice kept basically repeating itself after that. Trav reasoned that the voice was somehow connected to whatever had been pulling him to the mines in the first place. He wanted to find out what it was, but he had about forty cultists to deal with first.

As with several other times since he'd been in the tunnels, he acknowledged that running away would be the smart course of action. But his earlier realization that higher risk meant higher reward made him pause. Plus, something about this situation was resonating with his divine mantle.

The demon worshippers offended him.

He ducked back around the corner and briefly relayed what he'd seen to Yaakova. She stayed silent while he whispered, and when he was done, she didn't react how he'd expected her to. He'd expected a few questions or even a challenge to his ownership of whatever was in the emberstone cave. Instead, she just said, "I want to kill the warlock."

Trav frowned. "Didn't you come here in the first place for the power you were feeling?"

"Yes. But it doesn't matter anymore. When you marked me, you gave me everything I needed. Plus, you said it is surrounded by red stone, and it is next to that veil gate. I have no desire to die. Whatever is there has been looking at us, I can feel it."

Trav just nodded. He was glad he had to focus on the veil gate to feel the—wrongness—on the other side. This little adventure had been more than he'd bargained for. One thing was for sure—he was never leaving Narnaste behind ever again.

"Okay. Stand back." Trav drew his shiv and began slowly scribing rune equations on the rock wall where he was standing. This would be a similar working to what the Kin had done to the emberstone mine he'd worked in.

There was about to be a cave-in, a big one.

As he drew, he instructed, "Be slow and careful, but look around the corner and try to see if the robes people have any more living sacrifices."

"Why."

"Maybe we can save them."

Yaakova narrowed her eyes at him like he was stupid, but she made a face and complied. After that, Trav paid full attention to what he was doing. Yaakova was a wild card. The harpy was dangerous and stubborn but hopefully wouldn't turn on her new master. Trav's divine mark was potent, infused with divine magic, and the Kin woman had consented to be bound.

Worrying about Yaakova's loyalty was useless at this point and distracting. Trav needed to draw the rune equations as carefully as he could and only release magic at a small, constant rate. This method took a lot of control and massive amounts of focus. Luckily, he'd had several years of practice in single-minded patience.

Once he finished this rune working, it would automatically activate. There would be a drain on his power then, removing most of what he had left. This would definitely alert the warlock that he was doing something, especially since they were so close. If Trav ran away at that point, he'd lose any chance of finding out what was in the emberstone cave, and Yaakova would undoubtedly die. There was no way she'd just run away—no matter what, she'd probably still want to kill the warlock.

Kin were just like that.

Besides, Trav didn't have enough time to play argue-all-day-with-the-Kin. Time was not on their side. He couldn't talk while focusing on his rune working, but flashes of worry seeped around the emotional blocks he was using.

The idea of losing all of his remaining power for the day made him nervous. Logically, he knew he should feel lucky, though. Only the presence of so much emberstone nearby, and the magically-charged nature of the caves themselves, were allowing him to charge up such a powerful rune working. In essence, he was using the mountain to bring down the mountain, similar to how he'd destroyed the barrier on the prison cell earlier by turning it on itself.

He carefully drew a line terminating in a box and began attaching glyphs to the endpoint. This portion of the working would function as the fuse. After the rune working was activated, he'd only have about twenty minutes to escape. The continued chanting of the cultists filled Trav with dread and made his stomach turn. It sounded like their ritual had changed.

The harpy suddenly came back, leaning in close to whisper. "I just checked. There are no captives. In fact, the last sacrifice looks like it was one of them." Yaakova looked disgusted. "The witchcraft they are using is sloppy, inelegant. It's like using a large rock to stir a stew pot."

Trav nodded—his drawing was almost finished. "Alright, get ready. When this thing is done, hold back long enough to let me throw one of the stones in my pocket. Then you can kill anyone you want. Well, you might want to go after the warlock first."

"That sounds wonderful." The harpy smiled, her expression predatory and bestial. Trav was suddenly reminded again that earlier that day, she'd been ripping his pants off and would have gladly killed and eaten him.

Somehow, Trav was still surviving Asgard, barely—he was hardly comfortable, though. He doubted his benefactor, Odin, had ever gone through anything quite like this before.

Chapter 21

The rune working was almost finished, and Trav was sweating bullets. "I'm about to be done," he whispered. In the background, just a murmur now that he'd tuned it out, the voice from the emberstone tunnel still pleaded to be released.

He turned to look Yaakova in her unsettling, inhuman eyes. "Get ready."

"I am ready." The harpy stood crouched, watching their rear so nobody could sneak up on them. She practically trembled, she was so ready for violence.

Trav examined his entire rune working on the wall with a critical eye, making sure he hadn't left anything out. "And you will prioritize the warlock. He has to die as fast as possible."

"Yes. This is obvious, and you have already said so before."

"Okay, good." Trav felt strange doing so, but he whispered again, speaking aloud to the voice in the emberstone cave. He was fairly sure the voice was female, but he still wasn't certain. "Hey, you, the one who is trapped and wants to escape. I have heard you, but who are you? What are you?"

He was not surprised when the voice responded. *I am...Disir, I think she called me. Sigrun said she would have chosen me if I were not a woman. I lived in peace for a while in a grove of trees, and blessed warriors, but then one day I woke up in this...thing. I have been here for ages.*

Being trapped sounded fairly terrible, and it reminded Trav of his own imprisonment. He decided to speak his mind even while Yaakova glanced at him oddly. "I cannot promise anything, but I will try to free you. Now be silent."

I understand, said the voice, then it went still.

Only a couple lines remained of the last rune equation before the rune working would be complete. As he began scribing one of them, his mind wandered, thinking about the insanity of his current situation. A few minutes earlier, Yaakova had reported that the demon worshippers had been getting louder, and one of the women had thrown her robes off to be mounted by several men while the chanting continued. "These people were just born to be someone's noisy neighbor in an apartment complex," Trav muttered.

He gathered himself, mentally calming his mind once more. "Okay, here goes nothing." With one more movement of his shiv, he completed the entire rune working, which immediately started soaking up his remaining magic power. He'd been expecting it, so Trav didn't waste any time. After drawing a fire flower stone from his pocket, he primed the weapon and threw it right into the middle of the demon worshippers.

Even as Trav's rune working flared to life, the enemy warlock's head snapped around. The bald man shouted, "Kindred, the intruders have t—"

The rest of his words were cut off by the roar of Trav's enchanted stone exploding.

Charred bodies of demon worshippers were blown all over the room. The explosion had caught at least ten of them, stopped by the tightly packed bodies, but it had torn apart the unfortunates who'd been nearby.

A huge plume of fire blossomed in the midst of the cultists, and pieces of stone that hadn't shredded the robed revelers pinged off the ceiling. A few cultists screamed, but many kept chanting.

The robed worshippers who had not somehow ignored the blast turned to reveal feverish eyes. Trav figured they were all on drugs or being influenced by dark magic. Either way, none of these people were acting normally, or reacting how people normally would.

"Kill the warlock," Trav snarled, but when he turned, Yaakova was already gone. She'd dived forward into the mass of remaining heretics with savage glee, claws flashing.

"Block them! The ceremony is almost done!" screamed the warlock. His bald head reflected the room's witchlight, and he bellowed, "One of you go to the altar and give yourself to our lord!"

Trav ran into the room and shoved back one stinky, robed devotee so hard, the cultist collided with three others, falling to the ground. Smoke from the detonated fire flower stung Trav's eyes, and the haze in the air made the light reflect strangely, making the scene even more otherworldly.

The chanter that he'd knocked down rolled and the figure's hood dropped, revealing her as one of the women from the village. She looked dirty and terrified, but feral too. A murderous snarl crossed her face. Trav cocked an arm, ready to thrust with his spear, but he looked into her maddened expression and hesitated.

His inaction almost cost him his life.

He barely caught motion out the corner of his eye and turned in time to mostly dodge an attack by a tall man with a bushy beard. The villager's crude sword whistled through the air, just the tip managing to hit Trav, slicing through the meat on the outside of his arm. If he'd been slower, the attack would have taken off his entire limb.

While he reeled, the woman had produced a dagger from somewhere and lunged forward. She almost had Trav dead to rights, but his survival instincts had been honed in a hard school on Asgard. He dropped to the ground like a puppet with its strings cut. The woman howled as she overextended, hanging in the air over a very irritated Trav.

His system full of adrenaline, Trav kicked out as hard as he could with his superhuman strength, and the woman was thrown back like a rag doll. Before the attacking man could recover, Trav struck his spear between his enemy's ribs and ripped it out in a shower of gore.

He spared a glance for Yaakova and verified she was still alive, but the Kin was having a hard time getting through the press of bodies to the warlock. The dark magician frothed at the mouth now, screaming, "Midgard Children, stop them! Free the children of your lord into this world! We are so close! Don't let our sacrifices be for nothing!" The unkempt, evil man thrust a hand out at Yaakova, conjuring a purple fireball, but the harpy woman was fast. She grabbed a cultist and threw the screaming human in the path of the magic projectile.

Trav hissed as he caught another painful cut, this time to his leg. Focusing on his own fight had to be his priority for the time being. He darted back as another male cultist stopped chanting and tried stabbing him with a crude knife, made with an antler handle. Trav knocked the man's hand to the side with his spear before skewering him through the throat with his own shiv. As his enemy died, he noticed that the rail-thin man had been missing half his teeth.

The next few seconds felt surreal. Since Trav had upgraded himself with his new magic power, he'd only fought Kin or had killed animals for food. This was his first time fighting humans since then, and he wondered when regular people had all gotten so slow and fragile.

A woman with grey hair screamed as she clawed at his face. Trav stepped around the attack, grabbed one of her arms and broke it with a twist of his wrist. Then he thrust-kicked her into another group of cultists that seemed to be coming out of their stupor.

A couple more cultists rushed him, so Trav faded back toward the door, thrusting with his spear. The dwarven-made weapon had been designed to wound Restless, so human flesh offered almost no resistance at all. A flash of light out the corner of his eye preceded Yaakova screaming, "Dodge!"

With a curse, Trav dove to the side, barely avoiding a purple fireball that splashed against the stone wall behind him, burning a ragged hole. "Don't get cocky," he muttered to himself.

Yaakova finally broke through the mass of bodies to reach the warlock. She screamed in triumph and vindication as she used her great strength to tear him apart with her claws. Meanwhile, a cultist had climbed to the top of the altar. He threw his hood back, and Trav couldn't recall the man's name but recognized the village blacksmith. The scruffy, muscular, smiling man deliberately pulled out a knife from underneath his robe. He stared Trav right in the eyes, his pupils dancing, his face shiny with sweat—and cut his own throat.

"What the—" Trav began, but the handful of robed deviants who were still chanting redoubled their efforts, louder and faster. Trav could barely hear himself think anymore. All the cultists who were not screaming dark, guttural words suddenly dropped, arms and limbs moving jerkily.

The runes on the walls and floor around the veil gate began to glow red. Trav's eyes widened, moving from the dying man on the glowing altar to Yaakova. The Kin woman seemed as confused as he was. With one last glance around, Trav cursed as he developed a really good theory for what might be happening.

"Kill all of the ones that are still chanting," he yelled. "Actually, just kill all of them!"

"Are you sure?" Yaakova had been more than willing to kill cultists before, but she didn't seem to know what to do now that they were helpless.

"Yes! It's probably still too late, but who knows?" With that, Trav sprinted forward, conscious of the fact that the entire tunnel system would collapse soon. He hoped it would be enough to stop what the crazy warlock had started.

Trav deliberately did not look at the veil gate as he passed. The eldritch energies were growing and made his skin crawl. Instead, he darted into the emberstone tunnel, hoping that he could obtain some sort of benefit out of this messed-up situation. At the end of the tunnel, he found a table made of some material so dark it seemed to suck in all the light. On it sat an emberstone box about the size of a briefcase.

Oh, I can see you! You've come! Please, there is not much time! I can feel my connection to the gate changing!

"What?" Trav blinked dumbly at first but quickly understood what the voice had been talking about. The box, and actually the entire emberstone tunnel, had been connected to the mass of rune equations outside that stabilized and imprisoned the veil gate. He suddenly remembered that humans couldn't walk into a place full of emberstone like this without passing out and dying.

He briefly wondered who had built these tunnels, the gate, and the intricate rune networks, but shook his head. The voice had been right—there was no time. He grabbed the stone box, heavy enough that he would have had trouble with it before he'd attained superhuman strength, and ran back the way he'd come.

Trav stopped at the mouth of the tunnel, looking around. Magic was thick in the air, and writhing as several different, powerful rune workings ran their course. Yaakova grunted as she methodically slaughtered the remaining humans, and glanced up to look strangely at

Trav. He was reminded again that he was standing in a tunnel lined floor to ceiling with emberstone.

Then his world shook.

Something cold washed over his body, but also hot, igniting him on the inside. The feeling was awful, like a million tiny fingers with cracked nails all scratching at his soul. Yaakova whimpered softly, crouching down and putting her arms over her head.

Trav turned numbly. The barriers around the veil gate had been weakened so much they were barely there anymore...and a giant eye in the gate was staring back at him. The huge, awful pupil constricted, and the effect doubled. Intense fear, greater than any before in his life threatened to freeze his entire body, but his old stubbornness welled up.

Nobody intimidated Trav Sterling, dammit. At least, he would never admit it.

He grabbed the remaining fire flower stone out of his pocket, activated it, and threw it as hard as he could at the giant eye peering through the gate.

The effect was immediate and profound. A terrible shriek shook the air, making the entire tunnel complex shake. The veil gate had turned opaque again, even as the screaming continued, and Trav moved. He put his spear under an armpit and darted forward, grabbing the dazed harpy by the elbow, and practically dragged her behind him while running away.

"Fuck this, fuck this, fuck this," he panted. "Oh God, I hate Asgard." Then he remembered he was a god now, at least technically, and chuckled.

What a hell of a way to die this would be.

Chapter 22

The tunnels creaked around him as he ran, cracks splintering up the walls and the ceiling overhead groaning as the rune working took effect. Trav's magic had begun a chain reaction, coaxing the rock to break itself, creating ever-expanding channels of weakened, powdered stone—like a tree's roots.

Under one arm, Yaakova stirred but was still groggy. Trav briefly considered dropping her, leaving her behind to die. Even if she stayed loyal, which was a big if, the harpy was still bestial, wild, and dangerous. On the other hand, she was an asset.

"Just constant shades of grey," he growled in annoyance. Fear threatened to take over his emotional state, but he pushed it away. The tunnels really did seem to be much longer now that he was trying to escape, though.

At the mouth of the cave, before the door to the "mine," the witchcraft barrier still stood. It had seemed to exist before to alert the now-dead warlock of any intruders, but there was no way to tell it hadn't been changed since then. Trav didn't have time to study the fetishes, or for anything else. He gathered his remaining magic in one hand and with a surge of concentration, imagined a sigil in his mind's eye, projecting his power outward.

He'd had enough juice to break the barrier...barely. If the warlock had still been alive, this brute force method would have set up the equivalent of a flashing neon sign screaming, "I'm here!"

Trav ran forward, juggling the harpy, his spear, and the mysterious box, and kicked at the wooden door with all his strength. One board shattered, and the impact of his muscled body broke the rest that he collided with.

Behind him, the entire cliff was beginning to tremble, so Trav didn't stop. He got up and ran again, trying to regain momentum. "What is—" began Yaakova.

"Can you walk?"

"Yes, but—"

"Then let's go," snarled Trav, throwing the Kin woman forward to land on her feet as best he could.

She stumbled, but regained her balance, and took one glance back before running too. A few villagers outside goggled. One man ran at them with a pitchfork, but Yaakova almost casually destroyed the weapon with her feathers.

Trav hadn't been thinking about the feathers when he'd picked her up. It was good she hadn't turned them into blades while she'd been tucked under his arm. That would not have been pleasant.

Another villager, a teen, threw a rock. The stone hit Yaakova in the leg, and she cried out in astonishment. The villagers started to close in, faces full of fear and something else, maybe madness. Trav narrowed his eyes and hefted his spear, wondering if he'd need to kill even more people before the day was done. One villager began to move forward, the scrawny man wielding a cleaver, but then he fell down.

Everyone fell down.

Behind them, the entire cliff crumbled, billowing dust, the destruction sounding like the world was ending. Yaakova screamed in astonishment, fell back, and then Trav's jaw dropped as she transformed into a giant raven, winging into the sky. He blinked a couple times, but shook his head, getting up and running again.

The ground rumbled, and the area above the tunnels continued to crumble, sinking into the ground. The village's humble buildings and the solid walls fell, crashing down as the earth shook.

Trav fell and got up again before the earth completely stopped shaking. By this point, any of the villagers that might have still been thinking about attacking had decided to flee instead. Since Trav had no way of really knowing who had been in cahoots with the warlock and who might just be scared or defending their home, this suited him fine. He didn't have a problem killing people who had sacrificed children to dark powers, but he'd rather not wonder who had been who in the future.

A few minutes passed. Trav stood still, bracing himself with his spear and asking himself again if the village had had any children at all. As he wondered again what he'd stumbled in to, and if all of

Asgard was like this, he felt a burst of ruinous energy from the settling ground and the ruined cliff. "Uh oh."

The evil veil gate should have been destroyed, or at least filled in, but what if an unwelcome visitor had come through from the other side already? The earth began to move, mounding upward as something began to push its way out. "Uh oh," Trav repeated.

A huge, misshapen hand cleared the rubble, followed by an arm. Then what looked like a flayed giant pulled itself from the broken ground. As it bled, Trav realized it was actually a combination of multiple human bodies, pressed and bound together in an evil mockery of life.

"A giant flesh golem." Trav had never seen one before, but Odin's memory supplied the details. Whatever had been on the other side of the gate couldn't come through itself, or hadn't had time. It had somehow used its own power or sent an agent through to create a monster in this world using the bodies of the dead cultists.

Trav hoped they'd all been dead first, anyway.

The golem was constantly bleeding and would cease functioning in only a few hours, but that would probably be long enough to cause a lot of mayhem. As the monster's awful head turned and focused on Trav, he developed a pretty good idea of its purpose. The monster began lumbering toward him, and all of the human villagers who'd been hiding nearby fled, screaming.

So much for religion, eh? Trav was tired, wounded, and out of magic. He had no choice but to stand his ground, holding his spear in one hand and the emberstone box in the other. Whether emberstone would damage something that was already dead, he didn't know, but it wouldn't hurt to find out.

Suddenly, a stone hit the side of the golem's raw, bloody head with a sharp impact. Up in a tree, Yaakova wound up and threw again; her new projectile missed, and she cursed. The golem turned, heading toward the Kin in the tree. When it had gotten closer, Yaakova turned into a raven and flew off, easily avoiding the crushing hand that shot forward to decimate the tree.

When the golem turned, heading for Trav again, Yaakova landed on a tree to the other side of the creature, one that used to be part of Wall Home's wall. She wound up and threw another rock. When the unholy creature's steps faltered, pausing, Trav realized that the Kin was buying him some time. *Not that it would do any good,* he thought, exhausted.

Yaakova attacked one more time before the golem completely ignored her, centering its attention entirely on Trav instead.

OUR DREAD LORD ORDERS YOUR DEATH

The flesh golem thundered its proclamation. From a distance, the misshapen creation might have looked almost like a naked, dirty, fleshy toddler—with short legs, a big head, and long arms. But the closer it got, the more its horrifying, patchwork appearance became apparent.

Now Trav could verify that it truly had been fashioned from the bodies of the demon worshippers. One of the cultists he'd killed was part of the thing's chest, now just a dead, bloody face that moved and drooled. Torn bodies had been fused together, some with the dark robes they'd worn hanging out of the crevices in the patchwork body, grotesquely dripping bodily fluids as the monster walked.

Shit. Running away really wasn't an option. Despite its slow footsteps, the thing moved as fast as a horse. It was almost on him, and Trav hefted his weapons, hoping the emberstone would be enough.

What are you—began the trapped voice from the box. If Trav hadn't already been through so much in such a short time, the voice might have startled him.

"Be quiet," he muttered. The flesh golem crunched right through the remains of a building. Time was almost up. Trav reversed his spear and cocked back his throwing arm, waiting for the best time to attack. The gesture wasn't much, but it made him feel better.

He was not going to fall without a fight.

The fact that he'd chucked his fire flower into the gate made him chuckle. "Definitely worth it," he said. Nobody, not the Kin of Asgard nor any other bullying assholes were ever going to cow him again. He was free now, dammit.

And he was a god too...sorta. Let them all choke on that!

As the flesh golem stumble-ran forward the last few paces, raising one hand to squash Trav like a bug, he resigned himself to his fate. There was a chance he'd live through this, but it wasn't great. Trav stretched back, preparing to throw his spear, but suddenly he heard a familiar growl. A massive blur of snarling red fur jumped over some nearby rubble, snarling with primal, savage fury.

The eight-legged she-wolf clamped her jaws on the back of the flesh golem's neck and flung the unnatural creature like a rag doll. It crashed down, blowing dirt everywhere and impaling itself on broken trees. All the exposed human faces on its body cried out at once in pain. When it tried to get up again, Narnaste lunged forward, pounding it back into the ground with her front paws and dancing away before she could be grabbed.

Trav only spared a second to be surprised before roaring, running as fast as he could. Narnaste had flipped the abomination over and savaged its back, her eyes full of fire. The two warring giants stamped around, destroying puny human structures they bumped...and Trav was running right towards them.

He knew Narnaste would not be able to kill the flesh golem—she could only run out its limited life faster, but it wouldn't be enough. There were several ways to create such a thing, and Trav figured that the magic powering it was probably alien. If he had access to all of Odin's memories, maybe he would know a better way to deal with it, but right now, he thought his best bet would be a sealing glyph.

The golem's flailing fist almost crushed Trav, but he managed to dodge at the last second. "Hold it down!" he yelled. He hoped Narnaste's deeper growl meant she had heard him. With a few more running steps, he found the monster's head, reared back, and stabbed it as hard as he could with his spear.

A normal weapon wouldn't have had much effect, but Trav's spear was dwarven-made, a tool of power. The golem screamed, and the faces on its bulk joined its voice. This close, the many voices of the dead bodies bound in its body made Trav's vision blur. When one face opened its eyes, Trav kicked it as hard as he could. He jumped on top of the thing as it moved, trying to crush him where he had been standing.

After slamming the emberstone box down on the thing and verifying it had no effect, Trav summoned his shiv and began drawing a binding glyph. Lines of red light etched, smoking into the monster's disturbing flesh. This glyph was not very complex, or wouldn't normally be. It was a lot harder to draw on the back of a bucking flesh golem that was trying to reach back and crush him.

Trav didn't have any power left, but the binding glyph didn't require it. The basic rune working merely enforced the rules of the universe on a patch of space or an object, letting the world itself challenge any sort of magic or unnatural effect. In this case, the entire flesh golem had no way to resist and was bound.

The monster began to come apart as Trav leaped back. He didn't stop when his boot touched solid ground, but kept going. When the magically created creature exploded in a shower of bloody gore a few seconds later, he was grateful for his wariness.

Narnaste hadn't been so lucky. The huge wolf got hit by a shower of blood and offal, gagging as she shook her enormous head to get it out of her eyes.

Trav sat down. He'd need to retrieve the spear soon, but for now, he wasn't going to move for a while. The remaining human villagers were gone and probably wouldn't be back anytime soon. Besides, he had the Kin on his side...at least he hoped so. He was too tired to be worried about that anymore, though.

Yaakova winged down in her raven form and transformed back into a harpy. Her eyes danced, and she smiled without restraint. "I have always wanted to fly, to really fly." With a gentle touch one Trav would have never expected her capable of—she laid a clawed hand on his shoulder and gave him a meaningful look. "Flying has always been my dream, and now it has come true. Thank you. I will follow you. This was truly the best choice I have ever made." She gave the remains of the flesh golem a glance and shook her head, smiling wider.

Then Trav heard footsteps and turned. Narnaste had also transformed back into a woman at some point. She walked stiffly toward them, her entire body covered in blood. One hand had a white-knuckled grip on her seax sheathed at her belt. "Master, who is this?" she growled.

Chapter 23

Trav woke up feeling like he'd been run over by a truck. The morning light seeped through his eyelids, irritating him until he gave up on sleeping any further. The previous day had been intense in a way that he had never experienced before. Even escaping the slave mines hadn't come close.

I wonder if I can survive many more days like that, he wondered and rubbed his jaw.

The evening of the previous day, after they'd made decent distance from the creepy little village from hell, his little group had camped by a stream. The water had been liberally used for washing. Narnaste, in particular, had been filthy. Trav had been able to cobble together barely enough power to convert water into cleaning and purification solution before he'd finally passed out.

After walking some distance and relieving himself against a tree, Trav reviewed his available magic. Like he'd predicted, he had five available bars of magic power. Two more were tied up in permanent enhancements for a total of seven. He briefly checked his full list of available permanent rune equations he had access to now and shook his head—some of the most powerful required over one hundred bars, and even special or unknown requirements.

It was tempting to immediately use his newly replenished magic power to give himself another permanent upgrade rune equation on his body, but he calmed himself. Out in the middle of the forest, away from any civilization, and with a couple Kin women sleeping nearby, he probably wasn't in any immediate danger other than maybe from the Kin themselves.

That reminded him of the tense explanations he'd given Narnaste the previous day. For someone who called herself Faithful and thought of Trav as a High Master, she could be awfully set on getting her own way sometimes—and seemingly jealous. She hadn't trusted Yaakova and had been very vocal about this fact. Trav had hardly been in a place to tell her he agreed with her about the other woman when the harpy was standing right there.

What a mess.

Yaakova's joy with flight seemed to be genuine. She'd turned into a raven the size of a hawk multiple times, even landing on Trav's shoulder once. Of course, once she'd become a Kin woman again, she and Narnaste had begun trading veiled barbs. Trav had wanted to tell them that after almost being killed by a flesh golem, all other nonsense should be avoided for the time being, but he'd just been too tired.

His companions would have to wait. Trav still didn't know exactly what kind of status he wanted to cultivate with his new Valkyries. He didn't have any answers on that front, and they were still sleeping, so for now, he'd find out about the emberstone box and its mysterious prisoner.

The box itself had been placed outside of camp—the two Kin women had insisted. They hadn't expressly said so, but the emberstone obviously freaked them out. Not much really scared Kin, but emberstone was apparently nasty stuff to everyone except Trav.

He approached the box and thought about just talking to it, but that felt awkward. He didn't want to wake up the two Kin, nor be seen talking to himself. He shook his head—it felt weird of think of those two as his Valkyries.

After considering the situation for a second, he picked up the emberstone box and walked a few minutes upstream from camp. He found a good place to sit, propped his spear against a tree, set the box down, and sat. With a small sigh, he rested his chin in his hand. Figuring out all of his runic magic options concerning the box, if any, would probably take some time. His mind felt like it'd been expanding lately, and he decided to test it. Maybe he could comb through his magic knowledge or delve for more while having a...chat.

"Can you hear me?" Speaking the question out loud with nobody there felt strange.

Yes, I can hear you. I have stayed silent, hoping you would talk to me. If you hadn't taken me, I'd be buried right now, wouldn't I?

"Yeah, that's right."

You saved me twice then.

Trav nodded. "More like three times, but who's counting?" He cleared his throat. "I saw how the gate was draining you. Anyway, why don't you tell me who you are and fill me in on your situation, so I can figure out what to do with you."

I don't know where to start.

"How about with your name?"

After a pause the voice continued again, starting slowly but picking up to a normal cadence. *My name is Ysintrill. I was once known as a hero, a warrior, and before that, I was an apprentice apothecary on another world.*

"Another world?"

Yes. A long time ago, on my world, there was a war. A magician, a friend of my father's, tried sending me to safety when our town was about to be overrun. Instead, I found myself here.

"On Asgard?"

Correct. I was young when I got here. That was during the age that the gods of Asgard walked the land. Great adventures and explorations were common. My skill in medicines secured me positions on several exploratory teams, and a mercenary company. I discovered a small talent in runecraft as well, augmenting this world's magic with mysteries from my homeworld.

"Runes? What do you mean?" The disembodied voice had Trav's full attention now.

I never told a soul, but my homeworld had similar magic to Asgard's rune power. When I was an apothecary, I read a few books on the subject, and still remembered a few of the symbols. In Asgard, using them with what I learned or rune magic allowed me to grow in power. With the fighting skills I learned, I became a formidable warrior.

"Most magic from other veils doesn't work here, though, right?" That bit of knowledge seemed to be common sense, both after talking to Narnaste and based on what Trav could glean from his alien memories.

My knowledge allowed me to compete on the same level of those who would otherwise be beyond me.

The quiet confidence in Ysintrill's disembodied voice filled Trav with certainty that she was telling the truth.

"So what happened on Asgard?"

My friends and my family were betrayed. We fought bravely, but we were defeated. My betrothed was the first to perish. I was about to die and lay bleeding on the frozen ground when Sigrun appeared to me. The Valkyrie stared at me for a while before clucking her tongue. It turned out that she had a soft spot for female warriors, but since I was not born of this world, and I was a woman, there was not much she could do for me.

I was offered a choice to become a disir, and I took it. After that, my time as a human woman ended, but I remained alive, exploring this land.

"A disir?" Trav vaguely recalled the word, and Odin's memories helped fill in the gaps. A disir was a type of spirit, but there were dozens, if not hundreds of different types. "What kind?"

I was never truly sure. Some I encountered after that were frightened by my appearance, but others were merely curious. A few humans mistook me as an aelf. Eventually, I settled into a grove and made it my home. Over many years, travelers and heroes came to visit my home, searching for blessings. I was content, until one day I was visited by powerful visitors who meant me harm.

"What happened?"

My memories at this point are unsure, so I cannot rightly say. Whatever they did put me in this box, though. Since then, I have been trapped in the place you found me, tied to the veil gate.

"How long were you there?" Trav felt some sympathy again. Ysintrill had been a slave just like he had.

I had no way to note the passing of times. It was many years. I mostly focused on ignoring the veil gate. Sometimes, something awful would look through. I got the feeling it was always checking the wards around the gate to see if they'd weakened.

"Probably."

Now will y—

"Be quiet, please," muttered Trav, not unkindly. "I am thinking about what to do with you."

Understood.

Eventually, the way that Trav had dealt with the flesh golem gave him an idea of what to do. With an unbinding circle, which was simple in theory but actually a fairly complex rune working, maybe he could just reverse what had been done to the girl in the box. It seemed she'd been turned into some sort of mystical battery.

"I think I can free you." He stood up and grabbed the box, heading back to camp.

You can? Ysintrill sounded like she was suppressing her excitement, trying to temper expectations.

"There is a high chance, yes."

Will you do so?

"Probably, but I want to know what I get out of this deal." Trav's days of wide-eyed innocence were over. If he was planning to do someone a favor, he might as well get some sort of boon from it. It was still strange that the box itself had called so strongly to his divine mantle. Maybe Ysintrill had been imprisoned by another Restless. At this point, it seemed likely

But if so, why had the dark veil gate been established and helped open? There were mysteries involved here that Trav knew he wasn't qualified to solve yet.

After a pause, Ysintrill bluntly asked, *What would you have of me?*

"I want you to show me the unique magic you know. If I don't know it, I want you to teach me." The divine mantle that Trav had accepted felt more solidly connected now—it made Trav feel good. "I also want to create a rune connection, a bond with you that will give me a little bit more power."

Will this lower my power, if you can actually free me and do this thing?

"No, you will be mostly unaffected, but the actual mark will probably hurt."

Compared to an eternity of prison, that sounds acceptable. I agree.

"Okay, good. We have an agreement." Trav felt a sudden surge of optimism. He only had a few godly marks left, a limited number of Valkyries he could make, but maybe he could just keep marking subordinates to get more power! There were problems with this plan, not least of which was that he didn't even know if Ysintrill would give him any new magic in the first place, but it was worth a try. At the very least, it sure beat sitting around and waiting for random luck.

Now it was time to get back to camp, find a good place to do magic right next to the running water, and wake up the Kin. Trav wasn't looking forward to it. He had a feeling that Narnaste would have a lot of questions.

Chapter 24

Trav woke up this time in a jumble of bodies, his hand going to his head. In addition to a splitting headache, he had odd pains in strange places. A very long, very shapely leg lay across his own, and he gently, quietly disentangled himself, looking around while he did so.

He was surrounded by women, asleep around and partially on top of him. *What the hell?*

His thoughts slowly sharpened, and he realized that he was still at the campsite, but something had changed. For starters, it was twilight, almost night. The...feeling of the forest was different now too. Trav couldn't explain it, and he didn't even know what set of senses he was even using—normal or divine?

As he continued disentangling himself from the very naked, very female arms and legs he seemed to be tangled with, he counted one woman, two, and three—he did a double take, rubbing his eyes. There was Narnaste, her shapely breasts slowly rising and falling as she breathed. Yaakova was also completely nude, her beautiful, womanly hips jutting up in an interesting way as she slept on one side. But there was another woman too, a dark-skinned, straight-haired beauty whose lithe, athletic body reminded Trav of a figure skater.

When he looked closer, he noticed she had long ears, like an elf. Maybe she was an elf. Weren't elves a type of disir? *Seriously, what the hell? Was I drinking?*

He stared, trying to figure out who she was for a moment, his eyes moving to her plump, round, upside-down heart-shaped ass—and his breath stopped. A wolf mark, his divine mark from his ring, was on her lower back.

What the hell happened? What did I do? A hint of panic had intruded on Trav's inner thoughts, and he redoubled his efforts to free himself. He needed some space, some time to think. Asgard was a dangerous place. Losing control of himself was scary enough. But on Asgard...

Finally, he freed himself from the gaggle of bodies, looking down in fear and wonder. All three women were deep asleep. Narnaste was beautiful as always. Trav had to admit that Yaakova's alien, bestial appearance was softened by an amazing body, and he allowed himself to admit she was sexy in her own way.

And then there was the third woman. She had the kind of curves that he had admired in centerfolds back on Earth. She had a tiny waist; muscular, womanly thighs; and full, heavy breasts. Was that Ysintrill? The answer seemed on the tip of his mind. He just needed to give it some time. Hopefully.

Trav found his clothes outside, scattered around. He felt another surge of worry over what he'd apparently done but couldn't remember. His shirt had a new rip in it. He swallowed.

When he was about to leave camp, he remembered to grab his spear. Then, despite being freaked out, he settled on just moving a stone's throw away. Even though the forest felt strangely peaceful now, he couldn't leave the women unguarded. They were his Valkyries after all.

"Gaah," he said, running his fingers through his hair. What had happened? He hated feeling like he wasn't in control. Stuff like this was why he'd stopped drinking in his 20's.

With a sigh, he leaned against a tree and cleared his mind, doing some basic breathing exercises. As he calmed his mental state and let his magic flow through his body, he got another shock.

His magic had increased—a lot.

At first, his jaw just dropped, and he didn't know what to make of it. Then he pulled himself together and realized it probably had something to do with the third woman he'd marked. Ysintrill. Yes, that had to be her. In fact, now he could sort of remember something.

She'd been wild—

The stray thought intruded like an ice cube thrown into hot oil, but he shook his head and regained his senses. He definitely had more bars of available power now. Some memories were starting to trickle back. He'd used some magic, like two bars, while activating the rune circle to free Ysintrill—his memory of everything after that still hadn't returned, though.

"Strange." Normally, it took an entire day for his magic to return, or at least he thought so. Maybe it didn't actually need to take that long. Frowning, he left his thinking spot, heading back to camp, and located the remains of the magic circle. In the center, he didn't find anything but some scuff marks on the ground and three small pieces of emberstone.

With a thoughtful expression, Trav pocketed the crimson rocks and wandered back to the stump he'd found to sit on.

Did his nap that day replenish his magic, or did the emberstone? It had exploded, right? Could emberstone restore his magic—was it even possible to use it that way? His Odin memories were frustratingly silent on the matter.

Either way, regardless of how, he was back to full magical strength. Also, instead of five bars of available magic, he had eight.

"Eight. Holy crap!" he whispered, and slowly let his head fall into his hands. He stayed that way a while, just breathing, allowing himself to relax. Eventually, his memories returned.

He'd been emberstone drunk. Before now, he hadn't known that was even possible, but there was no other explanation for what had happened.

Yaakova and Narnaste had been skeptical of Ysintrill's story—against freeing her—but Trav had overridden them. He'd honestly been curious if his circle could undo whatever had put her in the box. Based on how he understood it, if it worked, the water from the nearby stream would work to help restore her form, too. He'd figured that if she'd been dangerous, or lying about who she was, his two Valkyries would help him deal with it.

Trav shook his head. Things hadn't turned out like he'd imagined.

Even as he'd activated the rune circle, he'd known something was different than he'd expected. Strong emotions had manifested, and he'd realized he was somehow feeling Ysintrill's emotional state. Infatuation. He'd saved her. She wanted to see him with her own eyes!

After that, he still only had flashes of memory. Magically enhanced, intense passion. Desire. Marking Ysintrill with connecting runes. Writhing pleasure. Gifting his new Valkyrie with the symbol of his office, then feeling a new, profound connection with all of them as he'd bonded with them, sampled them.

"I can't believe this." Trav rubbed his eyes and warred with himself. He had to be honest that part of him felt deeply satisfied. That part was further bolstered by the divine mantle he'd gotten from Odin, or at least he assumed so. But he partly felt a little bit of guilt too, mostly when he thought about his late wife. Coupling with Narnaste had been one thing, but magical orgies? *What the fuck?*

He laughed a little then, remembering Beth and what she'd actually say if he could speak to her again. She'd been amazing...and blunt. Her worldview had been straightforward in a way that only someone who had lived every day being reminded of their own mortality could manage. Beth had near-constantly told Trav that he carried too much baggage from his former life. Asgard was not Earth. She'd also forced him to promise her he wouldn't ever give up on life as long as he still lived.

Trav kicked a stick and realized that even if he could accept what had happened—the Valkyries did technically belong to him after all and had chosen that state of affairs—he didn't want to deal with the fallout. He'd never been particularly good with maintaining one relationship, much less three. Actually, on his road to godhood, he'd probably eventually bond more Valkyries.

"Oh God," he sighed—but he was a god now. Who could he ask for help? He doubted the creator he'd prayed to intermittently on Earth would have much to say to Odin's new incarnation.

Trav chuckled, soon transitioning to a deep belly laugh. His situation was utterly ridiculous. Most men would kill for three girlfriends, but his Valkyries were not girlfriends, and not even human women, they were Kin. *Well, I'm not sure what Ysintrill is.* He decided to think of her as Kin.

The Kin were all dangerous, all of them. Hell, this was Asgard. Even other humans here were scary and homicidal. His recent trials had proven that.

To survive this new life, he needed to be stronger. The raw power he had now was good, but it would be more useful if he upgraded himself some more. With that decided, Trav dove into his rune knowledge again, seeking to confirm the choices he'd made before on the subject. When he mentally went through his permanent rune paths again, his jaw dropped, and he ran through his magical knowledge several more times.

He knew more magic now.

At first, he wasn't sure how this was possible, but then more flashes of memory reminded him that Ysintrill had shared her mystical knowledge with him even as they'd bonded as master and servant.

He'd felt her emotions at the time. He'd saved her from an eternity of imprisonment. She'd give him anything now.

That kind of worried him. After being locked in the box for so long, he wasn't sure she was sane anymore, but that was a problem for later.

For right now, Trav grabbed a stick and decided to visually map out his most promising new upgrade paths. At this point, he was thankful that his friends and his cousin Ash had introduced him to video games back on Earth. Thinking about permanent rune workings, enchantments, as a magical skill or upgrade tree was already proving very useful. As Ash would have said, he was planning his build.

Without that former knowledge, Trav might have set himself up for long-term failure. For instance, if he'd chosen a pure strength or durability upgrade for his first enchantment, his choices as he continued to gain power would have dwindled. Many of the same rules for upgrading equipment with runes applied to his body, now. Some rune equations were incompatible with each other if they were applied one after the other, or needed to be supported by other runes.

In the case of the pure strength family of rune enhancements, they were powerful but didn't really support many other types of upgrades. If Trav had taken that route and had ever acquired hundreds of bars of power, he would have become incredibly strong, but have almost no dexterity—control would have been lacking. He would have also been left with bars upon bars of power he couldn't use.

Well, that's not true. Trav quickly amended his thought process. *I can always create enchanted gear to fill in for places that my other abilities are weak...if I have the power.* From his perspective, enchanted gear was inferior to enchanting himself, though. A crown or ring, or whatever he enhanced would need to be worn. These sorts of things could be stolen, and could even be used against him.

That's what had happened to the dwarves, after all.

Wait, what? Where did that come from? The random, alien memory had surfaced in a natural way. Not for the first time, Trav felt a niggling worry about how he was changing under Odin's influence, and if he'd even notice if he were to stop being himself.

But that was a pointless thing to dwell on. For now, it was time to draw upgrade paths.

After poking around in the dirt for a while, Trav narrowed down his most promising upgrade possibilities. His first permanent rune that had basically strengthened him to Kin-level physiology had been a wise decision. At this point, no other enhancements were really off the table.

One path he could take would eventually lead to shapeshifting. Odin had been able to change forms and disguise himself before he'd been killed. Trav actually theorized that the new mark of his authority that he'd created tapped into, or resonated with, his divine mantle. This would explain why all of his Valkyries could change form—unless Odin's had too in the past. Actually, maybe they all could, but Trav wasn't sure.

The problem with the shapeshifting upgrade path was that it was expensive, requiring lots of power. Most of the supporting rune workings to build toward shapeshifting were not all that helpful in the short term, at least not for surviving Asgard. For the first time, Trav felt a bit of jealousy that Odin had attained these types of abilities naturally. On the flip side, Trav would have more control over the evolution of his power, his progression. This was a positive side to being able to choose where he'd invest his power...if he survived.

Shapeshifting was only one of several more utility-focused paths that Trav could take. Some were very interesting, like camouflage abilities, or even invisibility at high levels.

He'd actually been thinking about investing in toughness or fighting-related abilities after the skirmish with Narnaste's old buddies. Two things had changed since then. First, Trav had just survived his experience with the dark, mysterious veil gate and the warlock. Second, he had new magic power available now.

The mystical knowledge of Odin's that he could access was so vast, he was able to quickly incorporate the new rune, sigil, and a couple glyphs into all the other rune equations he knew, and even create new ones. Then he was able to develop new permanent rune workings.

Most of the upgrade enchantments that had been available before had focused more on lowering magical costs for rune magic, or decreasing recovery time, or even allowing runes to be drawn faster. None of this had been all that compelling because Trav had his shiv, and he'd been more concerned with everyday survival.

But now his upgrade tree had grown. He had more options for temporary buffs now, even magic that temporarily increased one of his attributes, or even gave him new abilities for a time.

In the past, Odin had focused on stealth and deception-based abilities, or powerful magic that could take time to craft. Trav's personality was a little different, and he wasn't comfortable with relying on his Valkyries as much as Odin had.

The warrior-based upgrade paths were interesting, but probably not the best way to survive Asgard for the time being, and Trav was working from a disadvantage. He was just a human, not a god—at least he had been. Trav needed an edge, and just being stronger or faster was not enough—he could definitely see that now.

And unique magic was definitely a possible advantage.

Trav ignored the purely physical upgrade paths, instead exploring mystical options. He began carefully charting out the upgrade trees and possibilities available if he were to focus on his magical abilities.

This felt like the right direction to go for a few reasons. He still didn't know everything about the veils, or other worlds, but he knew that plenty of them had their own magic. He also knew that Odin had known multiple magic systems. Not all of them worked on Asgard, and Trav couldn't remember much now, but that might change in the future.

In fact, if he wasn't mistaken, he could access more of Odin's memories now since he'd attained more power. This was interesting, since the longer Trav was free, the more he felt a vague but powerful need to know and to grow. His original goal of revenge seemed small now. There were entire worlds out there, and more importantly, he believed that whoever or whatever had killed Odin was still alive and might come for him.

Trav wanted to live, and as he grew closer to accepting he was truly free again, he wanted to retaliate. Not just at the Kin, but at Asgard itself. He had power, real power now. Humans were treated like shit on this world and the depths that so many had fallen to offended him. Maybe Asgard needed a change in leadership. In fact, wouldn't that make his original revenge plan easier? Perhaps finding the village of the Faithful that Narnaste was leading him to could be his true rebirth, and where the beginning of an empire could start.

Maybe he could even save the other humans on Asgard.

But these were all just thoughts now, and wishes didn't get anything done. He'd definitely need to think about all of this later. On the other hand, now was a time for action.

He kept drawing in the dirt, fleshing out the magical upgrade paths he could give himself. Eventually, he decided he might have discovered the best compromise he could find. It had taken a while because the knowledge he'd gotten from Ysintrill seemed to affect runecrafting itself most strongly.

Two new abilities strongly interested him. One would allow him to draw runes at a distance. Another would allow him to draw them in the air. This would revolutionize the way Trav could fight, and also allow him to enchant himself, or buff himself on the fly.

The abilities were cheap and not super powerful to start with. For instance, the distance magic, what he thought of as ventrilomagic, would only let him cast magic about forty feet away if he started on that path, but he could grow his power and extend that reach. The ability to write in the air would not allow him to use large rune equations that way right away, just glyphs and such. Still, these powers would all be building blocks toward more strength. They were also abilities that Trav would much rather enhance his body itself with than enchant on a pair of gloves that could be lost or destroyed.

Taking this path, he'd still be able to pick up some combat and physical-related abilities in the future. Yes, this was probably the best compromise. He could almost hear his cousin Ash telling him that he was a "noob," but that he'd lucked into a good build.

Trav shook his head, wondering why he kept thinking of his family lately. It'd been years. Maybe he was just putting off the pain of upgrading. Last time he'd done this, it'd made him black out.

With an effort of will, he called his shiv into his hand. This was not going to be fun. After another last look at the ground, he reviewed what he'd chosen. He had eight bars of power to work with. One bar was going toward ventrilomagic, one bar for air scribing, and one more bar on a weak magic shield, which also gave him a bit of magic and physical recovery speed. It had seemed like a really good way to turn a single bar of power into a variety of abilities.

Last, he was going to spend two bars on magic recovery and focus. Based on what he understood, this would allow him to regenerate his magic quicker, and draw runes faster. The magic recovery also would give him an even more accelerated healing rate, which would be handy because he still had some nasty cuts from his fight with the cultists. The wounds weren't really slowing him down, but under his bandages, they itched like crazy. In the future, he might not be so lucky, either.

All of his chosen upgrades came out to five bars of magic, power he'd need to tie up into permanent enchantments, leaving him only three bars of magic free.

This seemed like a good tradeoff. Maybe in the future, he could keep adding an extra bar to his available magic pool every upgrade, meaning he'd slowly, steadily have more power to call on.

Trav looked at his scribbled notes on the ground one last time, trying to find any hole in his logic. There were other good upgrade paths, including flight, or turning extremely hard to kill. Most of those effects could be mimicked with temporary magic, though. If his experience with the flesh golem had proven one thing, he needed to be better in a fight, and keep a certain amount of flexibility.

"Okay, time to stop putting this off." Trav lifted his shirt and began drawing a series of complex rune equations on his body. This time, he knew to probably expect a lot of pain, so he mentally dragged his feet a little bit, crafting each line a bit more slowly than really required.

The first time he'd enchanted himself, the marks that had shown up on his body had faded over time, becoming barely visible. He hoped that this time, the same thing would happen. Otherwise, his upper torso was going to look like he'd been through a meat grinder.

When he was finally finished drawing the red, angry rune lines stretching across his chest, Trav connected the last circle and pushed power into the rune workings.

Everything hurt. The world was pain. He didn't even register when he'd passed out from mountains of pure agony assaulting his senses.

***

Trav awoke in a protective circle feeling great, wide awake. The three Kin women standing in a rough circle around him, facing outwards, made him feel guilty. They'd watched over him while he'd been unconscious, but he hadn't thought about them before putting himself out of commission. Who'd been protecting them while they slept?

Oh yeah. He realized he'd more than likely screamed, and they'd probably woken up. *No harm, no foul.*

With a shaking hand, he rubbed his head. "Master!" cried Narnaste. She knelt next to him, touching his brow and shoulders. "Are you alright? What happened?"

"Don't worry, I'm fine," Trav muttered. He mentally explored his magic reserves, checking to see if the enchantments had worked. It seemed they had. "I'm fine," he repeated.

With another glance around, Trav noticed that it was the middle of the night. He'd switched over to his emberstone eye to see without even thinking about it. That was interesting. The eye seemed to be integrating better with his body as he attained more power and kept upgrading himself.

To the side, Yaakova growled. "Without you, we will weaken, at least I think so. You are not allowed to take unnecessary risks, New One."

"Are you sure about that?" Trav asked.

"I don't know, but I don't want to risk it," gruffed the harpy. "I can finally fly. Don't go dying for no reason."

"Okay, okay." He rubbed a hand over his face. Then he checked his body, and sure enough, the rune equations he'd enchanted himself with had sunk deep into the skin.

The third woman, Ysintrill, shyly held her hands and watched him with wide eyes. He wondered if she could transform, and what she could transform into. Hadn't she said she'd been a warrior or adventurer in the past? There were so many things he didn't know right now and still needed to investigate.

But when Narnaste bent down and kissed him fiercely on the lips, muttering, "Don't scare me like that again," before she kissed him again, his focus wavered. Too late, he noticed the Kin women's dilated eyes and jerky movements. They were all probably still high on emberstone.

Okay, this makes no sense. Touching it hurts them, and getting cut with it can kill, but magic that disperses the emberstone is like Kin catnip? Even as the strange thought crossed Trav's mind and he shelved it for the future, Narnaste hauled him up and kissed him deeply again, leading him back to camp.

They guarded me even when they were high on emberstone? If they hadn't been Kin, Trav might have been touched. The fact that they cared about his safety so much would have been sweet. Instead, he knew they were probably running on instinct. Trav was not a normal man, and these three were magically tied to him, his Valkyries.

Part of Trav wanted to stop, take a second to examine the fact that he still barely knew Ysintrill, and that he was surrounded by inebriated Kin women, all of them dangerous. But then one thing led to another, and he had to focus entirely on the present.

His last coherent thought was that despite keeping strange hours for the last day, traveling at night was not an option, so maybe it was best to go to sleep anyway, just wait for morning. As it turned out, it was a while before he was allowed to actually fall asleep.

Chapter 25

"So you were trying to find some sort of new power or weapon to help your family fight, what, another family?" Trav swayed with the movement of Narnaste's easy lope. Ysintrill rode the huge red wolf behind him, and Yaakova sat perched on his knee, in her raven form as she seemed to prefer during the day.

"Yes. I also didn't want to complicate the succession if my family were to win the guiding tree." Like Narnaste, Yaakova's voice was different while she was in her animal form, but Trav could still recognize that it was her. Having a giant, talking raven around had only been strange for what seemed like a few minutes. This was Asgard, after all.

"So, what would you have done if you had found something, enabling you to go back and help them, then they'd won your tribe's leadership? Actually, is the tribe the same as your family?"

"No." The raven shook her head. "You call my people plains harpies, but we call ourselves Bernacians, after Bernacia, the first queen. We have three tribes in our territory, our land Demona, the Demona country. My family is the current ruling family of the East Tribe."

Trav blinked. "And leadership changes every ten years?"

"Well, it can. There is a contest for the guiding tree. Then after that, there is a contest for the royal tree between the Guides and their teams."

"So your entire leadership can change every ten years, like I said, right?"

Yaakova fluttered her wings. "It can but rarely does. Most families are in positions of power that have lasted generations. My family used to be the strongest in the East Tribe, but we have fallen on hard times. This year, we might actually lose our guiding tree. The North Tribe usually takes the royal tree."

Trav tried wrapping his mind around the strange system of government. "What would happen if your family won the—guidance tree—then won the throne, the royal tree? Who would lead your tribe?"

"It's 'guiding tree,' and the family that took second place during the games would advance to lead the tribe. This way, the top two families of each tribe will always work together to try winning the royal tree. At least, they're supposed to."

"And the royal tree harpy—"

"The Royal," Yaakova corrected.

"—and the Royal has lots of power?" Trav asked.

"She is in charge of diplomatic relationships, the overall Bernacian government, and holds two votes for all council voting. The guides have one vote each."

"And the council is all the guides and the royal?"

"Yes, although there can be special situations where others are given votes. It is rare, though."

Trav mulled that over for a while before asking, "All harpies are female, right?"

"Yes."

"So where do baby harpies come from?"

"Harpies get pregnant, obviously."

"How?" Trav met the raven's eyes.

"Most humanoids can be a father, but we keep human slaves."

"Ah. Thought so." Trav wasn't sure how to think about that. On the one hand, being a human slave in harpy land might be better than other places on Asgard, maybe not. Either way, a slave was still a slave.

At this point, he had a pretty good idea of how harpy society worked, at least among the plains harpies. He knew a fair amount about the Demona too, a race of Kin that looked or acted demonic, even by Kin standards. Apparently, they'd cobbled up their own country. Most of Trav's knowledge of Kin species came from Odin's memories, and he knew that during the god's time, Demona had all basically been leaderless savages regardless of what veil they were encountered in—

Veils. Every time Trav ran up against the subject of other worlds in Odin's memories, the flow of information would stop. This was beginning to get really frustrating, especially as Trav learned more and had been putting together how things had changed since Odin's time.

The last couple days of travel with his new Valkyries had been awkward at first. He suspected that they'd all been at least a bit embarrassed about their emberstone high-fueled hijinks. Trav had hardly been the type of man in his life to indulge in...sexual escapades like that, but he'd surprised himself by accepting the situation rather quickly.

Meanwhile, Narnaste had barely said a word for an entire day. Yaakova had seemed jumpy, and Ysintrill had been visibly out of sorts. Trav began to gather that she was also socially out of practice, and might not have been big on people skills even before she'd been killed in the distant past.

If he'd been honest with himself, he hadn't been feeling entirely normal either, not that he even knew what normal was anymore. While being intimate with three Kin women at once was just a drop in the bucket with Odin issues, Valkyries, and Asgard in general, he was reaching his saturation point for weird shit—he could feel it.

At least eating hadn't been a problem. Between Trav's magic and the three Kin women, finding food in the forest hadn't been terribly difficult.

He'd spent much of that first day of travel trying to talk to Ysintrill and admiring her ears. She really was a beautiful woman, one he had a hard time thinking of as Kin, especially since she might not actually be one. In fact, he wasn't sure exactly what made a Kin, Kin. They were obviously all different species of monsters. He was sure he'd figure it out eventually, but he hadn't gotten very far yet with talking to Ysintrill.

They'd mostly just traveled that day, warily observing each other. Trav had been glad of his new abilities. He'd used a few temporary glyph workings to help build camp, and his permanent upgrades had helped. Since Yaakova slept so lightly, and Narnaste could block the entrances with her huge wolf body, he'd created four rooms bored right into the side of a sandstone cliff.

Then he'd turned in for the night, planning to get up early and practice his magic. He'd been shocked when Yaakova had come into his cave, acting like she belonged there, and had made a place for herself next to him in his bedroll.

What had transpired then had been the strangest, most surreal apology Trav had experienced in his life.

"This is my night," the harpy had said in a matter-of-fact tone. She'd then explained that the Valkyries had decided that one of them would stay with Trav every night, for protection and company.

Trav had been impressed with how quickly the women had eventually adapted, but really wished he hadn't had to share a room with the harpy. Valkyrie or not, he didn't entirely trust her, even now. The way they'd met hadn't exactly been pleasant. He even thought about getting up and leaving, but he wasn't sure if that would create more problems.

At least now he didn't have to worry about being overpowered again. Even after Yaakova's increase in strength from their bond, Trav was much stronger now.

He'd tried to play it cool, suggesting they just sleep, that they'd had a long day, but he must have made a weird face. The Kin woman had looked away. "I know you probably don't want me here. When you met me, I was starving, and I attacked you. I thought you were just a human."

"Yeah, and humans are just slaves or should be slaves, right?"

"Well, not always, but you are different."

Trav had rolled his eyes at that. "I have power, so I can't be treated like shit, and that makes me different, huh?"

"No. You have strength. You are...unique. I," she'd paused, visibly searching for the words and continued, "regret that we met the way we did."

"So you don't respect humans, and I hate Kin, but we are stuck together, and now you can fly." Trav had practically growled the words.

Instead of being offended by Trav's tone, her eyes had lit up, and she'd lost some tension in her shoulders. She'd said, "Yes, exactly. We cannot choose our family, and this is true sometimes even later in life. I am not sure...about my place anymore, but I know that leaving would be a bad idea. This is a dangerous world, and I am Yaakova Vratsgadatter. I have already proven my worth. Do not disrespect me, now."

That had taken Trav aback, and he'd mutely nodded, then he had slowly lay down to sleep but had secretly crafted a few rune workings to last the night for protection. The harpy had given him a lot to think about.

The next day, while Yaakova had mostly flown around in her raven form, scouting ahead, Trav had noticed that tensions were easing in the group. He'd been a bit slow on the uptake, but he had realized that they must have been unsure about where they'd all fit in and had a bit more confidence now.

Trav had gotten a headache. Women were confusing enough. Kin women were on another level.

That night, Narnaste had visited Trav's bedroll in her woman form, and as usual, she'd been very straightforward with her intentions. Trav had found himself strangely relieved that she hadn't changed, and after their lovemaking, as the inhuman, murderous, faithful Valkyrie snuggled against him in the dark, he'd had an epiphany.

If Narnaste were killed, regardless of whether he'd lose power or not...he'd grieve. He'd had to admit that he cared about her, which meant that now Asgard had even more ways to hurt him. Hell, maybe by not keeping control of his feelings, he would be hurting himself.

But reality was reality, and Trav prided himself from not flinching away from harsh truths.

That night, after his heavy thoughts, Trav had put his arm around Narnaste, and she'd nuzzled next to him, wagging her tail in her sleep. Trav had been mesmerized, struck by how cute the simple reaction had been, and cursing himself for being so weak.

He'd turned into a Kin lover, literally. What was next? Actually, no, he'd made a mistake in his thinking. It wasn't Kin he cared about, just his Valkyries. That had made more sense.

So the next day, when he'd woken up, he'd decided to start being more proactive. He needed to learn more about this world, and about his companions. The fact that all three of them could easily talk while traveling on Narnaste's back had made chatting relatively easy.

Learning about Yaakova's country had actually been interesting and intriguing. Additionally, when he'd casually described a memory shrine and asked if there were any where she came from, she'd said she might have seen one before. Trav had made a note of that, and then their conversation about harpy politics had begun.

"So do harpy girls know who their fathers are?" Trav asked.

"Sometimes. It depends on the mother and whether the daughter is curious."

Trav's curiosity was piqued. "Do you know?" he asked.

The Kin-turned-raven froze to stillness before she answered. "Yes. This is a problem, in fact. I share the same father as the current Bernacian royal. As a result, she sees me as a threat, and my family wants me to try for the East Tribe guiding tree, and maybe for the royal tree itself. However, I do not want to compete against my sister, or replace my mother as the tribe's guide."

Trav shook his head. "And all this is because of who your father is? Why?"

Narnaste fluffed her feathers in irritation. "Superstition. My father was a powerful human warlock, one who was still allowed to practice magic even in our lands. It is most likely coincidental, but several of the daughters he has sired have become powerful leaders or magicians. As a daughter of Ruski, I am also considered to be marked for greatness."

Trav scratched his cheek. "Then it doesn't make sense for you to find more power." He shook his head. "Wouldn't your family expect even more from you then?"

"Yes and no. If I had more power, I could enforce my will and back my sister's claim."

Trav didn't know what to say to that. Kin were strange. "So how long will these games last?"

"They can be as short as a week or as long as a year. As far as I know, the tribes are all still holding the games for their trees right now."

Trav grinned. "So if we ever go to your home looking for a memory shrine, and I manage not to get killed or to kill all of your people, you might have to still get involved in all these politics, huh?"

He'd meant what he'd said as a joke, but he immediately knew he'd offended his Valkyrie. Trav cursed himself as the raven gave him a direct look before winging off into the sky. He really hoped he hadn't damaged his budding relationship with the dangerous Kin woman. He'd felt a mutual respect growing, one he'd like to cultivate.

"Damn," he muttered.

"You really have a terrible sense of humor, Master," rumbled Narnaste. Trav had forgotten she could hear every word spoken on her back.

"Yeah, well, nobody's perfect," Trav grumbled.

"Threatening to kill a girl's entire family is probably not a great way to continue a conversation." The voice had come from behind, and Trav whipped his head around in surprise.

Ysintrill smiled broadly, her eyes twinkling before she suddenly reverted back to her previous behavior, face smoothing and growing impassive. Trav shook his head, and grumped, "Seriously? Wow. Now everyone is a comedian. Fine, whatever. I made a mistake."

"Do you really hate Kin that much?" Narnaste asked. Trav thought she'd intended to speak softly, but for a wolf the size of a bus, this was probably not easy.

"Yes," growled Trav. "Think, Narn. You know where I come from. You know about what happened to my wife. If you were me, would you love Kin?"

"No, I suppose not," she said. Trav felt her sag.

"You should be gentle with Yaakova," said Ysintrill. "She is giving up a lot and accepting a lot of uncertainty to travel with you. Her life has changed."

Trav hummed then asked, "Why is she still with me anyway? I understand why you two are here, but Yaakova could just fly away and take care of her business with her family, right?"

"It's not that simple," rumbled Narnaste.

"Then explain it. I'm tired of being in the dark. If I have to start asking questions every five minutes, I will. I'm new to...whatever it is I am now, but I don't intend to keep living by the seat of my pants."

Narnaste flicked her ears before responding. "I have not heard that expression before, but I think I know what you mean. First, you probably don't know that harpies are obsessed with the thought of flying. Even plains harpies like Yaakova can spend their entire lives jumping off things to glide longer distances, or researching magic to truly fly."

"They have feathers. They can't fly?" asked Trav.

"No, not really, not like a bird," answered Ysintrill.

Narnaste said, "The other thing is—"

"You can say it," Ysintrill encouraged. Trav raised an eyebrow at that. This was the most he'd heard the elven-looking woman say at once in days.

After clearing her enormous throat, Narnaste finished her thought. "We all feel a pull toward you. We lose some or all of our new power if we do things we know you will not approve of, too. We've experimented."

"It's true," said the disir.

Trav had no idea how they could have figured that out but decided not to ask. Instead, he thought about the implications and said, "So for her to go back to her family, I'd either need to go with her, or give her permission, and she is probably too proud to ask. Otherwise, she might lose her new power, maybe even her ability to change form."

"Yes."

His eyes widened at a new thought. "If she reverted back into her normal form while she was flying, and since she can't truly fly as a harpy, that might be bad."

Narnaste chuckled. "See, Ysintrill? I told you he could be perceptive for a human."

When Trav said nothing in response, the three of them lapsed into silence for a while.

***

After stopping for the day to make camp, Trav walked off into the forest a ways to practice with his new abilities. He'd done the same thing the previous day, so it hadn't raised any eyebrows.

Now that he was by himself, he decided first to spend time loading more rune magic into his shiv, a daily habit. While he did so, he also searched his memory for rune equations that would synergize well with his new abilities.

He'd finally decided to name the shiv, "Hex." It had seemed appropriate. The name seemed to fit the little ill-fated blade and simultaneously wasn't too serious nor too goofy. Trav felt rather proud of himself for coming up with it, actually.

Hex's ability to memorize whatever Trav drew seemed limitless so far, so he continued to take advantage of it. Right now, he figured that the most useful rune workings for air scribing or ventrilomagic were magic traps. He could actually draw them in the air, use Hex to aim, and trigger them as soon as they materialized.

He'd also been focused on adding more temporary enhancements to his arsenal. Hex had been loaded with a wide array of buffs, and with air scribing, he could even cast them on himself while running or dodging.

After he was done scribing more runes and loading them into his shiv, he stood and breathed deeply. As usual, he held his spear. Nobody else was around, and he planned to use some flashy magic today.

When he felt the time was right, Trav ran forward, throwing his spear as hard as he could at a tree. Even as the weapon left his hand, he willed Hex into his palm, then mentally triggered a rune equation to appear in midair. The shiv generated the circular magic device at the tip of the blade, and he activated it. The magic sparked, expanding into a hissing wall of wind to one side, a barrier against arrows.

He jumped up as high as he could, much higher than a normal human could, planted his feet against a tree trunk, and launched himself back. While in midair, he pointed Hex at a different tree. "Lightning bolt!" With a flash, the magic pattern appeared and pulsed, generating a brilliant arc of electricity.

The attack hit the target with a brilliant crack, splintering the bark and burning the trunk. Trav wasn't watching the effects very closely, though. Instead, he pointed Hex at the ground he was about to land on. "Soften." The complicated series of glyphs that he'd willed into existence flashed on the ground, and when he landed, it felt like he'd hit a giant pillow, not the hard earth.

He scrambled up, positioned himself behind a tree, and pointed at the tree that his spear was still stuck in. "Explosion." This target was at his max range for ventrilomagic, but he could still just about reach it. The rune equation, basically a bomb trap, scribed itself on the tree trunk in less than a second, and Trav triggered it, ducking behind cover.

When the tree blew up, the world trembled. Trav was glad for the tree in front of him, especially if the spear had flown his direction, but apparently, it hadn't. Dust, splinters, and fine pieces of bark rained down as Trav stepped from behind his shelter. The top of the tree that he'd destroyed fell to one side, but he ignored it, instead pointing Hex upward. "Searching mist. Spear."

A tendril of fog shot out of the ground, moving outward, and Trav ducked behind the tree again. He'd tried this magic before but wanted to test its flexibility. In less time than he'd expected, the fog tentacle deftly moved around his tree, offering him his spear from wherever it had been blown to.

Trav didn't even bother examining the weapon—it would take a lot more than an explosion to be damaged. Then he threw Hex as far as he could in one direction and jumped to the side, running toward another tree before executing a series of blocks and strikes that reminded him of his time on Earth. Some of the techniques he'd actually learned from his cousin, Ash.

But then he transitioned to a more linear style of martial arts, one that Odin must have used. This style primarily used the blade of the spear and was very lethal.

Pretending there was an attack to one side, Trav dodged, letting his momentum carry him into a roll. He threw his spear at a different tree where it deeply embedded itself, and held out a hand, calling Hex. He pointed into the empty air, imagining a group of enemies rushing toward him. In his mind, they looked like the Kin he'd fought with Narnaste.

"Flamethrower."

Rune lines flashed, and a jet of flame rushed from the tip of Trav's dagger, forming a cone of fiery destruction that he maintained for several seconds. Finally, he halted the controlled inferno, sheathed Hex, and sighed.

Trav rolled his neck and took a minute to stretch before walking to his spear and pulling it out of the tree. Then he turned toward camp, beginning to head back. He figured he'd run into at least one of his Valkyries any second now, alerted by the explosion, searching for him. They'd promised earlier that they wouldn't bother him while he trained, but he still wouldn't be upset when they inevitably showed up.

The longer he was free on Asgard, the more he valued companions to watch his back, even if they did so out of self-interest.

As he walked, Trav's eyes lingered on the demolished tree trunk he'd blown up, and the top of the tree sagging against nearby supporting branches. He'd just used up a lot of power in mere seconds but felt deep pride, a sense of accomplishment. If he were to run into a group of Dacith again, they'd be fucked.

He'd come a long way.

***

That night, Trav retired to his room made of mud that he'd fashioned with magic. His magic recovery ability had really proven useful. Rest was fastest, but he didn't actually need to sleep anymore to regain his mystic reserves.

Earlier, he'd built an oven out of earth, and his little group had enjoyed some deer meat that Narnaste had caught, then cooked.

Trav's bedroll was looking awfully inviting, and he began getting ready for bed when Ysintrill hesitantly entered his shelter.

He didn't let his surprise show. "Hello, Ysintrill. How can I help you?"

"I was told that you understand the arrangement. Uh, I'm here to—stay with you. Also, if you'd like, you can call me Trill. That's what my friends called me. Well, before."

Trav regarded the disir woman levelly for a moment, openly studying her. She had flawless almond-colored skin and long, pointed ears that stuck out almost sideways. Her full lips were just a touch too low on her face, giving her a pouty expression, even while her face was at rest. Her straight nose supported big eyes with naturally long lashes. She was tall for a woman, at least by Trav's standards, probably standing five feet ten inches tall. Her body was lithe and muscular, like a soccer player.

He wasn't sure where she'd gotten her plain outfit from. When she'd been regenerated, freed from the box, she hadn't been wearing a scrap of clothing. Trav's memories from that time were still a little hazy, but he definitely remembered that. He also knew that she had pale areolas, and her breasts—

With a shake of his head, he focused back on the woman's— Kin's—face. Ysintrill was dangerous, at least to his emotional wellbeing. She definitely wasn't human, but he still wasn't sure if she was Kin. He decided to solve the mystery right now.

"Okay, Trill, could you answer a question for me?"

"Yes?"

"Are you Kin?"

The beautiful woman cocked her head and blinked at him. "I haven't really thought of it before, but no, I suppose I'm not. I was, am disir, technically a type of spirit."

"I know that." Trav gestured with his hand. "Doesn't that make you Kin, though?"

"No. Kin doesn't mean 'not human,' it's the term for people who have come from other worlds, veils that are compatible enough with Asgard that they could maintain their power."

"Huh?"

"You know how veils work, right?"

"I think so but remind me."

Now that she was assuming a lecturing stance, the tall, impressive woman lost much of her earlier uncertainty. "Most of the time, traveling between veils will sap a being's power the longer they are in a new world. The more powerful the traveler, the faster they lose their power. In fact, Narnaste told me that you witnessed an attack before you escaped slavery, right?"

"Yes."

"Those attacking, the humans, were probably from a different veil. They were also probably not very powerful for their kind. A truly powerful fighter will lose most of their abilities or magic the instant they transition. The only exception I know of is the gods."

Trav had grasped most of that, but now it made a lot more sense. "And the Kin?"

"Most of them were refugees from other veils, at least I think so. The first of them had begun forming settlements before I died." She paused for a moment, cleared her throat, and said, "Travelers from other worlds who were not compatible with Asgard moved on, or usually just died. There might be exceptions, or beings that didn't have any other power of note. Maybe the Dacith that you hate so much are an example of this scenario."

Trav nodded. He'd let slip the last few days how much he loathed the rat-like Kin.

Ysintrill paced a little. "Meanwhile, the majority of the Kin we see on Asgard now were able to retain most if not all of their power—Asgard must be similar enough to their homeworld that they didn't lose anything. At least, this is what the sages believed during my lifetime."

"So about that, you are dead, right?" Trav asked, and after summoning Hex, pointed it at the ground. He conjured a simple, flexible, and extremely convenient rune equation into existence, and willed a couple chairs to rise out of the earth.

Ysintrill nodded her thanks and sat down. "Not exactly. I was about to die, and one of Odin's Valkyries chose me, but because of my situation, I was denied Valhalla. As a sort of consolation, she used something to turn me into what I am now."

"Your situation?"

"Yes. Like I told you before, I am a woman not of this world. I was transported here...like I heard you were, actually."

Trav nodded. He wasn't surprised that the Valkyries had been talking about him amongst themselves. Now that his memory had been jogged, he remembered what Ysintrill had said earlier too. "Okay, yeah. So you transformed from an adventurer or mercenary to a...spirit. Why didn't you go back to your old life?"

"Times were different then than now. This was a human world then, and non-humans were not welcomed. Plus, I'd already lost everything. My family, my friends, my fiancé, they were all dead. I knew that I would have a long life, and I didn't want to ever go through that again, so I wandered.

"If I had one regret about all of this, it is just—" She trailed off, looking down.

Trav found her change in personality amazing. Just a moment before, he'd seen the strong, powerful, confident warrior she must have been in the past, but then she'd faded like a snuffed candle. "That box really fucked you up, didn't it?"

"Yes. Yes, it did."

Trav felt a sudden rush of pity. "What is your regret?"

"Honestly?" She looked up through long lashes and sighed. "I want my bow back."

"Your bow?" Trav blinked. That had not been what he'd been expecting her to say.

"Yes. After I was turned into what I am now, I journeyed far before settling down in my old grove. I found a bow at one point—dwarven make. The truth is that I am a terrible aim with a bow, but I prefer one for hunting and for combat. This one made it practically impossible to miss. I really loved it.

"When I was in there," she hissed, "the box, someone liked to taunt me sometimes. They said my bow had been sold to someone in the south, in a city called Vrasthath."

"I understand." Trav pursed his lips. "Well, I don't know where we are all going to go, but you basically work for me now. A good leader doesn't ignore his people. If we journey near this Vrasthath, or we can go there without jeopardizing something else we are doing, and if we are realistically able to do so, maybe I can help you get your bow back." He amended, "If it still exists."

"You would do that for me?"

"Of course. You fight for me now, more or less. Getting you the best tools available, and raising morale, all in one move? It's really obvious. Not only that, the way you were in that box...it was wrong." Trav felt the same pity from before, but also some respect. If he'd been imprisoned in a box, not being able to see, having nobody to talk to, only hearing dark cultists talk about sacrifices or whatever it is they did, would he have stayed sane?

The thought was so horrible, Trav said what was on his mind with no filter. "Whoever put you in there is a sick fuck, and I would help you kill them too. There are fates worse than death. I am glad we saved you from the tunnels collapsing. That would be—"

He was suddenly hit by flying feminine curves, a solid kiss placed on his mouth. *Oh yeah, she probably came here in the first place to spend the night.* He immediately regretted his snarky mental tone, though. Trill's emotions had been laid bare the moment she launched herself into his arms, and he couldn't deny what he'd seen. He could understand her feelings, too.

Trav knew what she wanted from him, and so he decided to give it to her. She'd earned his regard. Part of him whispered that he was biting off more than he could chew, even as he began undressing the elven-looking Valkyrie. But he was a god now, though not a very good one yet.

Ysintrill was his Valkyrie. She was interesting, beautiful, and Trav was tired of being hunted by bestial girls every night in his bedroll. This would be a welcome break from that. Yes, Trill may not be human, but he understood her, and at least she wasn't Kin.

That night, Trav comforted a hurting, broken woman who'd lost everything, and had almost lost her soul. With his newfound perspective, he felt truly lucky for the first time since he'd arrived on Asgard.

Chapter 26

If Narnaste had run, or even traveled a bit faster, the trip to the mysterious Faithful village would probably take less time. Despite Asgard being big—probably bigger than Earth—as transportation, the transformed wolf was really amazing. She was huge, tireless, and was only slowed down by wide rivers or thick vegetation.

But snow had started to fall, and Trav wasn't in any huge hurry to reach their destination. Now that he actually had some power to play with, he was growing in confidence every day. Experimenting with magic had become routine, as well as loading a growing number of runework into Hex.

Now that Ysintrill had come out of her shell, slowly healing from being trapped in her de facto prison, she'd been reverting back to the warrior and adventurer she'd been in the past. As a result, Trav wasn't entirely surprised when she'd suddenly tapped him on the shoulder and asked for some weapons.

In truth, their entire group was a bit lacking in weapons except for

Trav himself. Narnaste still had her seax knife, which she'd been using to butcher animals and do other tasks, but Yaakova only had a small belt knife she kept at her back, and Ysintrill had been carrying a club. She'd also found some flaky rock somewhere and had knapped it into a serviceable cutting edge. The group was making do, but if not for Kin biology, Trav's magic, and Narnaste's hunting, they would have been in trouble a while ago.

After the run-in with the demon worshippers, the group had been avoiding any signs of civilization while traveling cross-country. Existing out in the middle of nowhere had its drawbacks.

Trav thought about the weapons request. "Narnaste, could you take us over to that clump of trees near that big rock and the cliff thing?" Trav pointed, forgetting that his wolf-form Valkyrie couldn't see him, but her head swiveled around anyway, and she flicked her ears.

"Trill, what kind of weapons do you want?" he asked.

Behind him, the dark-skinned beauty replied, "I would like a bow, Chief. Perhaps some something else for my waist if you have time."

"Alright. Narn, what about you?"

The huge wolf shrugged her massive shoulders. "I think a simple spear will be fine, Master, more for hunting than anything else. During most fights in the future, I will probably be in this form, but having a backup would be nice. The seax is useful but not great for combat."

"I understand. You can't exactly be the wolf if we're in a cave again, either." He looked up, and shouted at the raven circling in the sky, "What about you, Kova?"

The dark bird fluttered down, settling on Trav's knee gently before speaking. "I believe I do not need any more weapons, New One. My claws have served me well before, and now I have my feathers too."

"What about clothes? A jacket, anything?" In her original form, the harpy still sported the revealing, fancy clothing that she'd worn when Trav had first met her.

"No, New One. The cold does not touch me."

"Okay." He didn't ask any more questions, just took her word for it, and moved directly to thinking of logistical concerns. Trav had knowledge from Odin about how to make crude, simple versions of everything that had been asked for. He jingled the items in his small, handmade bag and hoped it would be enough. "We have lots of sinew left from the deer we've eaten, right?"

"Yes," came Narnaste's answer.

"Good."

***

Trav glanced at the pile of materials off to one side and nodded. "I think that's everything."

"Will this take you long?" asked Ysintrill.

Trav shook his head. "No, gathering everything is what took a while. Where did Yaakova and Narnaste go?"

"Narn is hunting. Kova got bored of watching you and went to fly around."

"Got it. Well, that means you'll be the only one here to inspect what I give you and ask for any changes."

The disir woman chuckled. "Chief, I know you will make any changes the others ask for later. They know this too."

Trav didn't know what to say to that. He just grumbled, "Kin," under his breath as he finished organizing his supplies. That done, he got to work.

The large rock before him would be a work surface. He summoned Hex into one hand and pointed. "Soften like clay." The sigils danced over the surface of the stone, and Trav began shaping it with one hand while continuing to point the shiv. The stone still required a solid push to move, but it wasn't long before he had a flat working surface with a sunken, shallow, square portion. It looked like a mold...because it was one. With one more bit of effort, he created a channel to one side of the mold for excess material.

Then he produced the iron he'd pocketed from his bag and the handful of other iron bits that his companions had volunteered. Iron was not exactly rare on Asgard, but Trav didn't have a wheelbarrow full of it out in the middle of nowhere. He was making do. After placing all iron in the shallow mold, he pointed Hex and said, "Melt."

Magic flashed, and the iron almost immediately heated up, growing red-hot in seconds, and melting soon afterward. This magic effect was potent but used a lot of power. Luckily, Trav was only melting a small amount of metal and could cut back on the amount of magic it needed.

Soon the iron filled the mold, and some ran off through the excess channel. "Harden." The metal almost immediately began to cool, starting to form a sheet of solid iron. Trav nodded. This rune working would also make the iron as dense as if it'd been forged.

That done, he fashioned a new work stone and fetched some materials. First, he needed to prepare wood. Fresh-cut saplings were easy to work with, but as-is would not make good weapons. After placing a few green sticks on the new work stone, Trav used Hex and announced, "Dry." This magic had been incredibly handy over the last week, especially since the days had turned cold. Trav could place a glyph equation with a time limit in an earthen room, turning it into a drying chamber.

On a smaller scale, this magic seemed to be good at drying out saplings, too. Trav left the wood to cure and returned to the iron. Using Hex, he scribed lines of red, burning magic into the sheet metal, cutting out shapes he planned to use later.

After returning to the wood, he checked to see if it was dry and decided he could use it now. Nothing he was making would be an heirloom-quality weapon; it just needed to work for a week or so until they arrived at Narnaste's Faithful town.

He selected a fairly thick piece of wood and set it off to the side. Next, he bent a thin piece of wood and attached a string to both ends, making a bow. "Cut." The magic took effect, and now Trav had an incredibly effective saw for the next hour or two.

He cut a notch into the thick wood, making a handle for an axe. Next, he added four splints of iron to the haft—on the sides of the head, then one to the front, and one behind. He wrapped the weapon tightly with sinew, using a few holes he'd placed in the simple iron axe head to keep the whole contraption tight.

Next, he placed a plain leather wrap at the base for a handle and, using Hex, easily sharpened the iron blade.

Now Ysintrill had an axe. "Do you like it?" he asked, handing the weapon to the elven-looking woman.

"I am impressed you could make this so quickly. Yes, this will work, and thank you, but I need a sheath."

"Oh, okay. Just a minute." Trav quickly made a sheath for the new axe and then got busy again, creating new weapons.

He worked this way for some time, completely focused on what he was doing. Since he'd suspected days before that he'd need to craft something soon, he'd stored a number of utility rune magic in his dagger. Now he was able to cut a few corners, still working quickly and efficiently.

The bow was fairly easy to craft, at least with rune magic. After stringing it, Trav could actually increase the stiffness of the weapon, increasing its draw weight with a simple twist of his shiv, rotating a magic circle that hung in the air. He wordlessly handed the bow to Ysintrill to test several times until she liked the level of resistance, then he strengthened the wood, cut an arrow shelf at the appropriate point, and set it aside. Now it was time to craft arrows.

On Earth, making arrows would probably be fairly hard, but on Asgard, it was easy. Trav used a simple glyph to straighten each peeled, magically dried stick. Then he used another glyph to soften the wood like clay. The saw he'd crafted earlier helped with making a notch for the arrowhead and the nock. He'd punched a small hole in each arrowhead for the wood to meet and meld together through the iron. Once that was done, he wrapped below the iron and above the nock with sinew.

Finally, he used feathers he'd cut in half lengthwise, pushing them directly into the putty-like wood above the nock. After this, the arrow was finished, and he made fourteen others just like it. The entire time he worked, his long-eared Valkyrie watched him intently.

Now that the arrows were done, Trav crafted a simple quiver with leather he had on hand—most of it deer hide that he'd cured days before. Learning to cure hides with magic had been a necessity to create blankets and extra clothing as soon as the weather had begun getting colder.

He examined the quiver with a critical eye and slowly nodded. Then he handed the completed quiver, arrows, and bow to Ysintrill and shook his head. The bow probably had a one hundred-and-fifty-pound draw, far more than most humans could draw.

The disir accepted the weapons with a reverent air, and Trav smiled slightly. Trill was treating the weapons like some women on Earth would react to diamonds and rubies.

Trav returned to crafting and gave some thought to how he'd create Narnaste's spear. Since the Kin woman's clothing and anything she held disappeared when she transformed, bulk didn't seem to be a problem.

He made a face and decided to use the rest of the iron, cutting out a large, wicked-shaped spearhead. After that, it was a simple matter to craft the weapon, harden it, sharpen the blade, and even add a nice leather wrap for the grip.

"Okay, done." Trav nodded and felt a deep sense of accomplishment. He stretched and sighed. "Can you help me gather all this stuff up, Trill? We need to throw it back into those big saddle bags that Narnaste carries now."

"Of course, Chief."

The two of them began working, and after a few minutes, Ysintrill suddenly ran forward and hugged him. "Thank you," she said, rubbing her eyes and turning away. Then she began working again like nothing had happened.

Trav blinked a few times. He shrugged and went back to what he'd been doing.

***

The next morning, he could tell that Narnaste was feeling pleased with herself. She'd loved her new spear, and had spent that night with him. The lupine Kin woman had been practically bouncing all morning. Trav had to hide a smile a few times. Sometimes it was difficult to remember that she was Kin.

Their little group had begun traveling a little later than normal, and the clear, cold air felt crisp but healthy. Trav was beginning to enjoy the scenery and the smell of pines.

Suddenly, he cocked his head—he could feel something new. Without knowing exactly how, he knew that up ahead, somewhere in the sky, Yaakova had seen something strange and was sending the message to him for his decision.

Trav closed his eyes and caught flashes, images of what the

transformed harpy could see. Stone had been stacked before the mouth of a cave, effectively forming a stone home. The structure would normally be secure, probably even against most creatures on Asgard, but was currently surrounded by a disfigured pack of monsters.

"Narnaste," said Trav, his eyes still closed, "what kind of creature has lumpy brown skin and kind of looks like a man, but has claws and can walk on all four limbs? And also," Trav said, continuing to watch the vision in his mind, "have spikes on their elbows, big teeth, and long tongues?"

"Maybe Wild Ones, blood ghouls I think. Why?"

"Blood ghouls, huh? That sounds pleasant. Why are they called blood ghouls?"

"They usually pull their prey apart into small pieces and lap up all the blood first before eating the meat. They're really quite mindless. I believe they usually live underground in crypts, but sometimes they break out in a group, and a city's military has to put them down."

"Lovely." Trav continued to watch the images in his mind, observing with no sound as the creatures tore at the walls, trying to break into the stone building. One of them that had been beating on the door suddenly flailed back, a spear through its gut. Someone inside the house had skewered the creature through a hole in the door.

Then one of the monsters managed to bend a bar in the window, trying to force its way through the gap. It fell back too, screeching from a mortal wound in its neck. Whoever was inside the stone house was putting up a good fight, but the ghouls were obviously strong, determined, and not going away. It would only be a matter of time before they got in.

"This isn't my problem," said Trav out loud.

"What, Master?"

"Sorry, Narnaste, I'm thinking out loud. Give me a second, please." He felt a hand on his back and realized that Ysintrill was offering him support despite not knowing what was going on. The gesture touched him and helped him decided what to do.

Yes, some of the slaves back in the mines had been terrible people. Most of the Kin he'd met should be exterminated. The humans back in the walled village—praying to dark gods and sacrificing children—should have been flayed alive and tossed into a world of salt. But there were good people on Asgard, too. People like Beth had been. Some of the other slaves had shown true nobility, too. Then there was Ysintrill, and even some Kin like Narnaste apparently weren't so bad. Like it or not, all of his Valkyries were family now.

Part of him didn't want to put them in danger, but his honesty about the pockets of decency in this world added to his curiosity—who was living in a stone house out in the Asgard boonies? He sighed. It didn't matter what world he was on; it seemed he was destined to always do everything the hard way.

"Narnaste, head to the right, please. Turn on some speed, too. We're going to save someone—I think."

"Master, there is a fight?"

"Yes. We have some ghouls to kill."

"I hate ghouls. This is good," said Ysintrill. Trav didn't have to look to know she was probably adjusting her quiver.

As the huge, eight-legged wolf turned and began loping where Trav had indicated, following his directions, he wondered how Yaakova had communicated with him over such a long distance. Maybe the rest of the Valkyries were hiding things too, or had yet to discover them.

At least he knew now that all the Valkyries could transform, and what Ysintrill could do. He'd found out about it a couple days ago, and had a feeling it would prove handy in their coming fight.

Trav felt strangely stress-free as he rode toward yet another life-and-death struggle on Asgard. But he wasn't alone anymore, and he had a huge red murder wolf.

Some freaky Asgard monsters were about to have a bad day.

***

The ghouls didn't know what hit them.

Trav rode on the back of Narnaste, pointing with Hex. "Explosion." The ground between a group of the creatures violently erupted, sending the howling nightmares flying.

Ysintrill had faded to smoke, her shadowy figure running through trees before swarming up a large one. A moment later, she'd solidified back into her original form, drew her bow, and loosed an arrow. Despite her claims of poor archery skills, the attack had been deadly. Her simple equipment that Trav had made was not ideal, but the Valkyrie had made it work. A pebbly-skinned ghoul went down with a gurgle, an arrow through its chest.

Narnaste bent and chomped down on a monster holding a club. As she shook her head to kill it, Trav pointed again. "Lightning bolt:

forked." Jagged lances of crackling power lashed out, splitting the air and knocking over ghouls like leaves in the wind.

A small, black shape buzzed down from the sky, turning into Yaakova at the last second. The savage harpy woman laughed as she reached from behind a ghoul to tear out its throat. Her powerful leg lashed out, claws slashing the creature from waist to shoulder. She spun and solidified her feathers; the razor-sharp, iron-hard weapons cut the arm off another enemy. Then she changed back to her raven form, cawing in triumph as she climbed to search for a new target of opportunity.

Despite the danger of the situation, Trav's heart pumped in excitement, and he jumped down from Narnaste. The ghouls were undoubtedly dangerous. Each of them was probably the equal of a Dacith. A couple months ago, they would have been a deadly threat; a single one of them would have been able to completely overwhelm a group of humans. But Trav was not exactly human anymore. He'd changed, and backed by his three Valkyries, the blood ghouls didn't stand a chance.

One ran at him, screaming, its large teeth flashing. The creature's face looked human enough to be disturbing, but Trav was desensitized by Asgard. He didn't even flinch as he drove the point of his dwarven-made spear into its chest. The creature tried to pull itself forward, even as it died, but Trav wasn't just going to stay there and let it. He twisted the weapon, making the ghoul's terrible wound worse, and kicked it off the point.

He'd dropped Hex to fight effectively with the spear, so he

mentally willed the shiv into his hand again, pointed down, and said, "Gust."

A sudden howling gale erupted from the ground, and Trav jumped, letting the enormous air pressure carry him into the sky. After he was high up enough to see the entire fight, he located the largest group of living enemies. Maybe he could use a flashier attack now, one that used up more magic. "Cold scatter blast." A large rune equation formed in the air, triggered, and the moisture in the cool air immediately formed into small, deadly icicles that slashed downward.

The group of ghouls were hit, but only one went down for good. The rest of them had been injured but were still mobile. "Well, shit," Trav grumbled. "That attack sucks. What a waste of magic."

He plummeted downward. "Soften." Landing felt like hitting a trampoline, and he walked forward, deciding to use another powerful rune equation. The fight would probably be over soon, and he didn't get many chances to practice his destructive magic on actual bodies. His earlier experiment with the ice attack was exactly the type of information he was looking for.

A ghoul ran at him, screaming. It probably hadn't seen him in the sky a moment earlier, or maybe it had, and it was just that stupid. Trav didn't care. Now it was just a target. He pointed his dagger—and the monster went down with an arrow through its neck.

Trav was momentarily tempted to yell at Ysintrill in frustration but stilled his tongue. He glanced over and saw her in her smoke form moving down one tree, then swarming up another for a better angle. She was just doing her job.

Most of the ghouls were dead now. There wouldn't be any more of them to practice on soon. Trav sucked in a breath and ran toward one of them. It saw him and hurried to meet him, its crazed, inhuman eyes wide with adrenaline and rage. When it got close enough, Trav enacted his experiment.

He cocked back his hand holding Hex and held his other hand forward. "Accelerate." A circle-shaped rune equation formed in the air, and he threw the shiv through it, aiming carefully.

A sonic boom cracked as the blade was immediately catapulted to hypersonic speeds. The ghoul's entire chest practically disintegrated as the relatively heavy shiv zipped through its body at the speed of an Earth rifle round.

The impact from Trav's attack was so profound, that in addition to the giant cloud of blood and offal, half of the creature's body collapsed. One arm fell to the ground. The ghoul's hideous face stretched in a pained, surprised expression as it toppled over.

Behind the stricken monster, Trav's dagger rocketed forward, taking off another ghoul's leg at the knee, bouncing off the ground, and slamming through a tree with a hail of dirt, rocks, and snow it had kicked up.

Trav slammed his spear through the creature's corpse he'd just killed and called Hex back into his hand. The weapon suddenly appeared, clean, not a hint of filth on it. Trav still wasn't sure exactly how calling the soul-bound shiv worked, but he appreciated that he wouldn't get blood all over himself. He'd been barely able to avoid most of the brutal mist he'd created with his attack. *Good.*

Now he knew that he had a deadly kinetic attack in addition to the elemental magic he could generate. If he raised the power of this rune working, he could probably also make the dagger move a hell of a lot faster. Interestingly enough, since the shiv had already been in motion, the working hadn't actually required that much energy to activate. Magic effects needed more juice if they were acting against the natural world. For instance, forming ice blades on a hot day would be much more difficult than on a cold day like today.

Trav hadn't been fighting the physical world too hard for most magic he'd performed, but some of the abilities had still been somewhat flashy. He'd used up over one bar of power. *Wow.*

The last of the ghouls died, slashed to ribbons by Yaakova. She seemed to be enjoying herself. Trav cautiously walked to the door of the stone building. He stood to one side, out of the reach of any spear, and announced himself. "My name is Trav. We just killed all the ghouls that had been attacking—Wild Ones or monsters, whatever you want to call them."

The door swung open, and a fierce woman holding a spear stepped out. "There is no point staying inside, is there? You could just blow up my house." She warily watched all of them but seemed to be focusing most on Yaakova.

Smart, thought Trav. He examined the woman. She was Asian, or at least she looked Asian. Her long hair was held back in a flowing ponytail, and she wore loose-fitting, comfortable-looking clothing. Dark, almond eyes flashed with intelligence, and her generous mouth was set in a scowl. Her clothing was rough, practical and serviceable, but not very flattering. Trav got the feeling she'd be pretty if she cared about her appearance, but she obviously didn't right now.

"What is your name?" asked Trav.

"Jang-mi."

"And what are you doing way out here?"

She narrowed her eyes, but then her shoulders sagged, her expression turning resigned. "I am an escaped slave, and before that, I was living in Xing City. I was a martial artist and ability user."

"A what?" Trav placed his hands on his hips and met the proud woman's eyes.

"I come from another world. The Kin in this world call us Cultists. I may not be able to use my chi here, but I am not defenseless. If you mean me harm, then state your purpose and I will meet you appropriately."

Trav noticed her white-knuckled grip on her spear and the way she held her hand in a strange way over her chest. She was probably some sort of ability user who'd been on Asgard too long, and lost her power.

"I don't mean you any harm, but I'd like to talk. Are you going to invite me inside?"

"Why should I?" Jang-mi stood on the balls of her toes like she could move at any moment.

Trav rolled his eyes. "Because like you already said, I could just obliterate you right now, and there would not be a damn thing you could do about it." He was tired of playing games with people and needed information more than friends right now.

"Good point." She gave one last suspicious glance at the Kin woman and the slaughtered bodies of the ghouls. "I suppose you can come inside, Trav. Please leave these—ones—outside."

"Watch your tongue, human, or I might eat it." Yaakova smiled, showing off her sharp teeth.

"Calm down, Kova." Trav sighed. "Alright, Jang-mi, let's have a chat."

Chapter 27

The inside of Jang-mi's house was simple and austere but seemed more than livable. She'd obviously spent time to make the place feel like home for her. It looked like she'd built the place herself, too.

"How long have you lived here?" asked Trav. He'd been close enough now to tell she was probably in her late twenties or early thirties.

"Over a year by the way this world judges them."

"I see. How long ago did you get here?"

The proud woman sat on a homemade chair before she answered. "Two years ago. Why do you ask? What do you intend to do with me?"

"You could thank me for killing all those ghouls." Trav met her eyes. "If it weren't for me, you'd be food right now."

"I could have—"

"You would have died, and you know it. I don't need you to suddenly trust me, but a little respect would be nice."

Jang-mi stared for a moment before exhaling. "You are right. Besides, you have that giant red wolf. You truly have the power." She gave a lopsided grin without humor, and her shoulders sagged, but her eyes still glittered.

"Oh, Narnaste?" Trav mentally sighed. He'd forgotten the Kin woman was transformed. His group probably looked as nightmarish as the ghouls had been. "She is my...fighter. I was once a slave, too. In fact, I haven't even been free for a full month."

"You have monsters and Kin fighting for you. I have a hard time believing this."

Trav took a seat on the edge of a rough-hewn, wooden bench. "I don't really care if you believe me, lady. You don't have anything I need. Believe it or not, I just came to help—well, I was also curious. Why did you build your house in front of a cave?"

"I believed it would be stronger. The cave gives me more storage space and a place to train."

"So you're really out here by yourself?"

"Yes. The other slaves lacked spirit to save themselves, so I went alone. I was working in a mill. We were not always fed well. I used to be a warrior, and slavery was miserable. I doubt you'd understand."

Trav stared for a moment. He hadn't encountered any situation quite like this before. Back in the mines, most of the slaves had known who he was. After a moment's contemplation, he leaned his spear against the wall, then began undressing.

Jang-mi leapt back, aiming her spear at him. "So, your true intentions show themselves? If you—"

"Shut up," ordered Trav. "Just watch." Despite the cold, he removed layers of clothing, eventually standing bare-chested. He knew that from the front, his body was a bit ghastly, with all the obvious damage he'd incurred.

Then he turned and heard a gasp.

Trav had never seen them himself, but he knew his back was practically one mass of scar tissue. He'd been beaten and whipped so many times, he'd lost count. Since he'd never lost his sense of self, his pride, he'd gotten punished more often than the others, but that had been alright. At least when the guards had been hurting him, they hadn't had time to spend on the others.

He slowly turned back around, and in a deadpan voice said, "I doubt you have had as difficult a time as me."

"What happened to you?" Jang-mi's voice came out hushed, almost just a whisper. She seemed to see him again for the first time, her eyes traveling from his eye patch to his worn clothing, and the large, impressive spear he carried.

"Working in the mines, mining for red stone. For years."

"I heard of that, rumors. They say nobody survives long in the mines. How did you escape—oh, that's right. You have magic." Her eyes narrowed in suspicion again. "And Kin followers. How do I know—"

"Just answer some questions, and I'll leave."

The stubborn woman was silent for a moment. "Fine. Ask."

Trav had noticed her accent before and had finally made a connection between her appearance, how she held her weapon, and even what she'd said before. He would have figured she was not from Asgard just by the accent—hers was even stronger than his—but now he realized she reminded him of the people he'd seen during the attack on the mine.

"Tell me, the world you come from, do they wear gis or martial robes?"

"What?"

"Oh, hold on." Trav realized that since she didn't speak English, or even the native language that well, she might not know the words he was using. Instead, he muttered, "Image" at the ground while pointing Hex.

Jang-mi growled in surprise as the dirt floor began to move, resolving itself in a crude drawing of the kind of person Trav had seen attacking the mine. "Gis."

"Yes, this looks like it could come from my world. Why?"

"Interesting," said Trav. He rubbed his chin. "I think I might have seen some fighters from your world attack the Kin."

With a shrug, Jang-mi said, "Maybe so. They do that. Experts from various schools and families will go on raids through the veils. Beast people and Kin are desirable slaves."

"Slaves? How can you keep Kin..." Trav made a face and answered his own question. "They lose their power after enough time on your world, just like you have lost your power here."

"Yes. I am just a piece of the harmony. Hopefully, the universe approves of my new direction."

"Well, I wouldn't know." Trav stood. "What I do know is that your house is torn the fuck up, and I need to get going. We are heading to a village where Kin believe in the old gods. I'm assuming humans aren't all treated completely like shit there, but if they are, it will change immediately. I will make sure of it. You are welcome to come."

Jang-mi warily stood. "It is true that my dwelling will require many repairs. The ghouls attacking means there might be another group nearby, too. I should probably move. However, I have nowhere to go, and any creatures could probably track me.

"I don't trust you, though. Traveling with Kin is ridiculous, and I have no desire to couple with you. I have nothing to pay you with other than my body, but I am not willing to use that currency." She held her chin in the air, standing proudly. "What say you?"

Trav blinked, began to speak, but started laughing instead. Jang-mi frowned as he got himself under control. When he'd finished laughing, he said, "Couple with me? Lady, you have no idea how little I need that. No, I want more information. You will be free to leave any time you want, and I am fairly sure I can guarantee your safety at our destination. Either way, it beats walking around by yourself or living in a broken house with packs of monsters running around."

"I do not know if—"

"You need me more than I need you. My group will be leaving as soon as I exit this building. Make your decision."

Jang-mi searched his eyes for a moment before she shrugged. "You are right. I should be dead right now already. I will take this opportunity."

"Good. In that case, let's shake on it." Trav held out his hand.

The confident woman stared at the proffered hand for a moment before she hesitantly took it with one of her own.

"Master, are you alright? I hear—" Narnaste burst into the house. Her jaw dropped, and she growled. Trav didn't understand why until he realized he was standing shirtless with Jang-mi's hand in his own. *Really? Oh hell.*

***

A few days passed after Jang-mi joined Trav's little group, and she quickly adjusted. Trav made her a dwelling every night just like he did for the Kin women, and she kept to herself. At first, she'd seemed slightly curious, almost morbidly fascinated by the Valkyries, and openly shocked that they were all sleeping with Trav. She eventually grew accustomed to it and just ignored them all.

Not much seemed to impress Jang-mi in general.

Luckily, she didn't seem to mind talking if pressed, and he was able to grill her for information about her homeworld, and places she'd been on Asgard. He'd already begun picking up pieces of her language that she shared, too. Trav had never been much of a linguist, but Odin had been, and some of that was bleeding through from the god's mantle.

In some ways, it was nice to have another human around. Then Trav reminded himself that he wasn't really human anymore. The thought made him glum.

Trav shot a look at Yaakova in her raven form as she wheeled around up in the sky and signaled at her that they would set up camp soon. The transformed Kin cawed in acknowledgement and began a spiraling scouting pattern. Behind him, the others rode on Narnaste's back. Jang-mi had adapted quickly to traveling this way. She'd learned how to hang on to the giant wolf's back by grabbing her fur if she suddenly turned to run, and other necessary tricks.

Every member of the little group was physically superior to an average human, even Jang-mi, and setting up camp was routine now—it went quickly.

But today, after doing what he normally did to establish their little earthen rooms for the night, he realized that the others were all busy, and now he was alone with Jang-mi. At first, he thought it was coincidence, but he quickly realized that she must have wanted to talk. Rather than play coy, he asked, "What is it?"

The mysterious martial artist exhaled. "I have had time to think lately. This has been easy, strangely calm, and I have found perspective." She seemed to struggle to say the next words. "I am out of practice. I would like to work on my martial skills, to drill and perhaps spar, but I have been alone for a long time. Your group is the first I have been part of for a great while, but I cannot properly spar with any of your Kin...women."

Trav was tempted to disagree, but he thought about it first. Ysintrill was closest to a human in biology, and there was no reason she couldn't spar with Jang-mi, but the human woman was obviously uncomfortable with the idea. There was no point in pushing it. Instead, Trav took the opportunity to fish for more information.

"They are all stronger than a human, but you are not actually human, are you?"

She shook her head. "No, I am human. I can just cultivate energy."

"Is that why you are still so strong on this world? Well, strong for a human."

"I believe so. I think that by training in the mysteries, I have altered my body, made it stronger. This is good because without this advantage, I would not be here right now."

"What do you mean?" Trav asked.

"I do not want to talk about it right now." She obviously changed the subject and said, "So will you train with me?"

"I don't see why not. What do you have in mind first?"

She tossed him a stick about the thickness and length of a stave. "I want to see how you fight. No magic, no Kin bitches or tricks, just skill."

Trav frowned. "Those girls are my companions."

"So?"

Trav slowly nodded. "To put it bluntly, I trust them. I don't trust you."

"But they're Kin." Jang-mi crossed her arms.

"So?" Trav threw the word back at her.

The proud woman narrowed her eyes briefly before smoothing her face and nodding curtly. "Fine. But what is your answer?"

"I think I will exercise with you. We will only do this during the evening, though, and only when our chores are done."

Jang-mi gave a rare smile. "I agree to your terms. Shall we begin?"

Chapter 28

"That was good, but you need to keep an eye on my feet too." Trav nodded from the ground where he'd just been knocked on his ass. He levered himself up and warily got to his feet. His teacher beckoned, and he obliged by throwing a few experimental punches at about 50% effort, carefully watching how she avoided, blocked, or countered.

Jang-mi had actually proven to be a competent instructor. To be fair, she was more than competent. In addition to fighting techniques that she practiced herself, she'd even been able to teach theory and the basics of other styles she didn't actively use herself.

Over time, Trav had started to gather that Odin had been a decent warrior, but hadn't been an expert. Through the incomplete information he got from his borrowed memories, he figured the old god had possessed such overwhelming power, he'd never needed to rely on martial skills. Obviously, Trav had no such luxury, and he vowed that even if he attained all the power in the world, he would never forget how many times a rock or shiv had saved his life. Hex would help, his constant reminder of the mines.

Being taught by Jang-mi was a blessing. She would have been a great teacher even back on Earth, but Trav was also different now, a better student. These days, he felt like a sponge that absorbed information at a frightening rate. After only a few short days of training, he'd learned many new fighting techniques, and had refined what he'd known before—stuff that his cousin Ash had taught him.

Trav grunted and held his ribs where he'd just been kicked. During sparring, they both pulled strikes, but it still hurt to get hit. He made a face. "Let's take a break."

"Fine. Do you mind making some places to sit? I do not want snow to get my butt wet."

Trav grinned. "Sure. That makes sense." He pointed Hex at the ground and within minutes, had crafted a break spot in the middle of the forest.

While he was training with Jang-mi, the Valkyries stayed busy as well, often doing training of their own. Every once in a while, he heard the distant thrum of a bow, or noticed Yaakova glide through the sky overhead, keeping watch. Trav was a bit envious. The harpy loved to fly, so had fun while she practiced gliding, all while maintaining security for the group.

Jang-mi sat and took a sip of purified water out of an earthenware jug that Trav had made for her. "You know, I don't understand you."

"What do you mean?" Trav sat and gave her a level look. They hadn't known each other long, but he'd taken a liking to the prickly woman. In some ways, she reminded him of his mother. She'd always been blunt and no-nonsense as well.

The martial artist gestured vaguely. "There is no reason for you to be learning how to fight like this. You have power greater than I had before coming to this place. Three Kin willingly follow you—for reasons that I cannot figure out at all. You seem to lead effortlessly, in a way that most people would envy. While you have not said so to me, it is obvious that there is more to you than meets the eye, or at least your Kin believe so. You manage to be harsh and blunt while still being likeable.

"So despite all of this, having only been free for a short while, you've been traveling to a distant town that you barely know anything about—why? You could easily build yourself a home, no, a mansion. With magic, you are able to build us basic rooms in only minutes. In a couple weeks, I assume that you could create a castle or an underground palace. With your pet Kin to serve you, neither food nor protection would be a problem. But yet here you are. Traveling. I have a hard time understanding your motivations."

Trav slowly nodded. "That's fair. It's not like I haven't thought about some of this before." He sighed. "My original goal was revenge. My wife was murdered in the mines."

"I'm sorry to hear that." Jang-mi dipped her head.

"Yeah, well, thank you. The rage is still there, but it's like it can't get any momentum anymore with everything else going on. I'm still not at peace, I'm still mad as hell, and I still want revenge, but just charging around by myself doesn't make a lot of sense—even with my allies now. The Kin monster who killed my wife never goes anywhere alone, and while I can hold my own now, I'm not arrogant or stupid enough to think I can measure up to any of the stronger Kin, much less take on a whole city.

"As for disappearing into the wilderness...for what? There is a difference between living and surviving. Plus, what if my enemies come looking for me?"

"Enemies?" asked Jang-mi.

"Yes, enemies. I have made a few, and I've inherited some. When I was escaping the mines," he paused, trying to explain Odin and said, "someone—helped me and entrusted me with their work. This means I have some of their old baggage, too." Trav deliberately only used vague terms. He knew she must have noticed the way some of his Valkyries addressed him, but he didn't feel like explaining the Restless to her.

"I see."

Trav took a sip of water. "See, here's the deal, I've decided to keep heading to this town for three reasons. First, while Narnaste and I didn't meet as friends, she's never lied to me. Our relationship is based on a lot of trust, not least of which because I literally can't lie to her.

"Then there's the fact that I think continuing on this path is the right decision. About the same time I got my...power, and the baggage that goes with it, I've gotten weird feelings, too. I've only recently realized they were more than just hunches.

"Last, I have needed a goal, something to work toward. My time on Asgard has...not been good, but the last few weeks have been the most difficult of my life—I've had to adapt faster than ever before, except maybe getting used to the mines and slavery."

Jang-mi cocked her head. "A goal? What do you mean?"

Trav ran his fingers through his hair, trying to figure out how to explain his feelings in words. One advantage of having his Valkyries around was how they seemed to automatically understand his direction. This was the first time he'd had to communicate what was on his mind, and it was turning out to be surprisingly difficult.

He said, "I didn't have much power in the mines, at least no more than any other man. I did what I could to help people, devoted my life to it, actually. The only exception was my wife, but then she was taken from me. I had nothing, but then suddenly, I had everything, at least potentially.

"I was basically handed power, but it was at the whim of someone else, and it could only happen because I had already lost everything. You chose to come to Asgard and got lost, or captured, right? Well, I was just suddenly here. My family was gone, everything I ever knew was gone, and I found out what it was truly like for my life to have no worth. I've had to struggle to survive, to fucking kill people just to eat.

"Everything that happened recently has been overwhelming. I still don't know anyone on this world, and I definitely don't have many allies. To a normal human, I'm powerful, I'll admit it, but in the grand scheme of things, this is a world of Kin—half of them can bend steel without trying very hard, or they can use magic. On my planet, we have weapons called guns. They're powerful, but I saw a Kin guard throw a spear into the sky which killed a giant bird that was so high up I'd barely been able to see it.

"I need to get stronger. Camping out in the middle of nowhere is not an option. Stumbling onto civilization right now is not really something I can do, either. Recent events proved that even human groups can be murderous sons of bitches."

Trav met Jang-mi's eyes and sat forward. "I want to get revenge for my wife, but I hate to admit this—it won't be good enough. There are bastards, sick humans on this planet, but most people are still decent, innocent, and they don't have a chance right now. I want to help all those poor souls in the mines. This world is sick, but I have seen proof recently that it can get even worse.

"So for myself, for everything I want to do, I need to get stronger, and the only solid lead I have is what Narnaste has told me. Without some sort of direction, I'd be lost. Finding Narnaste's village is a starting point, the place where I can figure out what I'm going to do, and how I'm going to live...to do more than just survive. Beth, my late wife, made me promise that I would never give up.

"With all this new power I've found, taking an easy road would be giving up. I'm not a good person, not at all. But the only thing that this world hasn't been able to take from me is my pride, and I damn sure am not going to piss it away by just running, being a coward. When people hit you, you fucking hit them back."

Trav breathed heavily and realized he'd begun raising his voice. He made an effort to speak evenly. "It's a lot, I know. I just have to believe I can do something, have some sort of impact on this world, even if it's just putting the piece of shit that hurt Beth in the ground." He slowly shook his head. "Nothing is ever easy."

Jang-mi was silent for a few seconds. She said, "You are so strong. So very, very strong. I am shamed."

Trav blinked. "I don't know—"

"You are strong. You are full of energy, overflowing with yang. I see you, how your convictions fill you with fire. You very well may be destined for greatness. Meanwhile, I am average, just a mortal refiner who lost my power."

Trav slowly sat back. He hadn't expected Jang-mi to respond like this, and he'd been trying to pull her story out of her for days. She had his undivided attention.

The martial artist turned and began speaking while her eyes were averted. "I came to Asgard when I was young. I look older than my age now, I know. My power wasn't great back then, just mid-level first realm. I am a scion of the Ning family, in no interesting birth order. My destiny was not to be blessed by the heavens; I had no great talent. But I was still learning, growing.

"Then I came to this world on a raid, got lost, and just...gave up. I had no way to get back. If I'd tried harder, I probably could have avoided being captured. At least I can still be thankful that they hadn't known I was a cultivator.

"It took me an embarrassingly long time to escape. I just...I've never had any direction except for a general fear of disappointing everyone who knows me. When I got lost, I just stayed still. My whole life, I have been trying to move forward without knowing which way I was even supposed to travel. I think I envy you."

Trav raised an eyebrow. "What do you mean?"

"Well, you have your direction. You made a decision, and you are seeing it through, even though you don't know where else that first step may take you." She shook her head. "But that is not all; you also have power. It is true that I am fortunate to be stronger than an average human in this place, but I used to be so much more."

"How did it work?" Trav asked, cocking his head. "Your old power."

"I received energy from the world, refining it, shaping it through my dantian, letting it fill my body, and manipulating it to craft techniques and to affect the world. Every family and school teaches a little differently, but that is the best way I can explain it."

Trav crossed his arms. He didn't understand all of the terms she was using, but could follow what she was saying. "So what is the problem now?"

"My dantian is empty, bone dry. It is like...I can sense energy, but it just passes right through me. Trying to touch it is like grabbing at smoke."

Trav opened his emberstone eye wide in a way he didn't usually do because the input could be too confusing. But now, he focused on the eddies of power around her, how it seemed to be repelled by her. He hummed as he watched, tracing the mystical lines through her body, now barren.

"That is...actually really interesting." When the woman frowned, Trav quickly held up his hands in a surrender pose. "I am sorry for your situation and your loss, obviously...but—"

"But what?"

"I wonder if I can fix your condition, at least temporarily, or let you regain what you had when you first got to Asgard." Trav rubbed his chin, running through the magic formulas in his head. Some of what Odin had known was incredibly complex. Trav hadn't had a chance yet to update everything stored in his skull with the new information he'd gotten from Ysintrill.

Jang-mi's jaw dropped. "You can do what?"

"Well, I don't know for sure, and right now it's just—"

Trav suddenly stood as he heard familiar flapping. A black shape fluttered down from the sky, transforming in mid-air to become Yaakova. The harpy landed in an easy, predatory crouch. "I hope I am not interrupting anything?" she asked. None of the Kin particularly liked Jang-mi, but Yaakova, in particular, seemed to despise the human woman.

Jang-mi shut her mouth, her posture changing like she was about to angrily retort, but Trav spoke first. "Do you have a report, Kova?" He kept a cautious eye on both women. Jang-mi was brave, and undoubtedly a great martial artist, but Yaakova could tear her apart, literally.

"Yes, New One. I decided you would want to know what I just discovered."

"What is that?"

"I have located the town that Narnaste has been leading us to. It is more of a village. Either way, we will be arriving there tomorrow afternoon if we wake and travel as normal."

"You are sure about this? How did you know it was the right village?" Trav balled a fist. After so long, they'd arrived. Several strong, conflicting emotions warred for dominance in his heart, but he needed to verify the information first.

"Yes." The harpy's expression grew strained. "I met another flier in the air. She questioned me and told me the name of the village. Faith."

"What? Another flier?"

"Yes. She also said she could sense the divine on me and called me Honored One. I would like to bathe now. Her inquiries were beneath me."

Trav began to say something but stopped. "Are you being serious right now?"

"No, of course not. I am being dramatic and rather enjoying myself, but it is true that I was not sure how to react. Others recognizing my significant value upon first meeting has unfortunately not been the norm in my life."

Trav eyed her sideways, still not sure if she was joking or not. Dealing with Yaakova could be like this, especially if she was in one of her moods. Then he remembered her report and smiled. "We're almost there. Tomorrow we will finally reach Faith."

He turned. "Yaakova, you should go tell Narnaste, she—" Even as he spoke, the harpy had already transformed into her raven form, winging off toward their campsite.

Jang-mi raised an eyebrow. "You know she's an arrogant bitch, right? I mean, even for a Kin. I've said this before, but you keep really strange company."

Trav sighed.

Chapter 29

Trav had to privately agree with what Yaakova had said before. The town of Faith really was more of a village. His little group had walked into the open from the trail they'd found, and he'd gotten his first good look. After examining the place a moment longer, he conceded that while it didn't look like much, its security seemed pretty good.

All vegetation had been cleared around the village at least half a mile, creating a large, unnatural valley in the forest's sea of evergreen trees. The village had been laid out in a fairly long, narrow fashion, with one end near a lake at the base of foothills leading to a mountain. Small fields surrounded the village, and it looked like crops were grown in one consolidated area. On the other side of the valley, he could see livestock pens.

At first, he was confused by the lack of a large wall for security, but then he noticed how the defenses were actually set up. A large, deep trench circled the entire village, with a low wall on the other side that the defenders could hide behind. Nasty wooden spikes jutted outward from the fortification. Trav didn't understand the setup at first until he spotted an inhuman silhouette at the top of one of the guard towers.

Kin. He'd never really witnessed how Kin defended their territories, and it would make sense that they would approach security and war differently than humans. Now that he examined the defenses with fresh eyes, he spotted towers near the livestock and crops too. The guards there were probably skilled with ranged weapons or magic, effectively wielding the equivalent of heavy weapons on Earth.

He suddenly realized that his group was probably already being watched. Despite having traveled the worn trail and entering the valley that way on purpose, Trav developed an itch between his shoulder blades. He was really glad that his group had gone out of their way to not surprise any defenders.

The rest of the group must have felt the pressure too, and while Trav was confident they could probably escape if Faith turned hostile—maybe—he started feeling jittery from nerves all the same.

Then he took another step and almost fell over. Whether this place had a memory shrine, he wasn't sure yet, but there was definitely something powerful here. His Restless senses screamed at him, pulling him towards it. Whatever it was, the village must keep it very well shielded.

Trav hadn't known exactly what to expect while approaching the Faithful village. Their welcome party was still a surprise, though.

A gaggle of children, accompanied by a handful of adults, had left the village in the distance and the group was heading directly for them. "What are they doing?" muttered Yaakova. Then she groaned, "I want to be flying."

"Stay on the ground," Trav ordered with a frown. He turned. "Narnaste, what are they doing?"

"I don't know, Master. Like I told you, it's been a long time since I came here, and we went the long way around. I was with my parents, riding by carriage."

"That's right." Trav nodded, remembering Narnaste's stories. Based on what she'd said, there was a well-traveled road on the other side of the mountain. This meant Faith was remote, but not inaccessible for other Faithful.

"Can I at least take my bow off my shoulder, Chief?" asked Ysintrill.

"No. Everyone, just calm down. We're here to talk...because they're going to welcome us, right, Narnaste?"

"They should," said the canine Kin. "At least they would have years ago. You are a High Master, after all."

"Well, let's hope they're friendly," Trav muttered. "Jang-mi Ning, do you have something to say, too?"

"No," said the martial artist. She'd cleaned up during their travels, even finding or making some new clothes. She looked much younger now, closer to her real age than when Trav had met her. The direct woman announced, "But if they attack us, I am running away so fast, you will think I was a stepped-on cat."

"That's very reassuring. Thank you." Trav sighed. "Let's go meet this group and keep everything friendly. Everyone keep your fucking hands away from your weapons. I would rather not find out what those guards in the towers are probably pointing at us."

Everyone nodded and began slowly walking forward again. When the group of strangers was about one hundred yards away, he stumbled, almost falling over again. He'd just felt something he'd never felt before, but couldn't mistake for anything else.

There was another Restless nearby.

Suddenly, Trav broke out in a sweat, gathering power. He wondered what to do, even briefly considered running away. After sucking in a breath, calming his heart, he decided to keep moving forward. Showing weakness to predators was always a bad course of action, and even without another Restless involved, plenty of Kin were watching at this point—there had to be. He warred with himself about whether to tell the Valkyries what was happening, but as they got closer, he noticed them all startle, and turn towards him at almost the same time.

"That group has another like me," he said softly. "Stay alert."

"I don't think it is physically possible to be any more alert than I already am," growled Ysintrill. "I am about to piss myself now. Can I please take this gods-cursed, inaccurate bow off my shoulder?"

"I made it, so it's actually gods-blessed. But do you think it would actually do much good?" asked Trav in an even voice.

"No. But it would make me feel better."

"We made our choice the moment we stepped off the trail back there," said Trav with a shake of his head. "It's realistically not any safer to run away now than it will be later. We should find out who these people are and hear them out."

"Master, my skin is crawling," growled Narnaste. Yaakova stayed silent but flexed her claws.

Trav focused on breathing slowly as the two groups closed the gap. He observed carefully, his adrenaline keyed up as high as it would go.

The approaching group had about ten children, half Kin and half human. Flanking both sides were four adults. One was human, a man wearing light clothing with a rapier on his hip. The other three were Kin, two males and a female. Two of them were feline Kin, and the last male was a lizardman. These were all common species of Kin.

Walking at the rear of the little group, flanked by a child on either side was a human woman, at least she looked like it at first glance. But even without his divine senses screaming at him, Trav would have suspected there was something more to her. Despite the bright light of the noonday sun, she seemed to gather shadows, her aura as dark as her clothing was light. Trav didn't feel any ill intentions—in fact, she felt...friendly.

That's new, he thought. *I didn't know I could sense that.*

As he subconsciously relaxed, knowing instinctively that he could probably trust his new senses, he studied the new Restless. She was young, probably in her early 20's, around Jang-mi's age. She had blonde, elbow-length hair, green eyes, and high cheekbones. Her generous mouth had smile lines and sat beneath a thin, straight nose. She cocked an eyebrow at him as he studied her, and her eyes twinkled in a way that instantly put him on guard.

The woman wore a short linen dress that seemed native to Asgard, but Trav did a double take at the spandex leggings she wore underneath. Her little jean jacket, perfect for the cold weather, was very fashionable, but also not very Asgardian. *What the hell,* he thought.

With his emberstone eye open, he could see the swirling power around the woman, completely unique from anything he'd seen before. He wondered if someone examining him this way would see the same sort of thing. Her spiraling power touched the world and the people around her, and it flowed, creating random shapes, like stars, and concentric circles. Trav's inherited mantle responded to what he was seeing, and he decided she was probably more powerful than he was, but not by a lot. She had to either be newborn or must have inherited a mantle like he had.

When the two groups got close enough, everyone stopped, but the woman kept moving forward. Trav decided to follow suit. A few arm lengths from each other, she nearly startled him by loudly calling, "I knew that the children would be safe. Hello there! I've been waiting for you." She smiled. Trav noted she had dimples.

"Uh, hi."

Unlike Trav with his very obvious spear, the unfamiliar Restless carried no obvious weapons. But when she pulled a fan from her belt, Trav wasn't sure how, but he immediately recognized it as a powerful tool. He didn't make any sudden moves, even as she began fanning herself with it despite the cold. "Don't be so stiff, silly. I am hoping we can be...friends. It was a long journey to get here just to meet you, after all."

I think she's either showing off, threatening me, or teasing me. Two can play at that game. Trav scratched his beard and willed Hex into his hand to casually pick his teeth. The soul-bound weapon kept itself clean, but he still deliberately did not think about how many people the blade had killed before sheathing it again.

The blonde Restless clapped her hands. She turned to the human man in her group and said, "I like his style! The other one is so uppity and boring."

"I am glad that you approve, my queen." The man's voice was so deadpan, Trav almost smiled in spite of himself.

"Leonard, there you go again! You need to have—"

Trav interrupted. "I would like to know what is going on. Why did you come out here to greet me—us, I mean."

The woman raised her eyebrows. "Leonard, this one really is different, isn't he? The Oracle was right."

"You knew the Oracle would be right, Tiffany. That was why you consulted with it." The man's face was so impassive, it could have scratched steel. As he spoke, one of the three Kin in their group, the feline man, stifled a laugh. The children just seemed confused.

"Leonard, that's mean! You're supposed to be surprised, or at least act that way."

Trav watched them with glittering eyes, aware that they were pretending to ignore him on purpose. He knew why, and he also knew it wouldn't work. Unfortunately, Yaakova hadn't understood. She loudly hissed, "New One, they show disrespect. Shall I kill and eat them? That one in particular looks—"

The blonde Restless turned, and her friendly, somewhat silly demeanor disappeared. Her back ramrod-straight, the air around her filled with power and her voice cracked out, "Silence, creature."

Trav thought the cocky harpy might snap back, or even attack. He tensed to pounce on her, but Yaakova crouched, hissing as she backed away slowly. In fact, all the Kin took a step back.

"There we go!" said the bubbly blonde, her voice carefree and casual again. "Sometimes it is necessary to discipline a neighbor's pets if they don't."

"Who are you?" asked Trav.

"You first!" said the woman. She suddenly paused, holding up a hand and sticking her nose in the air to sniff. With a quizzical look, she cocked her head. "I can sense some sort of high-level transference on these Kin, something you have done to them. Wow. This is really powerful magic. Not many Restless could do this...hmm." She muttered to herself for a few seconds, openly studying Trav. "You interest me a lot more now, and you were already going to be my project for the next month."

"Huh?"

"I am going to toy with your heart and your time." The blonde smiled, dimpling, but Trav wasn't buying it.

"The hell you are. You are going to start talking straight to me and stop bossing around my subordinates, or I'm going to turn my scarred ass around and leave. If you represent the village, we will leave for good and the Faithful miss out on embarrassing one more High

Master. If not, we will wait until they kick you out before we come back. Simple."

She stared for a while, but Trav didn't back down. He met her eyes and made it very clear she didn't impress him. Even with only three bars of power available, he could make life very...difficult for her and probably escape. A line of explosions in the dirt that separated their two groups would help them run away, too. He really didn't want to hurt kids, but he was confident that he could tweak his glyph equation to make a lot of noise and confusion without being lethal.

Finally, she grumbled, "You are no fun. Fine. I'll go first, and we can be all serious about this. I hope you're happy. We'll have to be serious about the wars in the future; it would have been nice not to be that way now."

"Wars?"

The blonde ignored his question and introduced herself. "My name is Tiffany Erben. I have accepted the mantle of the goddess Zorya. May we know who you are?"

Zorya, huh? The name was vaguely familiar through Odin's memories but was not Aesir or Vanir. *She must be from a different pantheon of Restless.* Trav gave her a flat look. "And if I tell you, you will tell me what is going on?"

"Yes. Of course."

"And after I tell you, will you stop pretending you don't already know who I am?" He would have missed it if he hadn't been watching, but the adults in Tiffany's party tensed.

The little blonde blew air out the side of her mouth, lifting a lock of hair off her face. "You are still a clever one, eh, Odin?"

"The name is Travis Sterling now. You can call me Trav as long as we are not trying to kill each other."

"Ah, already moving to the threats then?" Her small smile had changed, becoming icy.

"Not as long as everyone keeps behaving. Did you really expect me to trust you when you were putting so much effort into acting silly and extra cute?"

"So you think I'm cute?" She smiled prettily.

He rolled his eyes. "Drop it. You were hoping I'd be stupid or innocent enough to easily manipulate, but I'm not. I'm not necessarily upset about it, though. Are we going to talk or what?" Trav's nerves spasmed. He was a hair trigger away from blowing the ground and taking off like a bat out of hell.

The goddess glanced at his Valkyries. "Can you vouch that your weapons will stay sheathed?"

"Yes." He turned just to make sure. "Girls, don't kill anyone unless they attack you first, alright?"

Narnaste nodded. Trav glanced down at the children and mentally chuckled. At least they had no idea what was going on, obviously bored with all the adults talking and using big words. There was no way he would have believed that Tiffany was just a silly girl when she'd come out using children as innocent little shields to prevent violence—or as a way to test him.

The move had been cold-blooded in a way that Trav might not have understood before coming to Asgard. Now he just admired how clever she'd been. He doubted she'd really believed that he would attack her, but if he had, he would have lost the support of Faith, and probably all the Faithful on Asgard.

This place was important. He'd long since realized he needed this village, as a base of operations if nothing else.

He still didn't have all of Odin's memories, but knew enough to not be surprised by Restless ruthlessness. Most of them were bastards in some way. Now that he thought about it, he wasn't even sure if they'd all died when Odin had or not. Strangely, he'd also never really questioned the fact that the Restless as a whole knowing where he was now would be bad, he'd just felt the truth of it in his bones.

"Alright, Trav, would you like to take a walk with me?" She glanced meaningfully at the others around them and jerked her head off to one side.

"Some Kin have amazingly good hearing. How are we going to have a private conversation out in the open like this?"

Tiffany began walking, not looking back. She held out her fan. "Come with me, worrywart. I will take care of it."

Trav stared for a few seconds but finally breathed in deeply and followed. Both groups watched him go. He hated being led around by the nose, not knowing what was going on. But realistically, if he wanted answers, he'd probably have to play by someone else's rules, at least at some point. He mentally prepared to summon Hex any moment, though.

Some distance away from the others, in a field with short, weak-looking grass, Tiffany came to a halt. She turned and showed him the fan. "I am going to make a bubble right now that won't conduct any sound. Please don't kill me."

Trav was taken aback, not only by the words but the sincerity and pleading in her eyes. He slowly nodded, finally understanding that she was far more afraid of him than he was of her. As he thought about it, he realized that he was physically a big, muscular man, and currently absorbing the mantle of a god who had ruled one of the most powerful and violent pantheons that had ever existed.

Tiffany had been putting on a show, a strong front.

He said, "Go ahead. Do you want some mist too, so nobody can read our lips?"

"Yes, if you can do that. Thank you."

"Alright, one moment." He turned toward his Valkyries and shouted, "I'm going to make some mist! Everything is okay. Stay there." Narnaste nodded, and he turned back. "Alright, go ahead."

Tiffany nodded and waved her fan. An intricate drawing flared to life on the fabric, blazing a pure, metallic silver. Through his emberstone eye, Trav could see the bubble that formed over their position. He pursed his lips in approval. Then he summoned Hex into his hand and pointed at the ground between where he stood and everyone else. "Mist." In seconds, a billowing carpet of grey fog sprung from the ground, obscuring his sight of the village, and diffusing the sun's light.

With the light dimmed, he could see Tiffany's dark, twinkling aura more clearly. It was really quite beautiful.

"Very impressive," she said.

"You too." Trav had put some things together, coming up with a reason for the charade. "You are not actually in charge here, but you want to be, and you need me for something, am I right?"

The goddess didn't beat around the bush. "Yes."

"Well, in good faith, why don't you tell me what I'm feeling from the village through my mantle, then?"

"That is the Oracle. It's almost dead and can only answer a total of six questions every year. I got to use mine mid-winter last year." She smiled, but now that Trav knew what to look for, he could see her nervousness. "I asked some questions for you, too, things you would want to know."

"What did you ask?"

"Before I answer that question, I have something to ask for confirmation, then something to tell you. How long have you had your mantle?"

"A few weeks or so. I haven't been tracking the days too closely."

She said, "I thought so. As for me, I accepted Zorya's mantle twenty years ago."

Trav processed that information and gave her a closer look. *I see it now.* Yes, she was definitely older than her appearance would suggest. "And?"

"I've only started remembering around the time when I, Zorya, died. For a long time, I was just absorbing star charts and celestial information since my mantle includes the night and the stars. The human brain can't hold all the information that a Restless acquires, so to fully integrate, our minds need to grow, to expand even as we relearn everything we used to know. This is probably happening with you, too."

"Maybe," said Trav. He wondered if he would ever think of Odin as himself. The thought disturbed him.

"The point is that even after absorbing all of that information, I have had more time to...get used to this. You still have huge holes in your other memories, right?"

"Yes."

"I understand. There is another Restless in Faith, in the village. He received his mantle differently than I did, and probably you too. I think we're all different in how we became what we are, but we all get more memories and knowledge over time. Do you remember how Odin died?"

"No, and I'm assuming that it's significant. Did you say there's another Restless back there?"

"Yes, Thanatos. He is an idiot and completely useless—you'll see. It's good he isn't a threat, but he won't help us either. But yes, the memories you are missing are significant." Tiffany sagged. "I don't know how to tell you this, or even where to start. I guess I will just...get it all out there. Is that okay?"

"I'll listen." Trav folded his arms and acted aloof, but he felt dread building in the pit of his stomach. Something was telling him that this might be a turning point in his life.

"Okay, before I start, I want to tell you that I have traveled, and I have met other Restless, some Originators, some Inheritors—what we are calling mortals who received a mantle. During my travels on

Asgard, I even met Fulla and Gna. I know where they are."

The names struck a chord in Trav, just on the tip of his mind, like they should mean something to him. He mentally filed the names and asked, "What about memory shrines, have you found any of those?"

"Yes, although none I could open. They are all for your Pantheon, here."

"Right." Trav didn't entirely understand, but now he knew the other Restless had probably seeded their own worlds with memory shrines. This was not surprising. The Restless were all born paranoid, after all.

"Anyway, I've been traveling because I have been avoiding death. On my homeworld, a seer told me that a powerful goddess wants me dead—an Originator, one of the ancient Restless. On top of that, she told me that my entire world is in danger and that only I have the power to stop it. Of course, this was said in front of several other Restless, and I was 'volunteered' to travel in order to save our world.

"I came to Asgard because of the Oracle. Not many know it even exists, much less where, but I was able to find ancient texts and figure it out. I never thought that looking human would be such a problem in this world."

"Tell me about it," groused Trav.

A smile crossed Tiffany's face, quick as a hummingbird, and she was back to business. "I will skip all of my journeys, trials, and hardships to get to the point."

"Thank you."

"You're welcome." The goddess sucked in a breath and began

speaking faster than before—like she needed to get the words out. "I had all day with the Oracle, and I used almost all of it, thinking about my questions. The Oracle is picky about what questions you can ask. Any question with an 'and' is usually just ignored, and you will have one less question to ask."

Trav asked, "What was your first question?"

"The first question I asked was what I should do to attain the power to avoid death. The Oracle's answer was that I should marry or join my life to another Restless to start a new Pantheon. When I asked who the best candidate was for me to marry, I was told Odin."

Trav raised his eyebrows at that, but stayed silent, listening.

Tiffany continued, "I asked how to find Odin, and was told that I would meet him if I waited in the village for a year. That seemed really straightforward, and was obviously correct." She gestured at the two of them.

"While I lived here, I began wondering what it would be like to meet Odin, one of the pantheon rulers. A king. I already knew that you'd been killed, in fact, that was one reason why I was marked for death, after all, Zorya had seen too much. In fact, it already cost Zorya Utrennyaya her immortal life. My sister is truly dead."

Trav asked, "What does that—"

"Please hold your questions until the end," Tiffany interrupted. "I just need to say all of this. When I heard what the Oracle said, I improvised, changing the questions I'd planned to ask. My next question was to ask what I could tell you that would make you more willing to listen to me. How I could get you to work with me." She met his eyes. "I don't understand the full significance of the answer, but the Oracle told me that members of your family still live and were transported through the veil like you were."

Trav's jaw worked, but before he could get any words out, Tiffany rushed to continue. "I asked the Oracle to answer the next question you would ask after I relayed that information. I got a response. So Trav, the answer to the question you have in your mind right now, probably, 'Like who?' is that you have recently been within a couple hundred paces of your cousin Ashley."

The sad grass on the ground softened Trav's fall, guiding himself into a kneeling position at the last moment. His knees had given out. After three long years as a slave, he'd refused to wonder what had happened to his family anymore, or even how he'd wound up on Asgard. *Ash is alive.* He could scarcely believe it.

Tiffany squatted in front of him, her expression like steel. "The next part is why we needed the eavesdropping shield up. Are you ready?" Trav nodded woodenly. She said, "With my sixth question, I took a gamble. Since I would be meeting you before I could consult with the Oracle again, and I only had one more question, I needed to make it count. If you would get no benefit out of working with me, joining with me, the next question would have been useless, but I would have gotten many other answers as well from the silence. I asked the Oracle why it was in your best interest to work with me."

"My best interest?"

The goddess nodded and pressed her lips together. Her words came more slowly now. "I memorized the Oracle's message. It said,

'Dark forces have unleashed the veil wraiths, Odin's chances of ever seeing his mortal family again will improve with your help, and Frigg plans to return to Asgard with an army to destroy it.'"

Tiffany closed her eyes, and her voice was labored. "Trav, Frigg is the Restless who wants me dead. One thing Zorya saw that got her killed was Frigg killing you. She stabbed Odin in the back, literally. Odin did something to bond her, to give her power, something she'd been asking for a millennium. After it was done, she betrayed you."

"Frigg?" Trav's mouth formed the somewhat unfamiliar word, but even as he said it, a torrent of emotions erupted from his mantle, making him go lightheaded for a second.

"Odin's past wife, the goddess Frigg, is coming to Asgard," said Tiffany. "And nobody will even talk to me about veil wraiths. I think they might be tied to the prophesied destruction of my world."

The blonde woman hit the ground in frustration. "Zorya had a smaller, minor mantle—a star goddess! I don't know how I got mixed up in all of this, but this is...so big. So I am here to meet you, and to ask you for your help. Please, join me and help me save my world. I am tired of pretending to be strong all the time in front of others, with no real confidences, no real friends. Please, I just..."

An ugly sob bubbled out of the blonde Restless woman's throat, and Trav automatically put an arm around her as she lurched forward. Her mantle might be ancient, but the woman beneath was probably barely thirty, and literally carrying the weight of a world.

His sympathy was overshadowed by shock, though. He believed that Tiffany had told the truth, and now he had a lot to think about. It felt like he'd still been a slave just yesterday, but now he was holding a crying woman delivering messages of doom.

He replayed everything he'd just been told. *She said Odin bonded Frigg—that sounds like what I've done to create my Valkyries.* Then he thought, *Odin's ex-wife killed him? Wow. Oh yeah, great.* Now Trav had inherited the old god's baggage. All power truly came with a price.

He hadn't even stepped foot in Faith yet, and he'd already been rocked to his core. For sure, he needed to consult with this Oracle as soon as possible—it sounded like that would be in two months or so. He wanted to verify the thing was real and functional as one of the first things he did, too.

There is a possibility I can see my family again. Ash is alive! Those simple, but powerful facts had opened up layers of scars on his heart, touching emotions he hadn't even known were still alive.

The old Trav, the Travis Sterling from America, might have been entirely overwhelmed in that moment, but he'd had survived the mines. Slavery on Asgard hadn't been able to break him and had pounded his pride and endurance into a solid sheet of steel with an edge. So as he knelt on an alien planet with a dead god's memories riding shotgun in his head, comforting a sobbing woman with crushing responsibility, a small, but strong part of him—his survival instinct—whispered. The voice inside kept asking the same question over and over again.

If I bond a goddess, I wonder how many bars of power I'd get from it.

End of Asgard Awakening,

Book One of Asgard Awakening

Trav's adventures will be continued in the next volume of Asgard

Awakening, book two!

Please read on for a note by the author, including multiple ways to

connect on social media.

...And don't forget to review this novel!

About the Author:

Blaise Corvin served in the US Army in several roles. He has seen the best and the worst that humanity has to offer. A sucker for any hobby involving weapons, art, or improv, he's a fairly hard core geek.

He currently lives in Texas with enough geeky memorabilia to start a museum.

Being a professional author, he must sometimes talk about himself in third person within author biographies.

It's all very eccentric.

Cheers!

To Readers,

You are wonderful and reviews are amazing for all authors, but especially indie authors like me. Your reviews help me pay the bills. Seriously.

If all you can think of to say is, "I liked this book, you should try it too," that would be awesome!

In 2016 I published my first book. Now I'm full time. This is pretty amazing, but also extremely scary. ...lol. A lot of writers don't admit to that. The uncertainty can be intense.

As a reminder, Asgard Awakening is part of the VeilVerse universe, a project that I started with my friend, William D. Arand. To read his current VeilVerse story that follows the life of Trav's cousin Ash, please check out Cultivating Chaos.

Ways to connect with me:

1.My Facebook fan group

Amazon and other distributors are pretty terrible at letting you know when my new books are out. For the latest news and updates, join my Facebook group:

Blaise Corvin Reader group

http://www.facebook.com/groups/BlaiseCorvinBooks/

2.My website

If you're interested in checking out my website, the URL is http://blaise-corvin.com/. You can find news, Delvers artwork, and maps.

The site is still a work in progress so please be patient with me.

3.These are my social media pages. Connect with me!

Twitter - @Blaise_Corvin
https://twitter.com/Blaise_Corvin

Facebook - Leave me a like on facebook!
https://www.facebook.com/BlaiseCorvinWriter/

GameLit Society Facebook Group
https://www.facebook.com/groups/LitRPGsociety/

Blaise Corvin Reader group (best place for updates)
http://www.facebook.com/groups/BlaiseCorvinBooks/

Harem Lit Facebook group!
https://www.facebook.com/groups/haremlit/

My Patreon!
http://www.patreon.com/BlaiseCorvin

If you really love my work and would like to support me further, Patreon offers a great way to help me pay the bills and keep writing!

My email
If you want to drop me a line for any reason, you can email me at:
Blaise.Corvin.Art@gmail.com

Until next time (--and please leave a review!--)

Thank you for joining me on this adventure! I couldn't do it without all the knowledge and encouragement I get on a daily basis from everyone I interact with.

I can't wait to spend time with you again with Trav, in *Asgard Awakening, Book Two.*

:)

-BC

The Veilverse Universe is owned by Blaise Corvin (that's me!) and William D. Arand.

Asgard Awakening follows the adventures of Travis Sterling. To read about his cousin Ash, please check out William's series, Cultivating Chaos!

Made in the USA
Middletown, DE
02 April 2019